T0060346

FOREST OF FORTUNE

JIM RULAND

TYRUS
BOOKS

F+W Media, Inc.

Published by
TYRUS BOOKS
an imprint of F+W Media, Inc.
10151 Carver Road, Suite 200
Blue Ash, OH 45242. U.S.A.
www.tyrusbooks.com

Trade Paperback ISBN 10: 1-4405-8907-0
Trade Paperback ISBN 13: 978-1-4405-8907-2
Hardcover ISBN 10: 1-4405-7989-X
Hardcover ISBN 13: 978-1-4405-7989-9
eISBN 10: 1-4405-7990-3
eISBN 13: 978-1-4405-7990-5

Printed in the United States of America.

10 9 8 7 6 5 4 3 2 1

Cover design by Sylvia McArdle.
Cover images © Adilfitree Prapruetsutjarit, Bram Janssens/123RF.
Author photo © Jason Gutierrez.

This book is available at quantity discounts for bulk purchases.
For information, please call 1-800-289-0963.

For J.J.
who laughed the laugh
that made death
tremble.

ACKNOWLEDGMENTS

I wrote an early draft of *Forest of Fortune* in late 2008. Then things got weird for a while. So many people helped me find my way back to this book that trying to acknowledge them all is an impossible task, but I'm going to give it a shot. Many thanks to: Michael Collier, Ted Conover, Alex Espinoza, Matt Mendez, and the mighty VOLTRON for helping me get my mojo back; Melinda Moore Baccanari, Marivi Soliven Blanco, Kathy Bucher, Kris Casselman, Lizz Huerta, Judy Reeves, and Sandra Younger and all of my colleagues at San Diego Writers for keeping the world alive; my Dub Club compadres Tammy Greenwood and Rich Farrell; Sean Carswell, MC Stevens, Todd Taylor, and the rest of the *Razorcake* familia for doing their part; Melissa Bell, Eric Bosse, Stephan Clark, Jason DeBoer, Pia Ehrhardt, Pamela Erens, David Fromm, Roy Kesey, John Leary, Danna Sides, and all of my Zoetrope officemates; Unice Arce, Cory Burke, Jen Mattuchio, Snowball San Nicolas, Kurt Otto, Fede Savinon, Doreen Schultz, Ryan Seaman, David Varela, Daniel Zamora, and anyone who has ever suffered the slings and arrows of the gaming industry; Porchista Khakpour and Mia Lipman for publishing an early excerpt in *Canteen*. Jami Attenberg, Matt Bell, Patrick DeWitt, and Scott O'Connor for showing me the way; Josh Mohr for wise words and terrible pants; the house arrest gourmet Josh Barnes for walking the crooked path with me; Erik Bitsui for being the student who teaches the teacher; and the legendary Legion of Vermin for endless insight and inspiration. I'd also like to thank my collaborators Peter McGuigan and Matt Wise at Foundry + Media for rowdy representation and Ben LeRoy and Ashley Myers at Tyrus Books for elevating the everyday to awesome. Lastly, mucho amor to my crazy family: the Carduccis, the Flanagans, the Guerras, the McKennas, the Nevarezes, the Rulands; and most of all to my wife Nuvia, who went down the rabbit hole with me and led me to the wonderland.

And as to being in a fright,
Allow me to remark
That Ghosts have just as good a right,
In every way, to fear the light,
As Men to fear the dark.

—LEWIS CARROLL

WINTER

YOU THINK YOU KNOW LUCK? *There are many kinds of luck, but those who come here to find fortune think only of the good. You can't imagine luck so bad it destroys you. You don't believe that such a thing is even possible. You think you are different. You think you are special. You wager what you cannot afford to lose. You do not consider the consequences of your actions. And then, before you know it, you are lost.*

It has always been this way.

I once thought like you, but the many years I have spent here have taught me that fortune may favor the bold, but it abandons everyone in the end.

You will see. I will take you to the other side of luck, the kind that is the opposite of chance. You will learn that luck doesn't matter when your fate has been sealed for centuries. Come with me and I will show you just how lucky you are.

ALICE BLINKED, LOOKED UP at the women peering down at her, every one of them a stranger. Old, wrinkled faces creased with worry. Inquisitive little monkeys who had climbed down from the trees, only the trees weren't real and neither was the forest.

"Are you okay?"

"You don't look so good, sweetie."

"Just be still for a while."

"I'm all right," Alice said to stop their chatter and suppress the panic rising within her. "I'm *fine*."

"I saw you go down," said an old white woman with a head like the tip of a cotton swab. "You were bucking around like a bronco." She laughed at her own joke and the other women joined in, their anxiety slipping away. Through the sound of their laughter Alice listened to the attract sequences of the slot machines: Cashylvania Castle's spooky organ, the frenetic four-note loop from Golden Gizmos. Usually she tuned them out, but today she found them reassuring because it told her where she was: on the floor of the Forest of Fortune, just inside the main entrance to Thunderclap Casino.

Alice sat up, steadied herself. Her underwear was only somewhat damp, thank God, but the shame clung to her. The Loot Caboose, the slot machine Alice was working on, hung open. She slammed it shut and the gamblers went back to their games.

Alice swept her long, dark hair from her face and tried to clear the cloud that had settled over her as tribal security arrived at the scene of the disturbance. That's the word they'd use when they filled out their incident report. Well, she was disturbed all right.

There were two of them this time: a man and a woman, Mike and Melinda. Both were big and beefy, the woman more so than the man.

Alice had seen her on her bicycle, patrolling the parking lots, telling the tailgaters and tweakers to move along, hassling team members for failing to display their Thunder badges.

"Are you all right?" Mike had kind eyes and sounded concerned. Most team members assumed Alice was Yukemaya. They went out of their way to kiss her ass until they figured out she was a different breed of Indian with no clout here at the casino. No clout anywhere. Just an ordinary slot tech trying to hold onto the few shifts she had left. Maybe this one was different. Alice hoped so.

"I must have fallen," she said.

"You had a seizure," Melinda said, eyeballing Alice's badge.

"No," Alice replied. "*Not* a seizure."

Mike looked surprised, Melinda not so much. "Who's your supervisor?" she asked.

Alice gave Melinda her supervisor's name and five-digit Thunder number. While Melinda sorted this out, Alice halfheartedly ran her small hands over her petite frame, checking herself for injuries. She was fine. Rattled, but okay.

The paramedics came in through the main entrance and set up their gear near the Loot Caboose. Slot players waiting to get on the machine whined in frustration. The machine had been on the floor a week and was fast becoming one of the most popular games in the casino.

"I don't need any help," she said to the paramedics. Because of her small size, people assumed they could tell her what to do, and she was sick of it.

"Uh, you have a thing," Mike said. He pointed at his cheek.

Alice touched herself there, and her fingers came back bloody. She relented and let one of the paramedics—a young guy with long-ish hair—look at her wound. She didn't know what happened. She'd opened up the Loot Caboose to check the paper in the printer when she caught a whiff of something weirdly sulfurish. She reached into the machine and . . . That was it. That was all she could remember.

"Don't worry, pretty lady," the paramedic said. "It's not deep enough to scar." Alice didn't care about scars. She had plenty already.

"You're gonna have to come with us," Melinda said.

Alice nodded and they escorted her to the tribal security office, the casino cop shop off the lobby to the main entrance. Cheap mismatched furniture filled the grim little room that buzzed from all the fluorescent lights. The place reeked of bad coffee and reminded Alice of the sheriff's substation back on the rez where she used to pick up her mother.

In the interrogation room, Melinda took charge. "Are you on any kind of illegal substance?"

"No."

"Have you been drinking today?"

"I don't drink."

"Good for you, but I'm going to need a sample."

"Whatever."

Melinda produced a bottle in a clear plastic bag and set it on the table. Whenever team members were injured while on the clock they got drug-tested. Alice understood. The world was full of people hell-bent on partying their lives away. Her roommate, Lisa, a cocktail waitress with bartender aspirations, was one of them. Lisa had trouble keeping her work schedule and her party schedule straight. But she wasn't Lisa.

Melinda told Alice to empty her pockets, and she dumped everything on the table. There wasn't much. A hair tie, a linty breath mint, a cheap Thunderclap pen. Melinda patted her down. Nice Mike looked and then looked away.

When Melinda was through, Alice took the collection kit into the restroom and closed the door. No mirrors, no trash bins, no doors on the stall. It must have been getting on four in the morning. Alice often thought about her mother in the hours before dawn. When she was a little girl she'd often wake up in the middle of the night and discover that her mother was gone. She'd toss and turn, wondering where her mother went, how long she'd be gone, if she was ever coming back.

Alice sat on the toilet, filled the bottle. She secured the cap and washed her hands with the pink soap that smelled like fake cheer. There were no paper towels. She didn't want to go back out there yet. She sat on the edge of the seat and cried into her dripping hands until someone came knocking on the door, asking if everything was all right.

DRESSED IN HIS LAST BLACK SUIT, Pemberton disembarked the bus and stood in the transit plaza on the frontier of the reservation. He squinted up at the towering mesa before him, first of many mountains, and let his gaze travel up the switchbacks carved into the canyon wall. A hawk drifted on a current of air, looking for prey. Pemberton shivered. He hadn't thought to bring a jacket.

The express turned around and rumbled back to San Diego. On the other side of the plaza, the casino shuttle was already boarding passengers. Workers bundled in heavy coats hustled aboard. He lifted his arm to catch the driver's attention, but he only made it halfway across the blacktop before the shuttle went roaring up the mountain without him.

Pemberton knew the Yukemaya Indian Reservation was 150 miles southeast of Los Angeles, but he wasn't prepared for *this*: a desolate, windswept, sparsely vegetated redoubt, high in the desert mountains. Leaving L.A. this morning, he'd imagined killing time before his job interview at the casino by exploring Falls City, but there was nothing to explore. Just a squalid-looking trailer park with a sign advertising DAILY, WEEKLY & MONTHLY RATES.

False City, indeed.

It seemed a shame to squander what little credit he had left on his card on a motel room, but he was exhausted and needed a shower. The first few drops of rain from a black quilt of clouds sealed the deal. He darted across the street and ducked into the trailer park's rental office.

A bell rang as he pushed through the heavy door. He set his valise down on the gritty wood floor so he could rub his cold hands together. The office was large, dark, cavernous, cold. Its barnlike features recalled another age. A map on the wall described the pseudo sprawl that was Falls City Vista, much larger than it appeared from the road.

"Welcome home!"

Pemberton jumped as an Indian fellow who looked to be in his mid-forties emerged from a side door marked Trading Post. Though he had always been high-strung, Pemberton was becoming increasingly more so since he lost his car, his job and, as of yesterday, his fiancée.

"Uh, yes," Pemberton said once the man was situated behind the counter. "I'm looking for a room."

"Are you a casino employee?"

"No. Not yet. I have a job interview today."

The proprietor smiled. "We handle housing for casino employees—for those who want it. Some opt to live off the rez. But we do offer single accommodations at day rates."

"I only need it for a few hours." Pemberton realized how bad this sounded as soon as the words left his lips.

"We don't rent rooms by the hour."

"Of course not, I only meant—" but the proprietor cut him off.

"I have a cabin you might like. Log cabin exterior, modern interior."

With all the latest amenities. A copywriter by trade, Pemberton knew brochure copy when he heard it yet was seduced all the same.

"How much?" Pemberton removed his credit card from his wallet.

"Forty dollars even."

"No tax?" Pemberton asked.

"Not on sovereign land."

"Right," Pemberton said as he filled out the paperwork, listing an address in L.A. he could no longer call home and a number for a driver's license that would soon be revoked. The proprietor handed him a key, an actual piece of notched metal, attached to a slab of molded plastic made to resemble a plank of wood.

"A real key."

"Ramona wouldn't have it any other way."

"I'm sorry?"

"All the cabins have names. Yours is Ramona. I'll show you." The proprietor removed a heavy winter jacket from a hook on the wall and put it on. "Where's your coat?"

"I don't have one," Pemberton replied.

"No coat?"

"No, I'm afraid I—"

"You gotta have a coat."

"Well, I don't."

"Here, I have an extra."

"I couldn't . . ."

"No charge," he said and thrust an overlarge anorak into Pemberton's hands. "Bring it back when you check out."

So much had gone wrong for Pemberton these last few days, he was overwhelmed with gratitude. He'd forgotten there were people like this in the world. Or maybe he'd just been in L.A. too long.

"Thank you. What's your name?"

"Sam."

"Thank you, Sam."

"No problem."

Pemberton donned the coat, retrieved his valise, and followed Sam outside. The wind had kicked up, and the two men huddled into their coats, saying nothing. Pemberton had no idea San Diego County could be so cold. The Thunderclap website featured a faux-pueblo casino done up in sandstone and turquoise—desert colors. Pemberton thought he was heading for heat and here he was dressed like an Eskimo.

He followed Sam down the gravel path. The trailer park complex spread out to the east, and several cabins scattered around a picnic area occupied the grounds behind the rental office. There was only one log cabin. It was darker and dingier than the others, and it squatted in the shadow of a gargantuan palm tree. Pemberton wasn't sure which looked more out-of-place.

Sam slid the key into the lock, opened the door, and ushered Pemberton inside: a small one-room affair with bare white walls, a kitchenette, and a bed. There was no television, no fireplace or stove, nothing remotely log cabin–like about the place save for an old photo portrait from the frontier days of a young woman with dark hair and stern features.

"Checkout is at noon," Sam said, "though I guess you'll be long gone by then."

"Yes." Pemberton took a closer look at the portrait. "Is this Ramona?"

"Thermostat's on the wall," Sam continued, ignoring the question. "The minifridge works, but you have to plug it in. Fresh towels in the bathroom. I'll be in the tepee if you need anything," he said as he backed out of the cabin.

Pemberton nodded but didn't take his eyes off the portrait until the door slammed shut behind him. Tepee? For real? Pemberton approached the thermostat and studied its markings. He clicked on the device and moved the lever from blue to red, setting the temperature at a comfortable seventy degrees, but nothing happened. He sat down on the edge of the bed without taking off his anorak, and waited for the chill that had settled into his bones to pass.

Leaving L.A. earlier that morning, Pemberton had felt like a criminal fleeing the scene of his latest transgression. This feeling persisted for many miles down the coast until he caught a glimpse of the Pacific, and the bright glittering blues buoyed his spirits. Everything was going to be all right, he thought. And for a while it was. At the bus station in downtown San Diego, he caught the express to Falls City, a speck on the map at the eastern edge of the county. The coach chugged through the suburbs and climbed higher and higher into the rough mountains. The towns got smaller and farther apart and then vanished altogether as they ascended into Indian Country. A fierce wind buffeted the bus and the glass windows were cold to the touch.

As the heater clicked on inside the cabin and warm air began to blow, regret spasmed through him and the doubts that had submarined his spirits returned. What was he doing here? How could he have let this happen?

He tried to stay focused on the positive. If the interview went well, he'd be back on his feet and in his fiancée's good graces in no time. He could turn things around. He *would* turn his life around, and today was the day.

The interview, however, was several hours away, and Pemberton was consumed with nervous tension and naked worry. To ensure that all went well, that today was indeed the day, he needed to straighten himself out. He needed, he conceded, a drink.

Although he'd promised himself he'd wait until after the interview, now that he was here he didn't see the harm in loosening up a little. He slid his valise under the bed and ventured out into the cold. The door slammed shut behind him. Did he bring his key?

Pemberton peered through the grimy window. Ramona glared back at him. The key was on the bed. Pemberton made his way back to the rental office. He went all the way around the building, but there was no sign of a tepee anywhere. He found the front entrance to the Trading Post, which must have been what Sam was referring to: *T.P.* not *tepee*. A little Indian humor at the noob's expense.

"Welcome home!" Sam exclaimed as Pemberton entered the store. The Trading Post's log cabin walls were genuine; it was a bit like going back in time. The shelves were packed with everything from Indian blankets, baskets, and war axes to frozen burritos, booze, and bootleg DVDs. Sam aimed a remote at an enormous big-screen television mounted on the wall behind him, muting a professional football game.

"I'm sorry to bother you," Pemberton began, "but—"

"You locked yourself out?"

"Yes, how did—"

"Ramona likes to keep her visitors on their toes. I'll let you back in." Sam reached for his jacket.

"Actually, I wanted to pick up a few things."

"What can I help you with?" Sam asked, anxiously fingering the remote.

Pemberton hesitated. He was reluctant to announce his intention of drinking before the job interview. "Just something to take off the chill . . ."

"Irish whisky, English tea, and honey harvested right here on the rez. Fix you right up."

"Sounds lovely."

Sam buzzed around the store, kicking up sawdust strewn about the floorboards as he retrieved the items. "You like football?" he asked.

"Not really, no."

"I can't get enough of it. Half-pint or a pint?" Sam held up a bottle for Pemberton's inspection. Chadwick's Unadulterated Irish Whisky, a brand he'd never heard of before, and he considered himself something of a connoisseur. A half-pint would be prudent, but since Sam already had his hands on the bigger bottle . . .

"Let's go with the pint."

"You're the boss."

"How long have your people owned this place?"

"My people?"

"You're, um, Native American?"

"I'm Armenian."

"Armenian?"

"Native of Armenia."

"I see," Pemberton said while Sam bagged the supplies. He'd been fooled by the man's checkered shirt and cowboy hat. Sam swiped his credit card and Pemberton rapped his knuckles on the counter—a miniature jig of joy—when the transaction went through. Sam insisted on carrying the groceries back to his cabin. The rain had come and gone. The light in the sky stabbed into Pemberton's eyes, brighter than it ought to be on a day so cold. Sam unlocked the door with a master key and pushed it open.

"Thanks again," Pemberton said.

"Don't mention it!" Sam replied and was off, back to his football game.

Pemberton unpacked his supplies and found everything he needed in a cabinet above the stove: cooking pot, coffee mug, whisky tumbler, spoon. He filled the pot with water and turned on the stove. The blue flames licking out of the burner lifted his spirits. He prepared the tea and honey, and when everything was ready, he broke the seal on the bottle and poured whisky into both the tumbler and the mug—one to shoot and one to sip. Tumbler in hand, he wandered over to Ramona. There was a vent in the ceiling above the portrait so it was warmer here than anywhere else in the cabin. He studied Ramona's features and confronted his own reflection in the glass. They both looked exhausted, frazzled, and sad, but perhaps he was projecting.

"Today is the day," he said as he raised his glass and looked Ramona in the eye to assure her that this time he really meant it.

Ask a shitload of questions. That was Pemberton's strategy for job interviews. Start with questions, end with questions, and cram more questions in between. Only the last time he'd used this approach it had worked a bit *too* well.

Pemberton had responded to an ad for a freelance-editing gig placed by a woman named Kiki. He hadn't done any editing since *You Had to Be There*—the online humor zine he cofounded in college, which had peaked at forty discrete visitors per week. Through an exchange of e-mails, he was able to ascertain that Kiki intended to write a book about her Korean boyfriend Ricky, who had a supersecret story to tell. Crime was involved. Money was no object. Would Pemberton like to meet at a coffee shop to discuss the details?

Absolutely, he replied.

Surprise, surprise, Kiki turned out to be a highly attractive Korean-American woman with long hair that kept drifting into her eyes. Ricky, predictably, was a thick-necked thug who, Kiki explained, spoke no English. Pemberton fired questions at his potential employer, and he learned quite a bit. Ricky was a gangster, a straight-up killer; Kiki was bisexual. Sapphic poetry was her thing, not criminal memoirs. That's where Pemberton came in.

"You're an amazing writer," Kiki gushed. "I can tell from your e-mails."

"Tell me more," Pemberton said.

"We're polyamorous. That means we like to fuck other people."

Ricky grunted. Kiki went on. She had a thing for massage oils. Ricky liked making home movies with his digital camera. They both enjoyed cocaine. Kiki offered these details in the unselfconscious way of someone auditioning for a reality television show. She certainly wasn't shy. She *wanted* the other patrons in the Beverly Hills coffee shop to hear what she was putting out there.

"What we're really looking for," Kiki confessed, "is a ghostwriter."

"I see," Pemberton said. "How do you propose we proceed?"

"Would you like to come back to our place and get to know one another better?"

Pemberton nodded his consent. Not because he was attracted to Kiki, though he was, and not because he needed the money, though he did, desperately, and certainly not because he wanted to put his relationship with Debra, which was already on life support, in further jeopardy. No, Pemberton accepted Kiki's invitation because he really, really loved cocaine—the ad man's drug of choice—and the prospect of getting paid an outrageous sum to do coke with a polyamorous bisexual Korean-American hottie made him weak with want.

They went up to the Hills in Ricky's limited edition Lexus. They lived in Koreatown, Kiki explained, but were mansion-sitting for a friend in the porn industry. The house looked like a wedding cake made out of birdcages. Floor-to-ceiling glass walls, fire pit in the parlor, infinity pool on the patio. The guest bathroom was a tribute to the 1970s. Pemberton wondered how many adult films had been shot here. They settled in a lounge strewn with sofas. Kiki fiddled with the stereo, asked Pemberton to fix drinks. He found the bar and made a Bellini for Kiki and poured himself a Scotch. He had no idea where Ricky had disappeared to.

"What I find exhilarating about *memoir*," Kiki said as if she were practicing her French, "is how naked you are. Just you, the page, and . . ."

"The pen," Pemberton offered.

"I was thinking thesaurus, but you're the pro."

Pemberton was ready for another Scotch.

"Can you handle that kind of nakedness?" Kiki scrutinized him over the rim of her cocktail glass.

"Of course, *I'm* the pro," he laughed.

"Let's do some blow."

Kiki dumped at least an eight ball on the glass coffee table. Pemberton asked more questions while she sculpted lines. "How long have you and Ricky known each other? What brought you to L.A.? You do know I'm heterosexual, right?" Kiki snorted a line of coke through an impressive-looking silver tube designed expressly for the purpose. The kinky couple from Koreatown was serious about their cocaine. Pemberton did one, two, three quick lines with a rolled-up dollar bill and levitated over to the bar to splash more Scotch in his glass while Kiki went back to work with her pretty little tube. Numb from the neck up, Pemberton could barely make out what Kiki was saying until she beckoned to him from the couch. He set his drink down on the edge of the coffee table and presented himself to her.

She slipped her hands inside his jacket and slowly undid the buttons of his shirt. Anything Pemberton might say would only wreck the moment, so he said nothing. She untucked his shirt and removed his white oxford and black jacket as if they were sewn together. Kiki knelt on the carpet and began untying his shoes. "Up," she commanded, and Pemberton lifted his legs one at a time while she removed his heavy wingtips. He caught his reflection in the mirror above the bar. He looked ridiculous. Blessed with broad shoulders and angular features, many of his girlfriends had told him he looked like a model—with his clothes on. Naked, he was gaunt and gangly, a starveling with dark floppy hair and a chicken chest.

"When was the last time you were totally exposed?" Kiki asked, looking up at Pemberton, eye-level with his crotch.

"Never," Pemberton said in a rare spasm of honesty that he instantly regretted.

Kiki eased his stiff leather belt through the loop and pushed it forcefully through the buckle. Pemberton closed his eyes. He felt Kiki's fingers tug on his zipper and pull on the waistband of his underwear, freeing him. In the mirror Kiki's black swamp of hair oozed over her shoulders and back. She was so close. Her breath warmed his thighs.

"Now you do me."

Kiki stood, twirled, and lifted her hair to reveal the clasp of her dress. Pemberton was careful not to touch her skin, only her clothes. A single button and a long zipper was all it took. She wore no bra. Just panties and heels. He got down on his knees and undid the straps of her shoes, which were more complicated than they looked. He rolled her panties down her thighs as if he were peeling an exotic fruit. There were no bikini lines, no tan lines of any sort, and her quim had been meticulously shaved so that it resembled an unblemished crease, a dimple really, and as he opened his mouth to ask if she was naked enough, she grabbed him with surprisingly strong hands and mashed his face into her crotch.

"Mmthmhmm?"

This wasn't at all what he expected. But now, with a mouthful of muff, he truly did feel naked and oddly vulnerable. With his face thrust into the essence of this gorgeous woman, Pemberton began to wonder and then to worry about the whereabouts of her gangster boyfriend. It just seemed too good to be true. So when Kiki relaxed her grip and said, "Easy, tiger," he was not at all surprised to see Ricky grinning at him from behind a digital camera, wearing a black silk robe that was much too small for him and revealed all manner of frightening tattoos.

They switched positions and Kiki took him in her mouth. Pemberton tried to angle his body away from Ricky, but the gangster circled the sofa to capture a better view with his camera. Though Kiki applied herself with admirable diligence, Pemberton felt detached from the proceedings. He couldn't see what she was doing down there and he felt jittery from all the coke. He couldn't tell if he was getting hard or not. He fixated on his drink, melting into the coffee table just out of reach. The ice cubes settled musically as if to tease him. He really, really wanted some whisky, but felt it would be rude to interrupt Kiki. He even considered asking Ricky to hand it to him but thought better of it. He closed his eyes to concentrate and his mind slipped away. Other women. Other blowjobs. Memories that weren't quite memories but bits of pornography that gurgled up out of his subconscious. He opened his eyes to discover Ricky plowing Kiki from behind. He was still wearing his robe, still filming everything with his camera, still grinning. Whether it was the coke or the camera or Ricky's terrifying tattoos, Pemberton's member refused to cooperate. Kiki addressed the problem with great gusto, kissing and licking and sucking and pulling on Pemberton's penis, but it was no use. Soft city. Kiki stopped. She produced a silver tube much longer than the first and handed it to Pemberton.

"What's this for?"

"If you can't service me," she said, "you can at least give my man what he needs."

"What?" Pemberton bleated.

"You blow."

Ricky got down on all fours and looked at him over this shoulder.

"I'm sorry," Pemberton said to Kiki. "I don't play that way. I thought I made that clear."

"No, like this." Kiki held the silver tube up to her mouth like a dart gun and slapped Ricky's ass.

Pemberton understood. He'd heard about this sort of thing, but had never seen the practice put into action. He accepted the tube and knelt on the carpet. He knee-walked to Ricky's backside and balked. Ricky's muscular cheeks gleamed with oil and smelled faintly of vanilla.

"Um," he said to Kiki, "can you give me a hand here?"

Kiki rolled her eyes. She crouched by Pemberton's side and inserted one end of the silver tube into Ricky's anus. Pemberton felt the first faint stirrings of arousal, but it was too late for that. Pemberton blew the cocaine that had been packed into the silver tube deep into Ricky's rectum. The Korean gangster howled as if he'd been jabbed by a needle. Or maybe he was singing Pemberton's praises as a cocaine delivery system. Unlikely, but the possibility couldn't be ruled out.

"What did he say?"

"He said he doesn't think you're the ghost we're looking for."

"I think I'd better be going."

"I think that would be best."

Pemberton pulled on his pants, slipped into his jacket, felt the reassuring weight of his cell phone. He wondered how many times Debra had called, and pushed the thought out of his mind.

"Say, do you think I could—"

Kiki slapped a baggie into Pemberton's palm. "Goodbye."

"Thank you."

"You were never here."

"Of course. And where are we exactly? So I can call a cab . . ."

Kiki backed Pemberton onto the porch. "If you contact me," she warned, "you can expect a visit from Ricky."

Pemberton tried to think of something clever to say as the door shut in his face. He was terrible at goodbyes.

He stumbled down the street, letting gravity be his guide. The moon! The stars! Three missed calls from his fiancée! Holy shit. He turned off his phone. He wasn't ready to go home. It was early, at least by coke-in-the-pocket-and-no-work-tomorrow standards. The interview hadn't gone well, but they weren't really looking for a writer. At least not one of Pemberton's caliber, in Pemberton's league. There was nothing left to do but hoof his way back to Hollywood.

After an hour of strolling shitfaced through the Hills, he ducked behind a recycling bin and keyed more coke into his nostrils to give the old boosters a boost. He followed the trancelike beat of house music until he stumbled upon a Halloween party in full swing. Canopies had been erected in the yard under which bartenders tended bar and DJs deejayed. All manner of people milled about. Freaks in capes frolicked with dwarves in drag. No one noticed him. The costumes made it difficult to separate the guests from the entertainers. In any other city in America a hairstylist, an actress, and a prostitute could show up to a party wearing the same costume and the guests would zero in on the pro. But in L.A., it wasn't nearly so obvious. Anyone who spent enough time in this town learned to stand out by disappearing into the role they'd come here to play.

Pemberton was precisely the opposite. He was only comfortable in his own skin when it was full of drugs. He got turned on to the pleasures of cocaine while interning at an agency his senior year of college. For the first time in his life, he was able to slip out of the stiff, formal creature he presented to the world, and he loved it. He'd dabbled in it ever since—though Debra didn't care for it. She called it a habit. He called it an accoutrement.

But he didn't want to think about his fiancée. He was considering turning on his phone when an attractive young woman dressed as Little Red Riding Hood told Pemberton she liked his costume.

"Thank you," he said, not bothering to ask who she thought he might be. "Cocaine?"

"Sure!"

"How old are you?" he asked.

"Old enough," she answered.

"You're not afraid of the Big Bad Wolf?" he asked.

"Little late for that." She showed off blood-red gashes on her neck that had been applied, Red explained, by a friend who worked for one of the studios as a special effects pro.

"Whoa! That looks infected."

"Look again," she said and offered her neck for inspection. The white globules deep inside the fake wound weren't just glistening—they moved.

"Maggots?"

"Animatronic. Aren't they awesome?"

Pemberton agreed that they were. Little mechanical maggots equipped with motion detectors programmed to wriggle and squirm whenever a potential admirer got too close.

"Charming," he said.

They slipped into a bedroom. Little Red Wolf Bait texted her friends and they were soon joined by Sleeping Pill Beauty, Zombie Bo Peep, and a couple of fairies. *This* was Pemberton's kind of party.

Except it wasn't. These people were too rich and too beautiful, and as soon as his coke ran out, they vanished. Pemberton wandered around the house, inside and out, to see if he could possibly score some more, but his new friends had all disappeared. He discovered a shed in the backyard decorated with plush carpet and a luxurious sofa that he wasted no time settling into. A single red light bulb hung naked from the overhead. Strange. He was joined by a middle-aged woman dressed in black boots and a velvet gown. She wore black nail polish that Pemberton suspected was part of her daily get-up.

"You wanna get high?" she asked in a way that suggested there was more to the question than she was letting on, and if the answer was yes, there would be strings attached.

"Depends," Pemberton answered.

The woman smiled and produced a pipe, which appeared to conjure a longhaired fellow in a slouch hat and a cape.

"There you are," he said, presumably to the woman, though he looked right at Pemberton. "And who is your darling new friend?"

"Out of here," Pemberton said and launched himself off the sofa, out of the shed, and away from the party. He'd lurched into that hour when nothing good could happen to an unhappily engaged man. He'd already crossed any number of uncrossable lines, the retelling of which would require an elastic relationship to the truth. Bottom line, he couldn't stay out all night with kinky Koreans, slutty coke-heads, and whatever those people in the shed were, and expect Debra to be cool with it. Even if, scratch that, *especially* if the relationship had all but run its course. But in Pemberton's mind, if he made it home before dawn, there remained a chance, however remote, that Debra wouldn't realize how late he'd stayed out. In any event, when they argued about it later, as they inevitably would, "staying out late" sounded a lot better than "staying out all night."

Unfortunately, the cab company he called to fetch him took forever, and by the time the driver asked "Where to?" the first rays of dawn were already lighting up the clouds to the east. So, fifteen minutes later, when he spilled out of the taxi on the other side of town, he wasn't really surprised to discover his belongings—his identical black suits, his paperback novels, his beloved experimental jazz records—scattered all over the lawn.

GUADALUPE MARIA GARCIA RACKED UP JACKPOTS on Golden Gizmos like it was her own personal ATM. She couldn't predict these hot streaks—no one could—but she knew what to do when they came: She played and she didn't stop playing until she cashed in. When she knew, she knew.

"Are you still up?" Denise asked.

"Dios mío! Don't sneak up on me like that!"

"Well, are you?"

"I think so." Lupita knew this answer would aggravate her friend. Lupita never asked Denise how *her* day was going, though today she looked like she was down. If Denise felt like telling her, she'd tell her.

"If you don't know where you stand, sooner or later you'll end up on your ass."

Lupita had heard it a million times. "You almost ready?"

"Yeah, my arthritis is killing me." Denise settled into an empty seat. Once upon a time, Slotville was decorated like a street in a Wild West movie, but the walls were bare and only the neon sign for the Slotville Saloon remained. The ceilings were low and the carpets musty. The rank odor of cigarette smoke was stronger here, even though it was practically empty. Lupita was convinced the machines in Slotville paid out better during the day, so here she was. The only other occupant was a young woman, her dark hair in braids. She played her game with one hand while rocking a baby stroller with the other.

"Just a little bit longer," Lupita said.

"I'm in no hurry."

Lupita and Denise made an odd couple. Denise was a brittle-looking white woman in her sixties; Lupita a curvy Latina thirty years her junior. But they'd been friends for almost as long as Lupita had been coming to the casino. Denise was the best video poker player in the Thunderclap Club Rewards program, maybe even in all of Southern California. She boasted that she'd figured out the algorithm for minimizing the casino's hold.

"Play the games the way they were meant to be played," Denise said, "and they'll pay."

Lupita had heard that one before, too. Denise came up with her system while she was in prison for killing her husband. She'd tried to explain it to her, but Lupita didn't have the patience to learn. When she wanted to play, she wanted to play, not do math.

Lupita had her own system. It was a flawed system, but she stuck to it. Otherwise, why bother? When she played a traditional three-reel slot machine, she started with a single-credit bet. If the first reel didn't put a symbol on the pay line—a seven, a cherry, a Golden Gizmo, whatever—she stuck to a single credit for the next spin. It could be a nickel, quarter, or dollar slot machine. The denom didn't matter. But if the reel put something on the pay line, she upped her bet on the next spin. It was all about that first reel. As long as it gave her a chance to win, she kept increasing the wager—all the way to the max bet—but as soon as the reel stopped cooperating, she dropped back down to a single credit. The way Lupita looked at it, she wasn't going to give her money away for nothing. The machine had to give her a shot.

This drove Denise crazy, which is why she could never watch Lupita play for long. "The thing about your system is it isn't a system."

"So?"

"When you press PLAY, what do you think happens?"

"Sometimes I win. Sometimes I lose." Lupita waited for the lecture she knew was coming.

"A random-number generator assigns a value that determines the position of the reels and dictates whether you win or lose," Denise said like she was reading from a manual. "Before the reels even begin to spin, the outcome has already been determined. The only part of the transaction that's not ruled by chance is the wager. That's why a serious player, a gambler who knows what she's doing, always plays max bet."

This wasn't what Lupita wanted to hear. That kind of talk could screw up a hot streak. Lupita cared about maximizing the *excitement*. That's what she loved best, the drama. If she got one Golden Gizmo, then a second, the anticipation she felt while she waited for that third reel to stop spinning was nothing less than delicious. She loved the possibility pulsing at her fingertips. The machine may have known the outcome, but she didn't, and that was good enough for her.

"Do you believe in luck?" Lupita asked as the reels spun. One . . . two . . . She almost had one there. She was getting close. She could feel it.

"Luck has nothing to do with it," Denise said.

"That's no answer."

"I'll tell you what I *don't* believe."

"What's that?"

"I don't believe luck is making these Indians rich. Do you think luck keeps the lights on at Thunderclap? Do you think luck pays the bills for their fancy cars and huge houses?"

Lupita let it drop. She couldn't imagine coming to a casino and not believing in luck. That was like going to church and not believing in heaven! As if to prove her point, the machine gave her one, two . . . .

"Tres gizmos!" Lupita shrieked. The woman with the baby stroller gave her a look full of envy and regret.

"Congratulations," Denise snarled.

Denise was once a very attractive woman, and she still played the part. She never left her house without her face on, and she got her hair done every other Saturday. Not like these cochinas in their tank tops and sweatpants that might as well have the price of doing business stitched across their asses. Some day, Lupita would be a once-beautiful woman, too, but she wasn't there yet. Not even close. Her figure may have been a little plumper than it used to be, but she still turned heads.

"I won a thousand dollars," Lupita said.

"Yeah, but you could have won three."

Lupita didn't care. With her system she was bound to miss out on a few paydays, but with all the money she saved by not maximizing her bet on wagers that never had a chance, she figured that things would even out in the long run. Denise shook her head in dismay.

"It'll even out all right—for Thunderclap!"

There was no point arguing with Denise. A number of elderly couples shuffled into Slotville using walkers and canes. They looked like they'd just stepped off the bus from a San Diego retirement center. Denise eyed them with disgust. She hated crowds. Something about her time in jail that she never got over.

"Can I ask you something?"

"Sure," Denise replied while rummaging through her purse.

"What are these gizmos supposed to be?"

"Hmmm . . . They're devices. Widgets. Little doohickeys. It's hard to explain . . ."

Denise didn't seem interested in their conversation. She didn't seem interested in anything.

"I know what the *word* means," Lupita continued, trying to engage her friend, "I'm talking about the gizmos in the game. What do you think they are?"

"I don't know what they're supposed to be," Denise said, "but I can tell you what they remind me of."

"What's that?"

"Have you ever been to San Francisco?"

"Yes, a long time ago." Lupita had been all over the country, but she'd never been to San Francisco. She didn't know where the lie came from, what purpose it could serve, but there it was.

"I went to San Francisco with my husband once," Denise continued. "He took me to a sex shop that had all kinds of gizmos and some of those gizmos had little gizmos on the end of them!"

"That's what you think about when I'm playing my game?" Lupita asked, feigning shock.

"Honey, that's what I'm always thinking about!"

Lupita laughed. She retrieved her card and cashed out. "Are you hungry?" she asked while she waited for the ticket to print.

"I could eat."

"My treat."

As members of the top tier of the Thunderclap Club Rewards program, they could take all their meals at the casino for a month, and Thunderclap wouldn't stop comping them. Still, it was a necessary gesture. Winners buy. That was the rule.

"Where do you wanna eat?"

"I don't care."

For Denise, food was the substance that allowed her to take her arthritis, heart, and who-knows-what-else medications. She carried her pills in a box that rattled in her purse like a maraca. Lupita liked to eat, especially after a hot streak. She could still feel her good fortune churning away inside her, anxious to get out. Perhaps after a bite to eat and a glass of Chardonnay, she'd be able to talk Denise into staying a little longer.

They made their way out of Slotville, back to the main hall where Denise had played Loot Caboose all morning. They followed the patterned carpet through the Forest of Fortune. It smelled better here. There was no smoking in the Forest of Fortune.

The Chop House was one of several restaurants arranged like a horseshoe around the backside of Thunderclap Falls, a massive artificial mountain with a waterfall that could be turned on and off. It was still early for dinner, late afternoon really, and they were the first to be seated in the casino's nicest restaurant. Their waiter, a young Tijuanense with black discs in his ear lobes, took their orders. Lupita selected an entrée of bacon-wrapped scallops in habañero cream sauce. Denise ordered a milk shake.

"I'm sorry, ma'am," the waiter said. "We don't serve milk shakes."

"Sure you do," Denise insisted. "I had one last week."

"Maybe at one of our other restaurants . . ."

"That must be it. I'll have a milk shake."

The waiter didn't get it. Though the casino had many restaurants, all of the kitchens were connected. Denise figured out a long time ago that she could order whatever she wanted regardless of which restaurant she happened to be dining in: dim sum at the Chop House; hot dogs at the Hong Kong Kafé.

Lupita intervened. "My friend doesn't mean to cause any trouble," she began, getting frisky with her eyes. "She just wants a shake, and if you can get it for her, there'll be something extra for your trouble."

The kid ran off to confer with his supervisor. Soon a balding man with a potbelly stuck his head out of the kitchen for a look and quickly whispered something in the waiter's ear. Lupita rearranged her purse, looking for a safe place to stash her winnings.

"Be careful!" Denise warned. "Don't let anyone see!"

"Oh, relax."

"I wish I could, but this heart medication they've got me on is like rocket fuel!"

They shared a laugh, but Denise was right. You never knew who might be watching, and not just the eye in the sky. Lupita had heard the stories: people who trolled the casinos for winners. Usually, the predators were women who used their charms on foolish men. They whispered sweet nothings in their ears and coaxed them out to the parking lot where there were plenty of cameras but never enough security. Just last month some poor man met a lady after a good run at the Pai Gow tables and accepted her offer to follow her home. Somewhere in the desert she pulled over, feigning car trouble. When the lucky fool got out of his vehicle to help, bandits brained him with a tire iron, took his money and his car, and left him in the desert to die. Lupita heard he was still in the hospital.

Easy come, easy go. But what did she know? People liked to talk about things they knew nothing about. Even here in the restaurant, diners whispered about her infamous friend. *There's the lady who whacked her husband.* This bothered Lupita, but it didn't really surprise her anymore. So what if her friend had made a mistake? She'd served her time, hadn't she? If the state saw fit to let her go, what business was it of theirs? It was almost enough to spoil her appetite, ruin her good fortune.

Their food arrived and Lupita tucked into her meal with some reluctance. Denise stirred her shake, which had been served in a Styrofoam cup.

"How elegant."

"Are you sure you're okay?" Lupita asked.

"I don't know. I had a strange experience on the floor today."

"Did someone . . ."

Denise shook her head. "I was playing that new game—Loot Caboose—and losing badly. I started with one hundred dollars and won a few credits early on, but then the machine went cold. It just wouldn't pay. I spent five hundred on that goddamn machine. It felt personal, Lupita, like it was holding back. But then, I did something I never do."

"What?"

"I changed my bet."

"You didn't!" Lupita exclaimed.

Denise nodded, deadly serious.

"I did. I played the minimum bet. It made me feel small. I wanted that fucking machine to pay, but I'd be damned if I was going to put in another hundred!"

The Chop House slowly filled and Lupita was certain people were staring at them. She hated making a scene, but there was something in her friend's voice, an urgency she hadn't known Denise was capable of.

"That's when it hit me. A terrible, terrible feeling." Denise lowered her voice and leaned across the table so that only Lupita could hear her.

"I felt like the machine was counting down not only my money, but my *time*."

"What are you saying?" Lupita asked.

"I was certain I'd lose. I could feel it in my bones. I knew that if I let my credits get down to zero, it would be the end of me."

Lupita laughed, but this wasn't funny. The scallop felt cold and muscular in her mouth. She raised the napkin to her lips and spat it out. "I'm not sure I understand," Lupita said. The scallop felt fleshy in her fist, like a tumor. She thought she might get sick.

"It felt like it was trying to kill me," Denise said with a crazed look in her eyes. "It felt like if I kept playing that fucking game, I would *die*."

TODAY IS THE DAY, Pemberton repeated to himself as the Thunder shuttle climbed to the top of the mesa. The bus made its final turn, presenting Pemberton with his first look at the casino. The weathered and wind-scraped walls needed paint. Cracks zigzagged across the stucco supports. Rock formations decorated the landscape, but the vegetation was withered, the soil eroded, revealing concrete posts where the fake rocks were anchored to the earth, like gums receding from a rotten tooth. The casino overlooked a pair of identical-looking mountains across the valley, the desert to the east, and the darkening canyons to the west. The casino was a dump, but at least the view was nice.

"Thank you for visiting Thunderclap Casino," the driver said as the shuttle wheezed to a stop. "Good luck."

Pemberton scowled. Luck was a commodity in a casino, and he'd take all he could get, but did he really look like he needed it?

Donna from Human Resources had instructed Pemberton to call her on the house phone when he arrived, and that's what he did.

"Mr. O'Nan will be right down," Donna said when he got her on the line.

"Great."

"You're lucky."

There was that word again. "Yeah?"

"He's in a good mood today."

The casino lobby was a small, dimly lit affair reminiscent of a budget hotel: pleasant but forgettable. Every so often glass doors whooshed open to let patrons in or out and the lobby filled with the musical chattering of the slot machines. Pemberton studied a floor-to-ceiling mural of a waterfall while he waited. It wasn't very good, but it wasn't terrible either. The left side of the booming falls tumbled into a forested canyon; the right side emptied into a mist-shrouded void out of which rose Thunderclap Casino.

Waterfall. Falls City. It was all starting to come together. But a waterfall way out here at the edge of San Diego County? Who knew?

He'd stumbled across the job opening at the casino on Craigslist shortly after he'd been fired. He'd filled out the application and sent it off but had never heard a thing. Donna from Human Resources had called while he was sifting through his stuff in front of his old apartment complex in L.A. It took him a while to figure out who she was and why she was calling, but once he did, she had his full attention.

"I'm looking at your application and I'm calling to see if you can come down to interview for a copywriting position I think you'd be perfect for."

"When?" Pemberton croaked.

"Can you make it down today?"

"How about tomorrow?"

"We'll see you then!"

Pemberton had no idea how he was going to get to San Diego, but he'd worry about that later. He'd just about talked himself into being glad the enormously complicated strain that he and Debra referred to as "their relationship" was finally over, but the sight of his shirts in the bushes, his shoes strewn across the lawn, made Pemberton realize the enormity of his error. He couldn't lose Debra. He just couldn't.

The Thunderclap gig would give him a chance to get away for a while, clean up his act, save a little money, and come back to L.A. a changed man. Thunderclap would save him. Save *them*.

After gathering up all his stuff and piling it on the stoop, he went up the stairs to beg for Debra's forgiveness. The door flew open just as he was about to knock. Debra's eyes were red—almost as red as Pemberton's— but she was dressed for work. She always looked her sexiest when she was on her way to the office where she was a media buyer. Debra had a closet full of tight-fitting blouses and pencil skirts. But this wasn't a good sign. It meant she intended to power through her day, get on with her life without him. He thought the end of their relationship would have been good for at least a sick day.

"Deb . . ."

"I don't want to hear it."

"Debra, I'm—"

"Sorry? Really? What exactly are you sorry for? Not coming home last night? Wasting almost *three* years of my life?"

"Well, last night for starters, but . . ."

"I'm done. *You've* been done a long time. That's perfectly obvious. Now *I'm* done. There's nothing left to say."

Pemberton felt absolutely wretched. His lips were dry, his throat parched. There was a good chance his legs would give out at any second. Debra was holding onto his valise, a worn leather satchel that looked like a country doctor's medical bag. He'd found it in a vintage store when he first came to L.A. and seeing it in her hand triggered a flood of memories.

"I'm sorry. I really am. I just got a job interview."

"Great. How long will you be gone for this one, a week?"

"Only a day. It's in San Diego. Outside San Diego really . . ."

"Stop. Just stop." Debra's eyes started to water. He had about twenty seconds, thirty tops, before her freshly applied makeup began to run, which never failed to trigger a tantrum that left him skittish and helpless. Pemberton was many things, but a fighter wasn't one of them. His flight skills, however, were meticulously honed.

"I'll go and we'll talk when I get back, but . . ."

"What?"

"May I have my bag back?"

Debra looked down at the valise, as if she'd forgotten she was holding it, the bones in her small hands standing out so beautifully birdlike. Her fragility, so out of sync with her tempestuous nature, was the thing he cherished most about her. Why did he keep forgetting that?

"Sure," Debra said.

Pemberton almost smiled. The amicable nature of their exchange gave him hope. It was something to build on, but before he could get a word out, she brained him with the bag and slammed the door.

"You must be Pemberton!" boomed an older man who was both short and squat and wore gaudy rings on both hands. Advertising was a young man's game, a fact Pemberton was acutely aware of now that he was in his thirties, but O'Nan looked like he was pushing seventy.

"Pleased to meet you."

"I don't know about you," O'Nan said, "but I'm starving. I've got another writer coming in an hour. What do you say we grab a bite? No booze though. The Indians are funny that way."

"Of course," Pemberton answered, forcing a grin to keep his anxiety in check. Another copywriter? That wasn't good news. And there was no way his credit could withstand a hundred-dollar hit at a steakhouse. O'Nan would probably pay, but what if he didn't?

O'Nan pushed through the doors and crossed the casino. Pemberton followed him into the fray. It was a bit like being dropped into a pinball machine. The patrons were old and beetled about at their own pace. The smell of cigarette smoke hung in the air like gas. O'Nan pointed out various features over a barrage of electronic bells and whistles: battered information kiosks, faded floor signage, threadbare carpet and a chintzy-looking high-limit area. Pemberton struggled to keep up.

The Chop House hostess greeted O'Nan by name and sat them in a quiet corner of the restaurant.

"Did you get a load of the rack on that one?" O'Nan asked after the hostess retreated to her station. "Grade A sweater meat."

Pemberton smiled. An image of Kiki bending naked over the glass coffee table swam through his memories. He urged himself to focus, to keep his eye on the prize, as they said. They ordered drinks and dinner—nonalcoholic beer and a porterhouse steak for O'Nan, sparkling water and red snapper served Yukemaya style for Pemberton—and got down to business. Pemberton fired the first salvo of what he hoped would be a long and one-sided campaign.

"How long have you been at Thunderclap?" Pemberton asked.
"Three months."

The answer took Pemberton by surprise. He should have known this, and he regretted not having had the time to research his potential employer. But it didn't matter. O'Nan was a talker. Within the first five minutes, he let it be known that he drove a Porsche, lived on a yacht, and owned a huge house in Las Vegas. (A mansion really.) He dropped three "fuckheads" and referred to one of his ex-wives as "a ferocious yap cunt." He said the word *Thunderclap* like it was a sexually transmitted disease. Pemberton thought this breed of ad man went extinct when the dot.com bubble burst and the Twin Towers fell, but the dapper little white-haired fire hydrant was just getting started. O'Nan had a knack for neologisms, an aptitude for slurs and slander, and an oddly willful kind of cluelessness when it came to the application of idiomatic expressions, which he called "O'Nanisms." (Oh yes he did.) All of which seemed at odds with the war stories he kept dredging up from the golden age of Las Vegas casino marketing back when dinosaurs still roamed the earth.

"Way before computers and sexual harassment and all that horseshit."

The food arrived and Pemberton received a small surprise: The fish still had its head attached. So that's what *served Yukemaya style* meant.

"I see you like a little head with your snapper," O'Nan said as he sawed into his steak. "Man after my own heart."

Pemberton poked at his fish with some reluctance, unnerved by the eye staring up at him. In his experience, fish eyes turned white when cooked, but this one gleamed with preternatural intensity.

O'Nan flipped through Pemberton's crude portfolio. "I don't see any radio here."

"I can assure you I have excellent references."

"References schmeferences. You know how to dominate a small market?"

"Frequency?" Pemberton guessed.

"Goddamn right. You plug the holes and you keep on plugging them."

O'Nan's metaphor conjured up images of Ricky screwing Kiki while his own penis impersonated a turtle retreating into its shell. This wasn't going well, Pemberton thought, and he was running out of time. He went all in.

"A man of your wisdom and experience. I'm sure I can learn a lot from you."

O'Nan liked this. He softened somewhat, and his voice lowered to a register Pemberton recognized—with a barely suppressed shudder—as paternal.

"I can be a prickly pear. I know that. But that's how I learned, and that's how I teach. Do you think you can you handle that? Because if you can't, you're wasting my time."

Pemberton nodded. He was a capacious nodder.

"Do you gamble?"

Only with my happiness, Pemberton thought. "Sometimes."

"Poker's my game. Terrible luck, but I know faces. You want to know what yours is telling me?"

Pemberton wasn't sure how to answer. His strategy had gone sideways. He should be the one asking the questions, not O'Nan. The last thing he wanted was a candid conversation. Being open and frank would get Pemberton nowhere.

"By all means," he croaked.

"You look like a guy on a bad run. I see it every day. Can't catch a break no matter what you do. Play it safe, throw caution to the wind, but nothing works. You know you're just pissing opportunities away, and there's not a damn thing you can do to stop it."

Pemberton chewed carefully so that when he swallowed the snapper had a chance of making it past the lump in his throat, and though he fought it, a wave of despair washed over him.

"Oh, you'll bounce back," O'Nan continued. "You always do. But you know that someday you won't. That day comes for all of us, the day we're forced to accept that things are as good as they're ever going to get and it's all downhill from here. I've had that day. But the question remains, Is today yours? How am I doing? Am I close?"

"You're not lying."

O'Nan laughed. "Guys like us in a place like this? I mean look around!"

Pemberton took a drink of his sparkling water. This wasn't nearly as much fun as his last job interview.

"Tell me something," O'Nan said. "If I were to offer you the position right now, you'd take it, wouldn't you?"

"Yes," he said with a dash of incredulity at having broken the unwritten rule of employment interviews.

"I knew it!" O'Nan pounded the table, made the silverware dance. "It takes guts to lay your cards on the table like that, and I appreciate it. I really do. So I'm gonna show you *my* cards and tell you exactly what's what. All right? Let's cut the bullshit and get down to brass tacks."

Don't. Say. A thing.

"I'm putting together an in-house agency," O'Nan continued. "I'm tired of getting gouged by third-rate shops downtown. Every time there's a problem they need a fucking meeting. Then they bill me for the hour it takes to drive out here and the hour to drive back. Fuck that. I understand that things are tough and the economy has everyone by the balls, but I'm not running a goddamn charity. The gravy train is closed. You know big-boy ad agencies. You know how it is. No one I've interviewed has half your experience. You're my guy. But if I let you walk out of here and go back to L.A., I'll never get you back on the rez again."

"There's always that chance," Pemberton bluffed.

"I know you're lying, but that's okay. At least you're trying. Here's what's going to happen next: I'm going to offer you the job, and you're going to take it."

"I am?"

"Yes, but on one condition. Your ass stays here."

"Excuse me?"

"After you sign your offer of employment, there's a waiting period while the gaming commission conducts a background check. You legally can't work during your waiting period, but I want you here in Falls City ready to go the second it clears."

"How long does that take?"

"A day. Maybe two. Sometimes longer, but rarely. It's just a formality. What do you say?"

There wasn't much to think about. Of course he was going to accept, but now that O'Nan had shown his hand, Pemberton was obliged to counter.

"I'll have to go back to L.A. to move my belongings. Say my goodbyes."

"Negative. Have them shipped. Make some calls."

"It's not that easy, there's a woman . . ."

"Send flowers."

"I'll need a relocation allowance."

"I'll give you a grand."

"Up front."

"Charge your expenses, and I'll make sure you're reimbursed."

"I can't do that," Pemberton confessed. "I'm flat-busted."

There. Now *everything* was on the table. O'Nan tilted his head down so he could peer at Pemberton over his glasses. Something like sympathy floated to the surface of his features, but it might be pity. Pemberton never could tell the difference.

"You really are a piece of work." O'Nan took some papers out of his jacket pocket and slapped them on the table.

"Read it, sign it, and bring it back tomorrow morning. I'll have payroll cut a check for you."

"Thank you."

O'Nan glanced at his watch. "I have to go."

"Your other interview," Pemberton said with a wry smile.

"What?" O'Nan snapped.

"The other candidate?"

"There is no other candidate, shit-for-brains." O'Nan got up from the table, peeled a hundred-dollar bill from his money clip, and tossed it on the table. "They're going to want a urine sample tomorrow, so don't show up drunk."

"Of course not," Pemberton said.

"Of course not, he says," O'Nan replied with a smile full of crooked tombstones.

Pemberton worked the numbers while he watched O'Nan leave. It had been less than forty-eight hours since he snorted the last of Kiki's cocaine. If his urine was tested, he would fail. He should just take O'Nan's hundy and make a run for it. But where would he go? And how would he get there? He should at least stick around until the relocation check cleared. That was the smart play. It was a shitty play, but it was the only one he had.

Pemberton was suddenly starving. He picked at the fish with his fork, but the fish was too lean, the meat overcooked. He jabbed the snapper in the eye in frustration. A black ichorous discharge spurted onto his shirt; it occurred to Pemberton that he was going about this all wrong.

"IT WASN'T A SEIZURE." Alice crossed her arms, dug in. She wasn't going to sign any paperwork until they showed her the tape. Until she saw what happened with her own eyes, she wasn't signing anything. She had been sitting in the tribal security office for over two hours, but she had no intention of backing down. She knew they had to resolve the situation before they could go home. She could see it written all over Melinda's square, mannish face.

Melinda scowled. Mike sighed. They agreed to let her watch the tape.

"You take her," Melinda said.

Mike brought Alice to Surveillance, a walk that involved an elevator ride up to the third floor, a part of the casino she had never been to before. Alice sensed an ally in Mike. He kept looking at her when he thought she wasn't paying attention. Not creepy, but concerned. Maybe something else . . .

Mike used his key card on an unmarked door and led Alice into a room with the lights turned down low. The computer monitors and video screens glowed in the gloom. Tinted one-way windows overlooked the Forest of Fortune and Thunderclap Falls, a mechanically controlled indoor waterfall that was the casino's pride and joy.

A white guy Alice's age sat at the console and manipulated the equipment. He had blond highlights and bleached teeth. She wondered why someone who sat in the dark all day would go to such trouble. She found an empty chair and sat down. Mike stood by the door.

"Here we go," the tech said.

The big screen came to life. Alice stiffened, her scalp tingling with anticipation. The cameras peered down at the machines in the Forest of Fortune. There she was, inserting a pass card into the machine. It felt so strange to see herself up there on the screen, like an out-of-body experience. Then all of a sudden she was writhing on the floor. Alice leaned forward to get a closer look. Loot Caboose was an endcap, a gaming device that sat at the end of a bank of slot machines in a high-traffic area. She watched herself roll into the passageway, where the cameras got a good look at her as she thrashed around on the carpet like a freak show. So. Embarrassing.

"It would have been a lot worse if you'd stayed between the banks," the tech said.

Worse than what? Alice stopped herself from asking, but she knew what he meant. The slot machines were made of metal and glass with lots of hard angles and sharp edges. Even the chairs were solid. Plenty of ways to crack a tooth, break a bone, or knock herself unconscious.

The seizure lasted less than a minute, but seemed much longer. As she watched, her eyes kept drifting to the clock at the right-hand corner of the screen, counting down the seconds. She wanted to scream. She wanted to run. The shame felt like it would last forever. But when the video ended, she asked to see it again.

The tech sighed, annoyed. Alice could sense them looking at her in the dark. She tried to focus on the screen but was distracted by the glare on the front of the Loot Caboose, a place where the belly glass caught the light and made the game glow.

"What's that light?" she asked.

"What light?" the tech asked, just to fuck with her.

"On the machine," Alice answered. "That glare."

"Hot spot. It's nothing."

It was *all* a big nothing. She was hoping to get a clue as to what triggered the seizure. Why here? Why now? But the video told her nothing. Alice was already starting to feel a weird detachment from the events on the screen, as if they'd happened to someone else. She was over it. The shame. The embarrassment. All of it. She studied her body as it rolled from side to side, her arms and legs flailing spastically about, a weird locomotion that God never intended. She was amazed by how much ground she covered. But toward the end of the video, Alice noticed something new. There was a woman standing near the open door of the slot machine, dressed in tattered rags like a homeless person, flickering in and out of the frame. There and not there. The hot spot, the glare, whatever it was, made it difficult to see her. The woman seemed taller than the other guests, clearly out of place. Then she got it: The woman wasn't *standing* there because her feet weren't touching the ground. She was *floating*.

Alice panicked. Didn't they see her on the video monitor? Couldn't they see the woman *climb into the machine* as the clip ended?

"Oh my God."

"What?" Mike asked.

"I saw something," Alice whispered, her voice barely there.

"You shouldn't even be here," the tech whined as he wiped the clip off the screen. "You had a seizure. Deal with it."

Alice felt like grabbing him by the hair and smashing his teeth into the monitor. The smart thing would be to let it go. She was pushing her luck. If they didn't see the woman climb into the machine and disappear, why bring it to their attention?

Because if they didn't see what Alice saw, she was in deep trouble.

"Just one more time," Alice pleaded.

The tech looked to Mike for support. Mike remained in the same spot by the door, arms crossed over his burly chest. "Play it for her."

The tech slowly spun his chair around, making a big show of his annoyance.

There she was again: Alice working, Alice opening the door, Alice flopping on the floor. It was all so *normal* looking. What had seemed terrifying a few moments ago had become dull. It was like she'd been given a window into the past, and the past was tiresome. She kept her gaze fixed on the Loot Caboose, but this time she didn't see the woman. She simply wasn't there.

"Did either of you see um . . . a woman?" Alice asked, her heart, her whole fucking rib cage, trying to muscle into her throat.

"Where?" Mike asked, but he was just trying to be nice, which was more annoying than the tech that was actually trying to piss her off.

"By the machine . . ."

The tech hit a button and the image froze on the screen, but there was nothing to see.

"*I* don't see anything," he said.

"Me either," Mike added, looking more and more uncomfortable.

"I swear there was something there," Alice said.

"There's nothing," the tech replied.

Alice stared at the screen, a million maybes swirling in her head. Maybe she was mistaken. Maybe it was only a hot spot after all. Maybe it was nothing more than a reflection in the glass panel. Maybe she hallucinated the whole thing.

"I don't want to be sick!" Alice shouted.

"Do you need a bucket or something?" Mike asked.

"Do I look like I need a fucking bucket?" Alice snapped.

The tech shrugged as if to say, You brought her here, she's your problem now.

"Let's see if we can find someone to take you home," Mike prodded, but Alice was no longer listening.

PEMBERTON WAS RELIEVED to see the lights on inside the rental office, but even though the door was open, the office was empty. This time Pemberton was ready for Sam the Armenian to appear through the side door, and he didn't have to wait long.

"You're back!" Sam exclaimed. "Welcome home!"

"Change of plans. I decided to keep my room."

A dark look crossed Sam's features. "I just cleaned it."

A sinking feeling settled into Pemberton's stomach as he followed Sam's gaze to a clear plastic garbage bag resting on the floor near his feet.

"Did you rent it out already?" Pemberton asked.

"No, but you checked out."

"If it's available, I'd like to check back in."

"Okay," Sam brightened, "that will be forty dollars."

"But I already paid for the night."

"Yes, but you checked out."

"I know I checked out, and now I'm checking in again. You told me you don't rent rooms by the hour, so my forty dollars should be good until checkout tomorrow."

Sam gave this some thought.

Pemberton didn't understand why this was so difficult. "Look, I'm still wearing your coat. I wouldn't have left without returning your coat."

This made sense to Sam. "Of course. No charge for you," Sam said, "but I have to get your linens." Sam left him with another registration form to fill out and disappeared through the side door.

Pemberton considered the possibility that Sam was not all there. Pemberton bent to the task of completing the form and accidentally nudged the trash bag with his foot. There was a whisky bottle in there. His bottle. There was still plenty of whisky left in the bottle and it wasn't too far down in the bag. About arm-deep. Easily reachable. Pemberton cast a glance at the side door and slipped his hand inside the trash bag. He reached between some empty soda cans and grabbed the bottle, but it slipped from his fingers as he tried to pull it out. He gave it another go and this time he got a solid grip on the bottle. Except it wasn't a bottle. It was something else. Something cold and furry and squishy. Something with a face. Something dead.

Pemberton yanked his arm out of the bag, scattering trash across the floor. He scanned the beer cans, tea bags, used-up tissues, but whatever he felt wasn't there. Nothing furry or dead. Just the bottle of whisky that he snatched up just as Sam came through the door with his linens. Pemberton was at a loss for words. What do you say when you've been caught picking through the trash? It was his own trash, but still . . .

"Here," Sam said, pushing a pile of sheets at Pemberton. The key to his room sat in the center like a bird in its nest.

Pemberton slipped the bottle into his coat pocket, wiped his hands on his pants, and took the linens. "Sorry about the mess."

"Checkout is at noon."

Pemberton nodded and scampered back to the cabin. He fumbled with the key at the door. The cabin was freezing, but he went right to the sink to pour a drink. Ramona scowled at him from the wall. The dregs of the whisky sloshed around the bottom of the bottle. Between two and three fingers: definitely worth the trouble, but not nearly enough to get him through the night.

LIGHTS WOBBLED ACROSS THE CEILING in trembling waves. A knot of anxiety worried loose, turned into something else.

Oh, no . . .

Another one?

No.

It was just her roommate pulling into the driveway. Alice lowered the volume on the television and listened to Lisa's approach: tires shifting gravel, emergency brake engaging, music thumping through car windows rolled up against the cold. Lisa was a cocktail waitress and a drug peddler. Alice didn't care what else she was so long as she kept it out of their trailer, but the boundaries were getting blurry. She liked Lisa, but she couldn't say the same about the company she kept.

The music cut out. Alice tensed. If she heard voices in the parking lot, she'd bolt for her bedroom. One set of footsteps mounted the porch. Keys jingled, the lock slid open, and Alice relaxed. It was only Lisa, no one else.

"What's up, kiddo?" Lisa seemed surprised to see Alice sitting on the sofa with a bandage on her cheek.

Alice didn't know how to answer, where to start, what to say. The words didn't come, only tears. Lisa stood in the open doorway. It was already ten degrees colder in their tiny shitbox of a trailer.

"You had another seizure?"

Alice nodded. "A big one."

Lisa shut the door, shed her jacket, joined Alice on the sofa. She tucked her legs under the blanket and touched Alice's face with her cold fingers. "Did you hurt yourself?"

"It's nothing."

"What happened?"

"I don't know," Alice answered, already a little exasperated by Lisa's barrage of questions, her own inability to answer them, the anger welling up inside her.

It had been months since her last seizure, but six weeks ago, Alice started getting headaches. Not the ordinary sinus swelling, but bullets to the brain that left her dizzy, nauseous, and weak in the knees for anywhere from three minutes to three hours before mysteriously going away. She tried to schedule an appointment with her on-again, off-again psychiatrist, Dr. Marcus, but he was booked solid until after Thanksgiving, so he prescribed a pain reliever over the phone.

"I don't normally do this," he said, "but I know how serious you are about your treatment."

Alice hated that word. She wasn't an alcoholic like her mother. The only thing she was trying to recover from was the shitty hand life had dealt her.

The pills didn't help. They didn't do a thing for the mind-scrambling migraines that came with irregular regularity. She didn't know what to do about them, where else to turn, so she did something she swore she'd never do: She smoked marijuana.

She didn't mean to get high. She was hungry and the weekend was opening up before her like a circus tent, a vast space she had no idea how she was going to keep from collapsing. The smallness of the trailer exasperated her. She wanted to go out and do something normal. Have dinner. See a movie. Go dancing. Then the headache hit, a knee-buckler that dropped her to the floor. The worst of it passed almost immediately but then little angry waves—like a radio station fading in and out—assaulted her for the better part of an hour. This was new. This was awful. This was fucking unacceptable.

Alice knee-walked to the sofa, reached underneath, and withdrew a dinner plate that held Lisa's stash: a small pile of weed, a ceramic bowl, and a lighter. The pungent green marijuana, so unlike the brown swag her friends in the desert used to smoke, beckoned her. She put a pinch in the bowl, sparked the lighter, and lowered the flame. She sucked for all she was worth and exhaled a funnel of smoke. At first she feared the smoke would linger, then she worried the smoke detector might go off, and finally she nearly freaked herself out imagining she would die in a fire because Lisa hadn't replaced the battery as she'd promised. Alice returned the bowl and the lighter to the plate and slid it along the carpet, which needed to be vacuumed, until it was safely under the couch, which needed to be replaced. How did the television get on? Alice couldn't remember. She tried to turn it off, but the remote was as complicated as a central processing unit. The TV screen seemed so big it could suck her right in and then where would she be? Alice didn't know. She couldn't recall Channel 6 being so interesting, nor could she remember pouring a bowl of cereal or opening Lisa's Oreos, but her headache had totally disappeared.

When her roommate returned, Alice confessed her crimes, which delighted Lisa, who told Alice she was a shoo-in for a medical marijuana permit. Something of a drug connoisseur, Lisa cooked up schemes for getting them both registered. Soon they'd be rolling in ganja. They laughed. A couple of trailer-park drug lords in tank tops and Old Navy pajama bottoms decorated with chocolate bars and bunny rabbits. But it only took a few hours before the remorse set in, then dread, followed by quick hits of fear as scenes flashed through her brain: Alice's mother emerging from under a filthy blanket to puke on the floor and return again to the cave of her mattress without cleaning up the mess; her mother crawling across the living room to drink the vodka one of her boyfriends had poured into a dog dish; her mother in the morgue, pieces of her anyway, after she was hit by a train.

Alice wriggled her toes underneath her roommate's blanket. "It was really freaky, Lisa."

"Freaky how?"

"I think I saw something."

"During your seizure?"

Alice nodded.

"Saw what?"

Alice hesitated. How do you put your worst fears into words? "A ghost."

"No way!"

"I'm pretty sure."

Alice nodded and tried to explain what she'd seen in the Forest of Fortune. She told Lisa all about the video, the hot spot, the woman, everything.

"Ohmygod! I totally have goose bumps!" Lisa made Alice run her hands up and down Lisa's arms. Her skin felt rubbery to the touch. "I always knew the casino was haunted. I bet all kinds of spooky Indian shit went down here. No offense."

Alice instantly regretted telling Lisa the story. Coming from her dope-smoking, conspiracy-minded roommate, what convulsed Alice with panic now sounded naïve, borderline stupid. That was when she remembered the drug test.

"Oh, shit."

"What?" Lisa asked, distracted by the plate of marijuana on her lap and her incessantly chirping cell phone as text message after text message arrived.

"That time I smoked your weed?"

"Yeah?"

"They tested me today."

"Oh, shit!"

"Yeah, *oh shit.*" Alice did the math. Twenty-five days. "How long does it stay in your system?"

"Like, a month."

"I thought it was three days?"

"That's coke or speed."

Alice tucked her chin into the collar of her oversize sweatshirt. "I totally nuked it."

"You don't know that. It's not like you went in there high or anything."

"What should I do?"

"There's nothing you can do. Except . . ."

"What?" Alice asked.

"Not worry about it." Lisa offered Alice the bowl she'd just packed.

Alice shook her head. Not worrying wasn't one of her strong suits. She fought off a twinge of low-grade jealousy as Lisa put the pipe in her mouth and flicked the lighter. The glow from the bowl illuminated Lisa's doll face and porcelain skin. She was beautiful. She deserved more than the guys who chased her could offer, and she didn't even realize it. The light dimmed; her eyes went glassy. Lisa looked up at the ceiling and fired the smoke through her nostrils. Lisa the party dragon. Alice watched the cloud drift and disperse. It was always at weird moments like this when she missed the reservation the most. The too-blue sky, the impossible clouds, the hills in the distance like a chain of elephants galumphing across the horizon. She'd give anything to go back, but going back was the same thing as going nowhere. The world spun so much faster now; she'd never make it. Alice clutched the seat cushions, afraid she'd be flung from the sofa. Somewhere out there a voice called her name, growing louder and more insistent.

"What?" she snapped.

"I didn't say anything," Lisa said.

"You didn't say my name just now?"

"You're kind of freaking me out."

"Sorry."

"You sure you don't want to hit this?"

Alice shook her head. She was so exhausted she couldn't say another word. She always forgot how tired the big ones left her, how wrecked she felt afterward. She needed less confusion not more. Alice pulled the sweatshirt over her knees, turtled her neck inside and willed herself to sleep.

Lupita woke on the sectional sofa in her living room, shivering under an Indian blanket. A crippling hangover and a deepening suspicion she wasn't alone competed for her attention. For the last hour or so, the former had held the upper hand, but now the dread was creeping in, too powerful to ignore. She tried to dismiss it as the remnants of a dream brought on by a late dinner at the casino and way too much wine, but the presence of an odor, sharp and feral-smelling, left her feeling violated.

She'd had another dream about Alejandro. They were making love on a table in his father's bakery. She couldn't see him, but she knew it was Alejandro by his rough touch. An explosion of flour, a swamp of sticky sweetness, the table galloping around the room from their exertions. When they finished, she tried to get a look at him but he no longer appeared in her dreams. Instead, she saw herself as he saw her, her brown body slick with sweat and powdered with sugar. She looked pale, like a calaquita. She awoke disoriented and confused because how could she be the woman on the table *and* the one looking down at herself *at the same time?*

She swung her bare feet onto the cold tile. There was nothing on the coffee table she could use as a weapon except the empty bottle of Chardonnay. It would have to do. She moved to the middle of the room to peek into the kitchen, brandishing the buttery-yellow bottle by the neck. The problem was immediately apparent: She'd left the sliding glass door to her patio open and some creature had crept out of the canyon that bled into her backyard and ransacked her kitchen.

She yelled to scare off whatever might be hiding in the corners, but nothing moved.

Lupita inched into the kitchen. She could smell it immediately: a musky piss-reek. There was urine all over the tile floor and on the throw rug she kept between the stove and breakfast bar. The trashcan had been upended, the refuse scattered across the kitchen. Muddy paw prints marked the path of a frenzied debauch, but she couldn't quite make them out. They could belong to a small dog, a large cat, or maybe even a coyote. Whatever it was could be lurking in the canyon, waiting for her. She skirted the stain to slide the patio door shut, making the odor that much more intense.

Lupita wasn't a morning drinker, but when she went looking for something to wash down the aspirin (well, not aspirin exactly) she found a screw-top bottle of cold Chardonnay in the fridge and poured three fingers into a clean glass. It didn't do anything for her hangover. If anything, being up on her feet made her feel worse. The light coming through the windows—it must have been close to noon already—felt like an assault, but the wine calmed her nerves and let her think clearly as she gathered her cleaning supplies.

She went upstairs to her bedroom to change out of the smoky clothes she'd worn to the casino and into a tank top and a pair of sweats. She wrapped her hair in a bandana. In the bathroom, she ignored how awful she looked and addressed her reflection in the mirror: *You can do this.* She returned to the kitchen to pull on a pair of yellow rubber gloves when her cell phone rang.

"Qué pasó?"

"Good morning, Lupita," Denise said in an uncharacteristically bubbly voice. "Just calling to make sure you remembered my appointment."

"Ai!" She'd forgotten she was supposed to take Denise to the doctor this afternoon. Denise was convinced she had cancer, but refused to get looked at by a real doctor. Instead, she'd been going to see a holistic practitioner every other week. This made Lupita crazy. Until her friend went to see a *real* doctor, Lupita refused to take the diagnosis seriously. The practitioner saw his patients in a trailer on the Indian reservation, for heaven's sake!

"Don't tell me you forgot . . ."

"I'm sorry, Denise."

"I know you don't approve, but I know what I'm doing, Lupita."

Lupita paused. Since when did her approval mean anything to Denise? "I don't understand why you're throwing money away on this curandero when you have health insurance!"

"He's a specialist, Lupita. A certified homeopath."

Denise went on and on about the "corruption of Western health care," and it reeked worse than the piss on her kitchen floor. When she moved on the deplorable state of heath care in California's prison system, Lupita lost her patience and told her friend she'd be there soon.

"My appointment is in an hour," Denise said in a clipped voice.

"I'll leave as soon as I can. I have to finish something." An hour wasn't enough time to clean up the mess in her kitchen, pick up Denise, and make it to her appointment, but Lupita didn't care. She ended the call, drank her wine, and splashed more Chardonnay into her glass. The wine wasn't very good, but it was cold and would speed up the medication she'd taken to relieve the pressure in her head, which just grew and grew and grew.

The door chime rang, and the sound startled her. Lupita crossed to the living room and peered through the window. It was her sister Mariana. They hadn't spoken in weeks.

"Oh, it's you," Lupita said when she opened the door.

"Just your overbearing big sister you never call anymore."

Mariana inherited their mother's imperious tone. She was the prettier of the two Garcia sisters. In her youth, she was like a sirena: Men drifted by, got sucked into her vortex, and floundered there like the helpless creatures they were. Many years passed before she settled down with her meek little husband from Mexico City, and now she had two beautiful niñas of her own. Mariana's skin was supple and smooth and well cared for. That was their mother's doing, and it was the only thing Lupita had in common with her sister. Though Lupita's features seemed to her crude in comparison—thick lips, wide nose, ridiculously long eyelashes, and eyes so big they bulged when she got upset—she possessed two gifts Mariana lacked: beautiful hair and a musical walk. Alejandro, the one great love of her life, was entranced by the swinging of her braids and the swaying of her rump, all that flesh in beautiful concert. Lupita didn't have particularly good teeth and for years she kept them hidden by not smiling. She would never let a boy see her smile, which had the effect of making her plainer than she already felt in her sister's shadow. *All women are beautiful when they smile*, Alejandro told her after they married, and it saddened her to realize he was right. All those wasted years . . . But it was true that Mariana envied her hair. Mariana's hair was a riot of curls she didn't have the patience to tame. But Lupita's hair had always been long and lustrous. *Like a living thing*, her mother often said. Taking care of her hair was how Lupita secured her mother's approval.

"To what do I owe the honor?"

"I was at the cemetery this morning,"

Last week was Día de Los Muertos. Lupita usually decorated their parents' graves, but time had gotten away from her. "I've been busy."

"Aren't you going to invite me in?" Mariana asked.

"No."

"That's really rude."

"I'm dealing with some things here. Besides I'm leaving."

Mariana looked her up and down. "Like that?"

Sometimes it felt like she and her sister were stuck in some weird adolescence, never deviating from the roles they'd been given when they were too young to know any better, but Lupita didn't take the bait. Although Lupita was older, they were so close in age she'd never had much authority over Mariana. If anything, Mariana was the favored one. Because of her beauty. Because of her height. Because their mother loved her more. Well that shit was going to stop.

"I have to take a friend to a doctor's appointment."

"What's going on, Lupita? The girls and I are worried."

"Oh, right. *The girls*." It was a wild thing, her anger. She'd managed to keep it under control, but she could feel it slipping its leash.

"What's that supposed to mean?"

"If you have something to say," Lupita snarled, "say it, but don't use *the girls* as an excuse to pry into my life."

"Who's prying? I'm just checking up on you. You don't return my calls."

Mariana never missed an opportunity to remind Lupita of her shortcomings. Lupita couldn't stand it, but she was too tired to keep fighting like this.

"Mariana?"

"Yes?"

Lupita hesitated. She was angry and annoyed, frightened and confused. She felt like she'd lost her grip on something precious while leaning over the edge of a cliff; as long as it kept falling she didn't have to deal with the loss, but once it hit bottom and was irretrievably gone, she didn't know what would become of her.

"How are they?"

"The girls? They're fine. Elodia's taking dance lessons, and Yasmina's excited about her birthday, but you'd know this if you'd spend some time with them."

"Tell them I'll come for a visit soon."

"When? You can't just—"

"Good bye, Mariana. I have to go."

Lupita slammed the door in her sister's face. They'd barely spoken since their big fight when Lupita told her she was "worse than Mom," and Mariana had to go and bring up all that bad business with Alejandro. But Lupita didn't feel sorry for herself. Instead, she crouched on all fours and bent to her task. She sprayed the brownish-orange stain with disinfectant and scrubbed it with a brush. This did the trick, made the mess easier to wipe up. But it also released an odor, stronger than before, which assaulted her senses made delicate by last night's excesses. After a few minutes of scrubbing, she began to feel woozy. Her head throbbed; her stomach churned. She gasped, trying to bring in more air, which proved to be a mistake. Her breath caught, her throat opened, and she spewed a vile yellow fluid that splattered off the tile and splashed all over her.

She scrambled to the sink, but when she realized her top was a lost cause, she yanked the sliding glass door open and stormed into the backyard as she peeled off her filthy clothes and hurled them into the canyon.

WHILE RIDING THE THUNDER SHUTTLE to the casino, Pemberton planned his strategy for winning Debra back.

On a hot summer morning that seemed like ages ago, his ex-fiancée informed him that when he came home from work in the evening she'd be gone. Debra didn't give a reason; she didn't need to. He'd gone out for drinks with some coworkers the night before, stayed out late, ignored her text messages and phone calls, and drove home under the influence. She'd had enough: *Your drinking is going to get you into trouble, and I won't be there to bail you out.*

Pemberton thought she was bluffing. Debra was a grandstander, a woman who ran on high emotion. She'd made threats like this plenty of times during the two-and-a-half years of their engagement, and he'd always managed to mitigate her concerns. This time, or so he'd figured, would be no different. Sure, he liked his liquor and suffered the occasional lapse in judgment. Who didn't? He was in advertising, after all. Excess came with the territory. But it's not like he was some hack with a bottle sloshing around his desk. He wasn't an LCD (lowest common denominator) or EDP (emotionally disturbed person). He was a *useful member of society.* Yes, he took long lunches at the cantina where Sharon Tate had her last meal before Charles Manson got hold of her. He often went out with coworkers to celebrate a new account, a successful campaign, or the simple drudgery of the day, and came home later than he'd promised and more inebriated than he'd intended to find the bedroom door locked and his pillow on the sofa. He went to the couch without complaint and in the morning tiptoed around Debra's frosty glare until her cold shoulder began to thaw. And it always thawed.

Pemberton went to work on the morning Debra announced she was leaving him and promptly forgot all about it. He'd been tasked with helping the production team put the finishing touches on a presentation and the hours marched along. When the presenters left to make their pitch, Pemberton went to the Irish saloon on the other side of the tar pits. He usually drank at this pub with his colleagues, including his supervisor's supervisor who shared Pemberton's weakness for spirits, but there was no one to accompany him that afternoon so he went alone. He sat at a cocktail table between oil portraits of Brendan Behan and Dylan Thomas and was well into his fourth whisky when he got the call: One of the presenters had become violently ill, and even though it was generally accepted that Pemberton was not a people person, he was summoned to the corporate offices of a massive Japanese electronics and entertainment conglomerate.

"Be right there," Pemberton slurred into his cell phone. "The cavalry is on its way."

Pemberton emerged from the murky pub without his sunglasses and squinted at the light slanting sideways from seemingly everywhere at once, wondering where the hell he'd parked his car. When he finally found it, an old Lincoln Continental, he slid behind the wheel and promptly careened into a slow-moving Cadillac, driven by the elderly wife of a prominent Hollywood producer with close ties to the very same entertainment and electronics conglomerate Pemberton's colleagues were trying to win over.

The repercussions were disastrous. Pemberton was arrested, dismissed from the agency, and harangued by Debra when she came to bail him out. "I *knew* this would happen," she said over and over again. Pemberton kept his mouth shut. A wrecked car, a revoked license, and blood alcohol twice the legal limit were not so easily explained away, but at least she didn't dump him.

Yet.

Debra handed down an ultimatum during breakfast the next day. "You've got three months to get your act together."

"What does that mean exactly?"

Debra let her spoon clank into her bowl of cereal. "Not six, not four, but three months."

"No, I meant the other part."

"What other part?"

"Getting my act together."

"You figure it out!" Debra stormed off and locked herself in the bedroom, leaving Pemberton to ponder his predicament over a bowl of soggy flakes barnacled with flaxseed and cranberry crystals.

Pemberton scoured the Internet, networked with former colleagues, fired off dozens of applications. After a month went by without a single job interview, Pemberton lowered his expectations and started searching for part-time positions, using L.A.'s criminally haphazard public transportation system to meet with prospective employers. After another month passed, he began scrounging for freelance work: contract proofreading, web portal editing, social media maintenance. Entry-level copywriting gigs that paid peanuts. He even applied for a position at a skin mag as a blogger. A *blogger*. It was all so disheartening. Pemberton began to question his usefulness to society.

Naturally, he drank more than ever. To avoid Debra's wrath he started earlier in the day, sometimes immediately after she left for work. The sad fact of the matter was that on most afternoons Pemberton could be found riding the bus with the rest of L.A.'s LCDs and EDPs: bitter, shitfaced, and borderline incoherent.

Then he met Kiki and Ricky, and that was all she wrote, but his three-month window of opportunity was still open, which meant his chances of reconciliation were, technically speaking, still viable. He'd feel a lot better with a thousand bucks in his pocket and decided to call Debra at her office as soon as he collected his relocation check.

The trip to the casino only took a few minutes—the bus ride up the mountain seemed shorter this time—and he rang Donna from Human Resources from the casino lobby.

"Welcome to Thunderclap," she said. Donna was a middle-aged Pacific Islander, which Pemberton hadn't expected though he couldn't say why.

"Thanks."

"It's a good place to work," Donna continued as she took him to the tribal security office, "though the first few weeks can be a trial."

"Oh?"

"You'll pack on fifteen pounds and get supersick from all the bad air and rich food."

Supersickness? Donna made the casino sound toxic.

"Mike will take it from here," she said. "I'm going to step outside for a smoke."

Pemberton assumed the overmuscled tribal security officer with the crew cut was Mike. He clutched the collection kit with a massive hand.

"Right through there," he said, pointing to a door at the end of the hall. Pemberton went into the bathroom and urinated in the piss jug. He was hoping all the whisky and tea he'd drunk had flushed the cocaine out of his system, but he was alarmed at how dark his urine was.

He handed the warm bottle over to Mike, now wearing black latex gloves, as if the toxic nature of Pemberton's urine sample could contaminate him somehow. Pemberton signed and dated a label on a sticker sheet and Mike affixed it to the bottle.

"Is that it? Am I free to go?" Pemberton asked.

Mike glared at him for a long moment and walked away without saying a word. Pemberton thought the cops would be mellower out here, or at least less uptight than they were in L.A., but apparently he was wrong. Cops were cops.

Donna from Human Resources was waiting for him in the lobby with his check. "Not a bad trade," she said with a laugh. Her smile reminded him of Kiki.

"Is there anything else I need to sign?"

"That's it."

"Then I'll see you soon," he said as he moved toward the exit.

"Hope so. The approval process can take a while."

Pemberton stopped. "What's a while?"

"Couple weeks. Longer if any red flags pop up."

"O'Nan said a day or two."

"Of course he did," she said with a hint of a smile. Pemberton got the distinct impression there was something she wasn't telling him. Her mobile phone lit up, and her expression soured as she scrutinized the message that popped up on her screen.

"I have to go."

On his way out of the casino, Pemberton considered what might constitute a "red flag" when he stumbled upon a curious scene near the exit. An elderly woman had fallen and the paramedics were trying to prevent her from getting up. Apparently she'd had some kind of spell. She seemed distraught. Something about the wildness in her eyes made Pemberton uneasy and he scurried through the door and into the cold.

He hopped onto the Thunder shuttle and took a seat near the front. The bright lights of the casino's video display towered above the freeway and he wondered how he'd missed it before. The sign featured a waterfall and the tagline: THUNDERCLAP CASINO: A ROARING GOOD TIME.

"Sorry I'm late," Lupita said as Denise climbed into her SUV, dressed in flowing robes of lilac and lavender. An enormous hat crowned her head and overlarge sunglasses hid her eyes. White gloves completed the ensemble. Lupita thought Denise looked just like Mrs. Fitzmurphy, the eccentric white woman who'd lived down the street from her childhood home in Chula Vista. The old lady loved nothing more than to spend the afternoon working in her garden, but the sun had taken its toll on her skin so she went about the orderly rows of peppers and tomatoes dressed like a white Muslim, a ghost in broad daylight.

Denise removed her bonnet.

"Your hair!"

"I shaved it off." Denise seemed pleased with her reaction.

"Is it from chemotherapy?"

Denise shook her head. "It's not that kind of cancer."

"What kind of cancer is it then?"

Denise was vague. Instead of talking about her symptoms, she went on and on about how her baldness was "a symbol of solidarity for her fellow foot soldiers in the war on cancer."

Lupita sighed. This was *so* like Denise. Last year it was rescuing feral cats, and the year before that it was prison reform. Such a martyr. Was it the attention she craved? Or did she get some kind of satisfaction being on the side of the righteous after the sins of her past?

"Do you understand how difficult it is to get an appointment with Dr. Rodriguez?"

"I said I was sorry." Lupita's hangover had finally subsided, but the pungent mix of oils and lotions Denise was wearing made Lupita feel sick to her stomach all over again. Although it was barely two o'clock, the sun had surrendered to an armada of clouds. "Tell me about this doctor."

"He's a wonderful, wonderful man. He does great work." Denise gushed like she was talking about the pinche Pope. "I've consulted with him on the computer."

"Ah, the computer," Lupita said, like that explained everything. "What exactly does he do?"

"He's an Ayurvedic specialist."

"No, I mean, what does he do during these . . . sessions?" Lupita struggled to find the right word, knowing the wrong one would set Denise off.

"I think he's wonderful, the first truly positive presence in my life since I was diagnosed."

"But wasn't he the one who diagnosed you?"

"Yes, and that's precisely the point."

"And you haven't sought a second opinion?"

"Look, a tumbleweed!" Denise exclaimed, clapping her hands as it rolled across the asphalt. "I love tumbleweeds. They're so . . . resilient."

Lupita shook her head.

"Where was I?" Denise asked herself.

"Your diagnosis . . ."

"Dr. Rodriguez doesn't just hand out prescriptions. He doesn't want to give me something that will zonk me out and turn me into a zombie. He interviews each patient very thoroughly and works up a chart for them."

"You mean like an astrological chart?"

"Oh, no. It's much more comprehensive than that. He's charted me, inside and out. He knows my *soul*, Lupita."

There was that tone again, and it made Lupita sorry she asked.

"He's going to read me my chart this afternoon. If, that is, he'll still see me." Denise glanced at her watch for the hundredth time, even though there was a perfectly good clock on the dashboard.

Computers? Charts? Denise might as well go to the botanica and pin a milagro to the altar like Lupita's mother used to do whenever someone in the family got sick. Her parents never went to the doctor and didn't seem any worse for it. Their eyes grew dim, their hearing faltered, and their organs would go into a kind of hibernation from time to time, but nothing ever prevented them from rising with the roosters each morning and finding things to fill their day.

"Next exit," Denise said, pointing to the green sign that told them they were now entering the Yukemaya Indian Reservation.

"Are you sure about this?" Lupita regretted the question as soon as it left her lips.

"I've never been more certain of anything in my life!"

Lupita sighed. Denise wasn't sick. This was a hedge against the emptiness inside her. Cancer for Denise was a pose, a badge, a stigmata, the latest stop on her journey to martyrdom. She'd attached herself to another lost cause, only this time the cause was *her*, and she paid a quack to affirm what she was so desperate to hear: She was special, one in a million, uniquely unique.

Lupita didn't want to hear any more. As they zipped past the billboard for Thunderclap Casino with its electronic waterfall, the beginning of a plan formed in her mind. While Denise was being evaluated, she'd run down to the casino. Denise could call Lupita on her cell when she finished her business with Dr. Rodriguez. Lupita would grab some take-out at the Hong Kong Kafé, and they'd have dinner back at Denise's house on the hill. In this way, the day could be salvaged.

At the edge of the reservation, Denise indicated an access road with a gloved finger. Another sign pointed the way to the RV park.

"Here?" Lupita asked as she turned the truck.

"Yes," Denise whispered. She was on the verge of becoming emotional with anticipation, anxiety, or something else.

They pulled into the parking lot and a tall, dark-haired man emerged from one of the trailers. He was young and lean with a mop of borderline inappropriate hair, but good-looking nonetheless—and so was the woman he ushered through the trailer door. They were both putting on coats. He walked with his palm pressed into the center of her back toward a small red sedan. A much younger woman—the patient's daughter?—sat behind the wheel, glaring at them both.

"Are you sure this is right?" Lupita asked.

"Oh, yes," Denise said, her voice barely audible.

"When do you want me to come back?" Lupita asked.

"Come back?" Denise asked, clearly puzzled.

"I'm going to pop over to the casino."

"You're not going to wait?"

"I'll be just down the road. I'll have my phone with me."

Denise scowled. She opened the door and set one foot daintily on the gravel. "Artemio!" she cried. The Ayurvedic specialist, whatever that was, appeared caught off-guard, but he recovered quickly and flashed a smile.

"Are you my one-thirty?" he called from across the gravel parking lot.

"Yes!" Denise exclaimed. "Yes, I am!"

"A pleasure to see you again, Ms. Cavendish!"

"You, too, Dr. Rodriguez!"

Ordinarily, this would embarrass Lupita, but she was transfixed. How could someone so smart inside the casino be such an imbecile out of it? Denise swept across the lot and embraced the doctor. Lupita rolled down the window. She couldn't hear what they were saying, but she could figure it out. The doctor fished a cell phone out of his pocket and consulted the time.

"Come back at four!" Denise shouted, giddy as a schoolgirl.

Four? That was quite an examination. If Denise wanted to pretend she had cancer so she could flirt with some New Age healer in his glorified van, it was no business of hers, but as Lupita drove away, putting the RV park in her rearview mirror, she couldn't shake the feeling that something terrible had gotten hold of her friend, and it had her by the throat.

"WE HAVE A PROBLEM," Sam announced when Pemberton returned to the Trading Post. Pemberton had a feeling he knew what it was. "My card?"

Sam was visibly relieved. He clearly didn't relish his role as the antagonist in the daily dramas that popped up at the trailer park. "Do you have another?"

"Actually, no."

Sam's expression hardened again. "Are you trying to take advantage of me?"

"No, not at all." Pemberton produced his relocation check from the casino. "I have this."

"Even better."

"Can you cash it?"

"Of course, of course. It is not a problem. Are you in the system?"

"What system?"

"The payroll system."

"No. I mean, I will be, but not yet."

"So that's a no?"

"Yes." Pemberton tried to keep the frustration out of his voice.

"Many of our resident team members have their rent taken right out of their check," Sam said, "but I cannot help you . . ."

"Unless I'm in the system?"

"That's right."

"Is there a bank where I can cash this?"

"Falls City Savings."

"And where is that?"

"In San Diego."

Pemberton wanted to know why Falls City Savings was located fifty miles from Falls City but sensed it would be pointless to ask. The panic Pemberton felt in the casino returned, a fluttery jolt that seized his stomach and assaulted his imagination with worst-case scenarios that all had the same ending: Pemberton stuck in this hinterland with no money, no job, no jacket, and Debra gone for good.

"I suppose . . ." Sam held the check up to the light.

"Yes?"

"I could open up a line of credit for you."

"That would be great."

"I'd have to hold the check."

"Of course."

"Deduct your room rate and whatever supplies you need until you get in the system."

"Where do I sign?" Pemberton realized this meant he'd be stuck here until the gaming commission approved his application, but what if they didn't? Then what?

He followed Sam next door to the Trading Post where Pemberton shopped to the soundtrack of a football game blaring on the big-screen television behind the counter. Sam must record the contests and watch them during the week. Pemberton purchased six cans of soup, a tin of crackers, a bottle of bourbon, and a candy bar. Sam marked it all down in a ledger by the phone book and wished him a good night.

Pemberton put some water on for tea and the cabin felt a little cozier. When he'd unpacked his meager belongings, he'd discovered a pillowcase that Debra had mistakenly thrown out the window with the rest of his things. The pillowcase was redolent with pomegranate, Debra's favorite scent, and he wrapped it around his neck like a shawl when he sat down to call her. As he dialed her number, another call came through from a number he didn't recognize.

"Hear anything from the gaming commission?" O'Nan demanded.

"Nothing yet."

"Must have hit a red flag."

It had only been a day. Less than a day. He wasn't expecting to hear anything until next week at the earliest. Looking through the bars on his cabin window, talking on a cell phone whose bill was nearly two months past due, Pemberton wondered what to make of these "red flags" O'Nan kept referring to. What, exactly, were the gaming commissioners looking for? Were they going to talk to his old boss at the agency? Was his DUI going to be an issue? Why did a cabin on the edge of the wilderness need bars on its windows?

"If this is going to be a problem—" Pemberton began before O'Nan cut him off.

"Goddamn right it's a problem! I've got a pile of work waiting for you!"

"I mean with the gaming commission."

"Have you robbed any banks?"

"Not lately."

"Then consider it a mental health day." O'Nan chuckled darkly and ended the call. Pemberton was beginning to think it wouldn't be such a bad thing if his application didn't go through, but now that Sam had his relocation check, he was stuck.

Pemberton redialed Debra's number. The call took a long time to go through, as if it were navigating the growing distance between them. Finally a connection was made, and a previously recorded message told him the number was no longer in service. The tea kettle whistled its alarm.

Pemberton's mental health day stretched into a week. Then two weeks. His court date for the DUI hearing in Los Angeles came and went. He was so broke he couldn't afford a bus ticket much less the court fee. He drank every night and ate poorly. His diet was reduced to what he could forage from the shelves at the Trading Post: cans of soup, boxes of pasta products. He felt decidedly unhealthy, mentally and otherwise. Debra would say he wasn't adjusting to his new surroundings, and she would be right.

Each morning he walked Falls City's mile-long stretch of state highway with the freeway entrance at one end and the trailer park at the other with lots of empty storefronts and boarded-up buildings in between. The dilapidated structures housed makeshift businesses that had nothing to do with the signs above their doors. A taco shop had been converted into a garage. A pawnshop did business out of a day-care facility. The library was housed in a trailer and was open four hours a day during the week and closed on weekends. A malevolent wind blew nonstop as if it had a score to settle. Wild animals Pemberton never saw ravaged his trash. Gargantuan vehicles dieseled up and down the drag, keeping him awake at night. The harsh voices of cackling women drifted from trailers whose lights burned deep into the night, filling him with longing. L.A. felt thousands of miles away. He felt Debra's absence with a pointed ache and consoled himself with what-ever booze was on sale at the Trading Post: Central California wine, Canadian whisky, Caribbean rum. Within a matter of weeks, Pember-ton went from being the type of person who took his meals in hotel restaurants to a guy who hoofed it to the library for fifteen minutes of free Internet.

He found an old antique record player at the Trading Post. Its turntable, spindle, and arm were housed in a well-traveled suitcase. Sam put it on his tab and Pemberton spent the night spinning the few albums he'd salvaged the night Debra tossed his collection out the window. As he dropped the needle into the dusty grooves, Pemberton announced the names of the jazz musicians, just to hear the sound of his own voice. He turned the pages of books about casino marketing he'd checked out of the library: *Dream Catchers: How Indian Casinos Are Reimagining the American Dream* and *Poker in the Tepee: An Insider's Guide to Indian Gaming*. He tried not to think about what would hap-pen if he didn't get the job. In his dreams, he fed money into an enor-mous slot machine whose reels spun round and round.

On the eighteenth day, O'Nan summoned Pemberton to the casino. It was ten o'clock in the morning. The thermometer nailed to a post on the porch read twelve degrees. He'd just washed his dishes. In the beginning, he spent his afternoons pacing the cabin and burning off his anxiety by listening to records and completing mindless chores. After his first week in captivity, he started worrying about money again and drank to convince himself everything was going to be fine. Before long he was starting his day by polishing off what was left from the night before. His one good whisky tumbler sat glistening in the sink next to his alcohol supply. The dregs of last night's fun called out to him from the heel of the bottle, *Drink me!*

Pemberton obliged, and when the liquor was gone, he suited up and headed for the casino. He arrived at half-past ten; O'Nan made him wait until noon. In the lobby, Pemberton watched the people come and go. He studied decorative dreamcatchers and elaborate axes, which the faded cardboard placards identified as Yukemaya artifacts, until he felt he could close his eyes and describe every detail from memory: a museum of the mind filled with dream axes and dream dreamcatchers. The sameness of the people shuffling into the casino made him drowsy. He lost himself in the waterfall mural. Pemberton had never seen a real waterfall before, not even from a distance. It wasn't something he recognized as missing from his fund of experience until now. He would very much like to see one up close, not just as a spectator but to be immersed in the waterfall, to feel the spray on his skin, the force of all that falling water. What would that be like?

"Pemberton!"

Pemberton roused himself. "Good morning," he said to O'Nan, who looked shorter, rounder, and older than he remembered.

"Still with us, I see. I was afraid you'd taken a powder on me."

"I wouldn't do that."

"Save it. Come with me." Pemberton followed O'Nan through a door marked TEAM MEMBERS ONLY! The little man took the stairs two at a time. On the landing, a message above a mirror urged team members to START EVERY DAY WITH A THUNDERCLAP! Pemberton was more than a little dismayed to see team members actually clapping their hands as they went up and down the stairs.

O'Nan presented his badge for the casino cop's inspection and pushed through a door to a long subterranean passageway that connected the casino to the team member parking lots.

"Where are we going?"

"My car. Have you heard anything?"

"Nothing," Pemberton said.

"Well, it's out of my hands. It's those cocksuckers in gaming."

The Thunder tunnel ramped downward for two hundred feet and then headed up again, so Pemberton couldn't see the end until he was almost at the middle. Fluorescent lights flickered unevenly and massive banners declared inspirational messages. The one that marked the midway point stopped Pemberton in his tracks. It featured a smiling Korean-American actress named Jenny Parks, whom Pemberton had worked with on a television commercial in L.A. Jenny was murdered a few weeks ago, another Hollywood stalker story with a horrific ending. The caption read THUNDERCLAP TEAM MEMBERS ARE #1!

"Is something wrong?" O'Nan asked.

"I think I know her."

"Who? This chick?" O'Nan jerked his thumb at the supergraphic.

"Yeah, I worked with her."

"No kidding?"

"Toothpaste commercial."

"That was you? I remember that one."

Pemberton felt a secret thrill at having his work recognized by O'Nan. Every time one of his spots aired on TV or the radio, he was overcome with a desire to tell someone he'd written it, but whenever those opportunities arose he was invariably alone.

"She was one of my first spots for Thunderclap. Shot her right before she croaked."

As they continued walking through the tunnel toward the parking lot, O'Nan told Pemberton he never used employees as talent in advertising because it always backfired. The employee/actor inevitably did something scandalous, making the employee's appearance in even back-of-house signage an embarrassment. The most famous example was a Las Vegas blackjack dealer who was in cahoots with a team of card cheats. The dealer's grandfatherly mug was plastered all over town. After the collusion was exposed, it took weeks to track down and remove all the ads. Pemberton began to tell O'Nan about a similar situation he was involved in with a spokesman for a hotel chain, but O'Nan wasn't interested.

"We need to talk about your application."

"Okay."

"Is there anything you want to tell me?"

"Me? No." Technically, it wasn't a lie because Pemberton didn't *want* to tell O'Nan anything.

"Are you sure about that?"

Pemberton wasn't sure what he was sure of, but the longer this went on the more certain he was that O'Nan had found out about his DUI. They moved out of the tunnel and into cold sunlight. For the first time Pemberton could clearly see the surrounding mountains and the desert beyond. It was beautiful, breathtaking even.

"Is it unusual for applications to take this long?" Pemberton asked.

"Unusual? Yes. Unheard of? No." O'Nan pressed a button on his keychain and the lights on a red Porsche flashed. He opened a door and tossed his briefcase in the passenger seat where Pemberton would sit if O'Nan intended to take him somewhere.

"I know creatives," O'Nan continued, "because I am one myself. Our imaginations are our lifeblood, but sometimes they get us in trouble. If there's anything on your application you were a little *too* creative about, now's the time to tell me."

"There's nothing." The lie came easily, without effort.

"Good," O'Nan said, "I believe you."

Meaning he didn't. This would be more meaningful if they were in a field other than advertising.

"Hang tight," O'Nan said as he climbed into his Porsche. "Something's bound to shake loose soon."

He slammed the door, cranked the engine, and roared out of the parking lot like a teenager. Pemberton turned in time to catch his vanity plate: CAPN ART.

This was what O'Nan summoned him out here for? To make vague threats and show off his Porsche?

Pemberton walked back to the Thunder tunnel and stared at the supergraphic. Jenny's smile was enormous. Each tooth was as big as his head. Her lips were the size of a small love seat. He could see every pore in her face, and her eyes reflected something cloudy and out of focus, something hidden in the shadows of her nonexistent future. Pemberton didn't belong here. He belonged in L.A. with Debra, the woman he was supposed to marry, the woman who wouldn't respond to the messages he left on her voice mail. He thought being away from L.A. would provide clarity, but all it had done was underscore Debra's absence, the distance he'd put between them. Mountains. Deserts. Miles of freeway.

He wished he could get through to her somehow. And then he remembered her BlackBerry, a number Debra forbade Pemberton from ever using while they were engaged. He looked up the unfamiliar number and dialed.

"This is Debra."

Pemberton's pulse quickened at the sound of her voice. "I've made a terrible mistake."

"Pemberton?"

"I can't do this anymore." He searched Jenny's gigantic eyes, found something that gave him the courage to continue.

"I'm working, or will be as soon as my application clears. I—"

"I can't do this now," Debra said, her voice taking on an all-too-familiar edge. "I can't do this *ever*."

"I want you back."

"It's over. There's nothing you can say or do that's going to change my mind. I've moved on. I suggest you do the same."

"But Debra."

"I'm hanging up the phone."

"But—"

And then she did.

While riding the Thunder shuttle back to his cabin, the call Pemberton had been waiting for arrived: His gaming license had been approved. He was to report to the tribal security office for his Thunder badge the following morning. Pemberton took this as a sign that his luck had finally turned around and stopped off at the Trading Post for a bottle to celebrate.

ALICE SAT IN HER PSYCHIATRIST'S waiting room, fingering the scar on her ankle. When she was seven years old she got bit by a rez dog. The wound bled badly, worse than any cut she'd ever had before, but her mother refused to take her to the ER. She was drunk of course. Her reasoning became clear when one of her boyfriends rode up to the trailer on his motorcycle. When he found out why Alice was so upset, he shot the dog with a pistol and took her mother away on his bike. The dog's body lay in the dirt for weeks, buzzing under a shroud of flies, a symbol for something Alice still couldn't explain. That night she had her first seizure.

It was a tiny room in a building that had once been a house with chairs and tables wedged into three of the corners of what was once the parlor. On the rez, Alice was referred to neurologists, brainy men who studied brains, but they didn't have those kinds of doctors in Falls City. If she wanted to see a *neurological specialist* (just the way the lady at the insurance company said it made it sound expensive), Alice would have to take three buses down to San Diego and three buses back. Once she figured out that this other kind of doctor—the kind who asked her how she was feeling and offered to make her a cup of tea—could give her what she needed, she stopped worrying about finding a specialist. Besides she wasn't an epileptic anymore.

Sometimes Dr. Marcus wrote what she said in a book he kept in his lap during their sessions, a book that looked like it should contain lines of poetry. Sometimes he didn't write anything at all. Sometimes he closed his journal and wiped his glasses with a patch of cloth. When he held the frames up to the light and peered through them without looking at anything and announced *Yes, yes, I see*, she knew their session was nearly over.

His name was really Mark Marcus. Why someone would do that to their kid was anyone's guess, but the name suited him. Roman nose, square jaw, cleft chin, the works. A professorial bearing, though she could picture him in a toga. He looked like the kind of man who exchanged his long hair for a beard when he finished grad school. He could pass for an athlete, but she imagined his body had gone soft under the corduroy and tweed. Not that she thought about his body. He was her doctor, after all. Would she want him imagining what she looked like underneath her clothes? Did he?

She hoped so. But the name ruined everything. Maybe his mother was drunk when she picked it out. Alice pushed the thought aside. She hadn't talked about her mother much and didn't intend to today.

She picked up the book on the table at her elbow. *Alice in Wonderland.* How predictable. Kids teased her about it on account of her name. She'd seen the Disney version—parts of it anyway—but didn't care for it. Alice wasn't interested in white-girl problems.

"Good afternoon," Dr. Marcus boomed as he entered the room, startling Alice.

She collected herself, tossed the book on the table, and smiled weakly.

"Come." He held open the door to his inner sanctum. Did he call it that once, or was it something she made up? The lights were dim, the sofas low. His massive desk was pushed up against the far wall. When he was seeing a patient, Dr. Marcus moved to a wing-backed chair with doilies on the armrests. Doilies. Diplomas she'd never bothered to read hung between an oversize tie-dyed tapestry (a relic, she presumed from his hippie days) and a samurai sword. Doilies and decorative swords. That was Dr. Marcus in a nutshell. He probably owned a cat.

"So, you had another one?"

Alice nodded.

"Tell me about it."

Usually Dr. Marcus's mood was light and jovial, but today he was all business. Alice was comfortable talking about her seizures with Dr.

Marcus. They shared a vocabulary that made it easy to be precise—or at least as accurate as her memory would allow. But Dr. Marcus wasn't interested in the seizure so much as what led up to it. For him, it was all about the triggers. What was she doing? Was she under any stress? What was the setting like? Did she introduce anything new to her environment? Dr. Marcus was trigger-happy.

She told him everything. Almost everything. She didn't mention the ghost, and Dr. Marcus zeroed in on the omission.

"Is there something you're not telling me?"

Alice looked away, at the spines of the books on the bookshelf, the way the light caught the gold-framed prints on the wall, at anything but his eyes, which were an incredibly pale shade of blue. Dr. Marcus may have had terrible taste, but he was no dummy.

"This only works if you confide in me completely. I'm not a miracle worker, Alice. I can only go as far as you'll let me."

"I smoked pot," Alice nearly shouted. She'd had enough of Dr. Marcus's journey-to-the-center-of-the-mind routine. "And your office decor totally sucks."

Dr. Marcus smiled, caught himself, wrote in his journal. "Now we're getting somewhere," he said. "Is this a regular thing for you?"

"No!" Alice said, more forcefully than she intended. "Only once."

"Only once this week? Since you've started seeing me?"

"It wasn't this week; it was over a month ago."

"How many times would you say you've experimented?"

"It wasn't an experiment."

"Alice . . ."

"One."

"One?" Dr. Marcus seemed almost disappointed.

"It was my first time. I was getting these headaches, the ones I called you about. The medication you prescribed didn't help."

Dr. Marcus flipped through the pages of his journal until he found what he was looking for.

"Ah, yes," he said in that *now-I-remember* tone she found so annoying. *You don't remember,* Alice thought. *You're reading what you wrote down so you wouldn't have to.*

"I was worried anything stronger might interfere with your other meds."

Alice rolled her eyes in a way that was meant to get on Dr. Marcus's nerves. It didn't seem to work (it never worked), but he got the message: *Get on with it.*

"It could be the marijuana that triggered the event, but after so many weeks it doesn't seem likely." Now it was Dr. Marcus's turn to stare off into the middle distance, which he did for some time, long enough for Alice to wonder if *he* was on something.

"You don't like my office?" Dr. Marcus asked with a smile.

"No."

"Not even the wall hanging?"

Alice took another look at the tapestry. She'd never noticed the silhouetted figure in the center of the design before: a hunchbacked caterpillar atop a giant mushroom.

"I said *no.*"

"You know who Lewis Carroll is?"

"Duh, he wrote *Alice in Wonderland.*"

"And *Through the Looking Glass.*"

"That's good to know," she snapped, losing her patience.

"He had epilepsy."

This she didn't know.

"By all accounts he suffered from a very mild form. His seizures were unusual in that they weren't disruptive per se but would cause him to perceive things differently."

"Like a hallucination?"

Dr. Marcus nodded.

"What kind?" Alice asked, her mouth suddenly chalky and dry.

"Sometimes objects would appear disproportionate to their size. That is, things would seem either very, very small or very, very large. Sound familiar?"

Oh God. What if her illness wasn't the terrible affliction Alice thought it was, but some terrifically hokey cliché? That would be beyond unbearable. "What's with the history lesson?" she asked.

"I wanted you to know there's a precedent, that your condition can be managed."

"I don't want to manage it. I want it to go away."

"So do I, Alice. But I hope you take comfort from Lewis Carroll's example. You can lead a normal, productive life with epilepsy."

Alice shrugged. Comfort was a cousin to pity, which she despised. She didn't pity her mother, who certainly deserved it though she brought her suffering on herself, so why should anyone pity her? She wasn't pitiful.

"So what do we do?" she asked.

"You know what I'm going to say."

"I know, I know," Alice interrupted. "I should be seeing a *neurological specialist*." No way was that going to happen. The last neurological specialist Alice went to wanted to put electrodes in her brain to see where the seizures were coming from. She could see herself, wired up like Frankenstein, *fourteen days per lobe*. As if. Then, if they were able to figure out where the seizures were occurring, they'd excise the lobe, which sounded suspiciously like a lobotomy to Alice. She never went back to that—or any—neurological specialist again.

"First," Dr. Marcus continued, "we up your dosage."

"The blue ones or the yellow ones?"

"The yellow ones," he answered, not convincingly.

The yellow ones made her itch and something else she couldn't remember. Insomnia? Vivid dreams? Name a side effect, and she'd had it. She didn't like the yellow ones.

"Are you sure about this? Because sometimes it feels like you're just making this up as you go along."

Dr. Marcus's demeanor went from puzzled to professional. "Alice," he repeated, choosing his words with care, "we have to be aggressive. We've tried the wait-and-see approach. I'm not ready to throw in the towel. There may come a time when we have to accept the best we can do is address your quality of life between seizures, but that's for a neurologist to decide."

"I told you, I'm not ready to go there."

Dr. Marcus smiled. "Neither am I. That, to me, would be an admission of defeat."

Alice nodded. If she spoke, she'd sob. It was hopeless. Absolutely hopeless. She pulled her legs up and her fingers drifted to the scar, the place where the rez dog's teeth took hold. Dr. Marcus watched, and her hand jumped, like a bird knocked off a wire. She could feel Dr. Marcus peering at her with his iceberg-blue eyes. She looked at the sword on the wall. She ought to kneel on one of his atrocious pillows and let him whack her head off with it. That was one way to solve all of her problems.

Sayonara, Alice. Off with your head!

SPRING

I was born unlucky.

My sister and I were taken from an orphanage in Mexico City and sent across the sea to live with a family in California. Our father was a foreman at a rancho that stretched for miles and miles. His wife, our mother, was capable and pleasant, though she favored Ysabella, who was younger and prettier. They had no children of their own. We lived in an adobe house that sat atop a hill overlooking the valley. From the window in our room we could see the long road that followed the river between the mountains and the sea.

Life at the rancho suited us. Being orphans, my sister and I longed to marry, to start families that we would attend to with religious fervor. Ysabella's desire was to find a soldier who would take her back to Mexico City when his contract ended. But I wanted to stay here in this wild new country our new father was struggling to tame. Even then I think I knew he'd never succeed, but I loved our house on the hill. It was better than any home I'd dared to dream of while at the orphanage, and I wanted to keep it.

Ysabella was promised to a captain, a gallant-looking officer who was as eager to return home as she was. As for me, those who came calling took no interest and were quick to retreat. Some didn't even stop to dismount before guiding their horses back down the hill to the river. They say a girl who comes of age in an orphanage is destined to become a spinster. If that was to be my fate, so be it, but there are two kinds of fate: the one you don't know about and the one that comes for you out of the darkness with a scream.

Our cook, an old Indian woman from the mountains, told me someone would come for me in a fortnight. I laughed, taking comfort in her good intentions, but she knew not of what she spoke.

One afternoon my father summoned me to the livery. A suitor was coming to see me and he wanted me to be ready. This man has a reputation, my father said. Don't pay any heed to what the others say.

What do they say about this man? *I asked.*

Don't you worry about that.

Does he have a name?

Gamboa, *he said with some reluctance,* Sergeant Gamboa, *and sent me on my way. I went looking for the cook to help me prepare a bath, but she was nowhere to be found.*

At the appointed hour, Gamboa arrived and my father invited him into our house. He was short and stout with a thick beard, nothing like Ysabella's captain. His boots were cracked and his jacket was stained. He did not strike me as a suitable prospect, but I had no say in the matter. Gamboa came into the parlor to have a look at me. He inspected me up and down like a horse. When he was done, he shook hands with my father, and in that instant my life changed forever.

There was a disturbance in the courtyard as Gamboa made ready to leave. One of the sergeant's men had overheard our cook passing a message to one of the young native boys who went back and forth between the ranchos. The soldier brought the boy to Gamboa and told the sergeant what he'd heard: The natives were planning a raid. The boy was defiant. Gamboa brought out his sword and struck him with it, slicing off one of his ears. Gamboa skewered it with the tip of his blade and waved the ear in the boy's face, warning him that he was looking at his supper if he didn't confess. The boy refused. Gamboa struck him again and killed him. This was the reputation my father had warned me about.

Father made a scene. Where there is law, there must be justice!

The law of the sword is the only law these heathens understand, *was Gamboa's reply.*

He promised to return for me after he secured more horses for the coming campaign. He told my father to send all his Indians away and move his family. We were not safe in our home.

All of this excitement left me agitated and confused, and I hoped things would soon return to the way they were, but the hateful expression on the cook's face told me I'd spend the rest of my days in the shadow of this terrible crime.

Our father hid us in the tanning shed down by the river. It was an awful place filled with the stench of cowhides and the droning of flies. Mother took ill at once, and we looked after her. We were not a true family, but we did the best we could. Ysabella was of little use and fretted about her captain. I feared she might go mad with worry.

On the seventh night, we heard the sound of riders approaching. We hoped it was Father with news that the danger had passed. The doors crashed open in a shower of sparks. Torches sailed through the air, setting the hides alight. The red men of the mountains welcomed us with axes and clubs, wet with blood. Mother tried to protect us, and they cut her down with the same ax they had used to kill her husband, our father who was not our father, their blood mingling one last time. The natives took us away from the rancho, away from the sweet water of the river valley, away from the life I barely knew, a life I still dream of reclaiming.

PEMBERTON WAVED HIS THUNDER BADGE across the sensor and listened for the telltale click before pulling on the warm, germy door handle. He'd been on the job for two months and although winter had sledge-hammered Falls City, the illness Donna from Human Resources had warned him about failed to materialize. Aside from the occasional hangover, Pemberton remained reasonably healthy.

The same could not be said for his coworkers. It was so bad, the marketing department had become something of an infirmary, a place where sick people gathered to comfort one another in their illness and make each other sicker.

Everyone knew Cassi the advertising coordinator was having prob-lems at home so she brought her cold to work. Shortly after word got out that her husband had left her, she went out and bought breast implants, and for a while, it was all she talked about. Cassi always ate at her desk—they all did—but Cassi went after her food like a fifteen-year-old at an all-boy's-school cafeteria. She was terrible at hiding her feelings. When she got upset her face turned into an angry smear, like a brake light in the fog. She was obviously medicated, but Pemberton suspected if someone asked her what she was on and at what dosage, she'd have no idea how to answer.

Amy, the leader of the events and promotions team, had the snif-fles, which she blamed on her chronic allergies. She lived in the trailer park, not far from Pemberton's cabin, which he retained on a month-to-month basis. Amy didn't smoke, but she took frequent trips to the parking lot, and when she returned she looked like she was about to cry, yet remained strangely energetic. Pemberton had suspicions about Amy's so-called allergies.

O'Nan was the sickest of the bunch. He called it "the crud," and instead of blowing his nose, he loudly sucked the mucus back into his sinuses during meetings. This grossed everyone out, but O'Nan didn't seem to care. Forty years in the trenches of Las Vegas casino marketing had left him a crusty, irascible creep, but beneath the saurian exterior was an exhausted wretch propped up with pharmaceuticals. O'Nan carried his singular brand of assholishness with astonishing vigor, but the side effects were killing him. He complained he rarely slept, seldom moved his bowels, and couldn't remember the last time he'd gotten an erection. His hair-follicle stimulator made him pass gas, and he was always excusing himself from meetings to break wind in the hallway, which earned him the moniker Little Chief Thunderclap.

But it was Barbara who terrified the staff with her violent barking spasms that seismically shifted the phlegm in her chest up to her throat and back down again so she sounded like a seal gagging on a piece of blubber. The diminutive Filipina administrative assistant had been like this since Pemberton started, and her illness worsened through the unusually wet winter, but she refused to take a sick day. One by one they had all manufactured excuses for moving their desks to the other side of the cubicle warren, to workstations they imagined were beyond the reach of her honking fits, and donned headphones to be spared that awful gelatinous quack that sounded like an oyster sliding through a trombone.

Even though the weather had turned, Pemberton feared he wasn't out of the woods. It was only a matter of time before it caught up to him. He imagined his coworkers' illnesses mingling and merging, metastasizing into a kind of supersickness expressed as invisible vapor, like a creeping green finger in an old cartoon—if it touched you, you were done for. Sometimes Pemberton imagined a hamster trail, a network of microbes traveling like worker germs on a subway, Barbara's pneumatic hacking propelling them along to their final destination. Next stop, Pemberton's immune system. Listening to the chorus of coughing, sniffling, and sneezing, Pemberton had to fight the urge to flee the office and walk the floor for a while, smile at the guests, listen to the music of chance, but if the marketing department was a contaminated subway car, the casino was Grand Germ Station.

Pemberton spent the better part of the morning ignoring a headache brought on by too much whisky and too little sleep while rearranging the keys on his keyboard, which one of the graphic designers had cleverly reconfigured so the home row read

PMBRTONSUX

This wasn't the first time Pemberton found himself the target of such juvenile pranks, and he was vaguely aware that he brought it on himself. His less-than-firm handshake and unnecessary formality of dress marked him as peculiar. (Pemberton wore the same ensemble every day: black slacks and off-the-rack sports coat with a white oxford.) In L.A., such quirks were encouraged, especially among the creative classes, but in Falls City, this trailer park collective that masqueraded as a village, eccentricities were forbidden. He figured if he ignored the shenanigans, whoever was pranking him would grow bored, but his indifference had only egged them on. He was almost finished fixing his keyboard when he became aware of a dark presence standing in his cubicle entrance.

"I need you to whip up a press release," O'Nan said.

"A press release?"

"You do know what a press release is, don't you?"

"Of course."

"You sure about that?" O'Nan asked, making it clear he wouldn't tolerate another interruption. He seemed more frazzled and on edge than usual—a terrifying possibility.

Cowed, Pemberton nodded.

"It's the one-year anniversary of the Yukemaya Peace Park. Channel 6 News is sending a crew out. They should be here"—O'Nan shot his cuff and glanced at his Rolex—"any minute now. Find a copy of last year's press release and freshen it up. I need this quicker than quick."

O'Nan rocked on his feet. Pemberton got the impression he was trying to make himself taller. He was like a species of reptile that flared its gills when threatened, except O'Nan was *always* like this.

"Chop chop," he said as he headed for the door, "that copy isn't going to write itself."

"CREATOR, WE HUMBLY ASK YOU to bless this land, this sky, this wind, and this water. Guide us, Wise One, so we many continue your noble work and praise you through our actions all our days."

Chairman Cloudshadow stepped away from the microphone and bowed his head. The Chairman was a massive man, a giant of an Indian who carried the weight well. He was always impeccably dressed but never wore a tie, favoring silk mock turtlenecks, like a gangster in a made-for-television movie. From what Pemberton had seen, the Chairman was always serious but seldom somber. He was also one of the most handsome Indians on the reservation.

It was a small gathering—just a handful of Tribal Council members, a smattering of shoppers, and Pemberton—but the producer from the television station had them bunched tightly together to create the illusion of an assembly. The cameraman made last-minute adjustments with his equipment but otherwise remained still. Behind him, the reporter rifled through her oversize purse. A fountain gurgled. Birdsong filled the trees.

Pemberton could feel a headache coming on. O'Nan was supposed to be here but had sent Pemberton in his place. "To represent," O'Nan said and raised his fist until Pemberton, with profound reluctance, bumped it with his own. Pemberton generally didn't go for this kind of easy intimacy, and he immediately went to the bathroom to wash his hands.

The Chairman shook hands with members of the Tribal Council, the inner circle of the Yukemaya government that presided over all aspects of the tribe's enterprises, and popped a cough drop into his mouth. The reporter was an attractive woman in her forties named Jill D. Dean. Pemberton was hoping Channel 6 would send Pat Hamilton, a fixture on the L.A. morning show circuit who'd been exiled to San Diego on account of his extracurricular shenanigans. He'd gotten into the habit of dropping a lot of money at Indian casinos and writing off the losses on his expense account, a practice that came to light after he punched a transsexual prostitute in his hotel room and was subsequently banned from Indian gaming establishments within one hundred miles of L.A. Although the tribes took their sovereign nation status seriously, they circled the wagons in a crisis. If you messed with one tribe, you messed with them all, especially if you were a Caucasian fuckhead like Pat Hamilton.

Jill D. Dean looked a lot older in person than she did on television. She'd clearly had a ton of work done, which struck Pemberton as sad. She was tall and gaunt with expensive white-blonde hair and a tiny waist. Her big green eyes lit up when she greeted Chairman Cloudshadow.

"If I could have a few minutes of your time, I'd like to take a walk through the Peace Park with you and ask a few questions about its significance."

"Of course, Ms. Dean," the Chairman replied, "I'd be happy to walk with you," but his body language said otherwise.

"Please, call me Jill," she said, selling it with the eyes.

Jill conferred with her cameraman, and they worked out a plan to tour a scenic stretch of the park. Pemberton lagged behind to make sure he stayed out of the shot.

"I'm here with Chairman Cloudshadow to celebrate the first anniversary of the opening of the Yukemaya Peace Park at Thunderclap Casino," Jill began. "What can you tell us about this amazing place, Chairman?"

"We built the park to honor the land our ancestors roamed for centuries," the Chairman replied, and the rest was tribal boilerplate: maintaining the land, preserving the tribe, giving back to the community. No mention was made of the fact that the Yukemaya Peace Park was nothing more than a glorified jogging trail that encircled an outlet center with over a hundred retailers. They did this several times, walking down the same stretch of path, repeating the same words. With each take, the Chairman increased the Yukemaya's claim on the land from centuries, to millennia, to all time. He closed with some claptrap about "harmony with the land as a means of bringing peace in the universe," prompting Jill to close with "and that, my friends, is what it's all about."

Pemberton, being a stickler for such things, wondered what exactly "it" was supposed to mean. He didn't grasp how selling sneakers made in overseas sweatshops and hamburgers from cows raised on clear-cut rain forests, et cetera, et cetera, constituted *harmony with the land.*

When they were finished, Jill consulted with her cameraman who whispered the bad news: They were going to need another take. Pemberton could sense the Chairman's annoyance. He seemed immune to the TV reporter's charms. Apparently high-strung white chicks weren't his type.

"What seems to be the problem?" Pemberton asked.

"Well," Jill said with a nervous laugh, "it's the park. I'm having trouble hearing the Chairman over all the birds." She looked everywhere but at Pemberton.

"The birds?" Pemberton asked, and as soon as he did, he could hear them squawking in the trees.

"I can take care of that," the Chairman said.

"You can?" Jill gasped.

"Yeah, no problem. Old Indian trick."

"That's incredible!"

"It certainly is," the Chairman agreed. "Our comprehensive sound system covers the entire park. Now if you'll excuse me."

"Of course," Jill said while the Chairman whipped out his phone and gave the order to shut off the birdsong soundtrack, like a forward observer calling in an air strike.

Jill fussed with her bag to conceal her embarrassment. She sought and found reassurance in a compact mirror.

The Chairman put his phone away. "I'm afraid I have—"

"Time for one more take!" Jill linked arms with Chairman Cloud-shadow, Silencer of Birds.

"One more," the Chairman warned.

They went back to their marks. "And one," the camera operator said, but before Jill D. Dean began, Pemberton felt a feathery tickle in the back of his throat. He attempted to stifle it, but the harder he tried to suppress the cough, the more it wanted to come out, and when he finally opened up his mouth to suck in more air, a greenish-yellow charge of sputum splashed onto the sidewalk.

Everyone looked, then looked away.

The supersickness. It had finally caught up with Pemberton. Suddenly, O'Nan was there, decked out in a ridiculous full-length fur coat, slapping him on the back.

"You aren't going to die on us, are you?"

Pemberton tried to answer, but the slaps kept coming, hard and violent. O'Nan hooked Pemberton's elbow with one hand, and kept whacking away with the other, until it felt less like a friendly gesture, and more like an assault.

"Good, good," O'Nan said. "Now why don't you get out of the shot before you hatch any more chest oysters on these nice people!" O'Nan shoved Pemberton away, disguising his aggression with an extravagant good-old-boy smile. "And clean up that mess you left on the sidewalk before a guest slips in it!"

Pemberton withdrew a handkerchief from his breast pocket, and stooped to make the stain disappear. O'Nan regaled the Chairman with a joke that Pemberton didn't quite catch. He strained to listen, but he couldn't hear it over the sound of sprinklers whirring all around him, spattering him with a torrent of water, like waterfalls that ran in reverse.

WHEN LUPITA GOT LONELY, she went to the casino, but she decided instead to head down to San Diego to visit her nieces in Chula Vista. She hadn't seen the girls in ages and she was determined to disprove Mariana's claim that she never made time for them. She called her sister as she pulled up to their house, but she could tell before the phone began to ring that no one was home. Mariana's car wasn't in the driveway and the lights were all off. Lupita ended the call without leaving a message, but she wasn't giving up that easily. She'd get a cup of coffee and wait. Rather than go to the coffee shop by the freeway onramp, she pulled into the parking lot of the panadería where she met Alejandro. A new sign hung above the door and another in the window read UNDER NEW MANAGEMENT. Alejandro's father must have died or retired or sold the place, which meant it was safe to go inside. She suddenly longed to take in the bakery's warmth, savor its sweet-but-not-too-sweet smell.

She smiled for the boy at the register as she ordered a cup of café con leche and a pink conchita she didn't really want. The boy smiled back. He reminded her of how Alejandro looked before he joined the air force. She was against it from the start, but she couldn't talk him out of it. They were always fighting, even then, but it got worse after he enlisted. One time she wanted to have sex in his car during his lunch period at school, but he didn't want to risk it. She stopped talking to him for a week. She had already graduated from high school, was four years older than Alejandro in fact, but they worked together here in his father's panadería. He was a baker; she was a cashier. When Mrs. Diaz, a regular, asked Alejandro why he was looking so sickly, he answered, *Guadalupe won't talk to me, Mrs. Diaz. Why won't she talk to me?* Right in front of all the customers! Alejandro had a big heart and a bigger mouth that got him into plenty of trouble. Mrs. Diaz told his father who forbade Alejandro from seeing Lupita. If he was smart, he would have fired her on the spot, but he didn't and had to wait until after he caught Lupita and Alejandro having sex on a pile of empty flour sacks. The whole neighborhood found out about the scandal. Alejandro was coerced into joining the air force to get him out of Chula Vista and away from Lupita. Her mother was outraged, Mariana even more so. This left Lupita with just one option. When Alejandro finished recruit training and was sent to Tucson, Lupita followed.

"Will that be all?"

"Sí," she said with a smile. Lupita enjoyed being looked at, studied, desired. She'd always wondered what it would be like to be an artist's model. Only she wouldn't want to see the drawings afterward. Dios mío, no. That would spoil everything.

Lupita had been giving her admirers plenty of reasons to look at her: flashy necklaces, expensive blouses, and a diamond tattoo on the inside of her wrist for luck. She had achieved a kind of reversal. She was more beautiful than she had been as a girl, and it had nothing to do with her looks. If she knew then what she knew now, she could have spared herself so much trouble. When a woman stopped looking at herself in the mirror, she was truly alone.

The inside of the panadería hadn't changed. Her father used to take her here when she was a little girl. He let her buy whatever she wanted. One, two, three pieces of pan dulce. It didn't matter. They'd sit at a table outside, and he'd read the headlines and smoke cigarettes, one after the other. Sometimes he'd look up from the paper and repeat something he'd read, and she'd think he was the wisest man on Earth. Or the saddest. He was the one who got her the job. He was the one who came for her when Alejandro's father called her a putana after he found her fucking his son.

Alejandro.

He inherited his father's temper, that's for sure. The first time Alejandro hit her she went into the bathroom of their apartment on the south side of Tucson and looked in the mirror to inspect the damage, and she was both surprised and relieved to see there wasn't any. Wild with anger, she went into the living room, picked up the keys to his truck and when he tried to stop her from leaving, slashed him across the face. She drove to Sloppy Joe's—a bar near the base that air force wives frequented when their husbands were deployed—and got stupid drunk on daiquiris. She let herself be picked up by an officer. Once Lupita was certain he knew she was doing him the favor and not the other way around, she took him to Alejandro's truck and fucked him in the cab. His name was Lawrence. He had blue eyes and white-blond hair. He wasn't wearing a wedding ring, but that didn't mean anything.

Too drunk to drive, she took a taxi back to the apartment. Alejandro asked where she'd been. "Sloppy Ho's" she said, using the moniker that the airmen employed, and threw his keys on the table. Alejandro didn't say anything. That was one good thing about him. He didn't prolong their fights. When it was over, it was over. He had a deep scratch on his cheek that Lupita didn't apologize for, then or ever.

Alejandro never brought the incident up, though he had to have known what went down in his truck. The passenger seat was cranked all the way back. Her shoes were on the floor mats. She was pretty sure there was a condom wrapper down there, too. She never did anything like that again. The next time she cheated on him, she waited until he was deployed. She often wondered if his last thoughts were of her. Some days, like today, she thought it would be a comfort to know.

Dios mío. The dull horror of daydreams. The stupefying sun like a sugar skull in the sky. She shouldn't have come. Too many depressing memories. Even the television screen mounted in the corner above a case of conchitas, the sweet breads arranged like breasts, pink and brown and white, depressed her. There were too many televisions these days: in waiting rooms, baños, even cars. People used to smoke everywhere, now they watched television.

Lupita waved goodbye to the boy behind the counter, but was distracted by the cards hanging below a take-a-number sign by the door. To the best of her knowledge, these numbers had never been used, but they'd always been here. There were only a few left. The next number was 33. Her number. She took this as an indication that good fortune was coming her way. Ever since she'd turned thirty-three, she'd been telling whoever would listen that this was her year, the year she won the big one. People looked at her like she was crazy. *You'll see*, she told them. *You'll see*. Before she could stop herself, she reached for the number. She could see her hand slowly moving toward it as if it possessed a will of its own. Lupita plucked the card from the nail and stashed it in her purse. Embarrassed by her impulsiveness, she pushed through the door and made her way across the cracked and pitted parking lot. A child on a motorbike blasted up the street, its overworked engine bleating like a goat.

"Guadalupe?"

Lupita turned and there was old Mrs. Diaz, waddling up to the door.

"What a surprise to see you here!"

Lupita read Mrs. Diaz's eyes for signs of scorn, a mocking kind of mirth, but the old woman seemed genuinely happy to see her. She reminded Lupita of her mother.

"Do you live here now?" Mrs. Diaz asked.

"Oh no, I'm just visiting my sister."

"But I'm sure I heard you'd come back."

"I moved to Falls City."

"And what do you do all the way out there?" Mrs. Diaz shifted her enormous purse from one shoulder to the other.

"I am a gambler," Lupita answered.

Mrs. Diaz hooked an eyebrow. "And do you win?"

"Always."

ON HIS WAY TO WORK, Pemberton experienced what a less cynical person might call an epiphany. After the eleven o'clock status meeting, he was going to ask O'Nan for a raise. When the bully from Baton Rouge demanded an explanation, Pemberton would tell him he was hired under false pretenses, promised one thing and given another, the old bait and switch. Pemberton had written copy for freeway billboards, in-house signage, pole banners, table tents, and even matchbooks ("CLOSE COVER BEFORE STRIKING IT RICH!"). Scores of postcards, letters, self-mailers, and other direct-mail devices had sailed from his keyboard, one laser-printed page at a time. He'd cranked out ads for the publications that pass for newspapers in this ultrarural shithole, and contributed articles for the team member newsletter, *Falls City Rumblings*. He'd written everything *except* what he was hired to write: radio spots. This was not a satisfactory situation. Ergo, he demanded compensation. Pemberton wouldn't say how he really felt: He had come to hate his boss with debilitating ferocity.

Just this morning, he dreamed up a compelling concept: casino promotions broadcast as fake weather reports. *I'm here at Thunderclap Casino with your winner fore-cash: Thunderclap just got hit with a blizzard of bucks!* If only he could push a few of his ideas through, a raise would be a mere formality . . .

He inspected his desk for signs of sabotage—he'd identified the prankster from the graphics department as either Jasper or Kyle or possibly both—but found nothing amiss. Pemberton removed his notebook and pens from his briefcase and arranged them on his desk while waiting for his computer to warm up. There were no messages. Once he'd logged in, Pemberton checked his casino calendar and T-mail. Using an ultra-fine-point black pen, he wrote "check calendar and T-mail" in his notebook, and promptly drew a line through it. For Pemberton, the appearance of orderliness was more desirable than actual order.

Pemberton kept a photograph of Jenny, the dead model whose supersize image he walked past every day, tacked up on his cubicle wall. In the picture, she was posing with an account exec from his old agency. The photo was taken at a holiday party. Whenever someone asked him who they were, Pemberton always gave the same answer—*That's my old girlfriend Loren Ipsum and her sister Dolores*—but no one ever caught the joke or recognized Jenny from the Thunder tunnel, not even the guys from graphics, who helped install it.

The phone rang as he finished the assignment he'd been working on. He lifted the receiver and experienced a sensation of primordial terror as something slimy pushed into his ear canal. Pemberton screamed the only way he knew how: like a ten year-old-girl at a slumber party.

"Yeeeeeeeaaaaaah!"

Cold, dead squid tentacles dangled from the earpiece, secured by a precisely cut rectangle of duct tape. Jasper. Or Kyle. But most likely Jasper. Unless it was Kyle.

"Pemberton?" O'Nan shouted. "Are you there?"

Pemberton maneuvered the phone so he could speak into the mouthpiece without putting the receiver to his ear again.

"I . . . I . . ." Pemberton stuttered, but what could he say? He was scared shitless by a piece of sushi?

"I want to see you in my office!"

Pemberton removed the squid, carried it into the men's room, and flushed it down the toilet. He spent a full minute furiously scrubbing his ear and wiping his hands with alcohol swabs from the first-aid kit. When thoughts of torturing Kyle and eviscerating Jasper stopped flashing through his mind, he returned to his cubicle to print the document and proceeded to O'Nan's office.

Pemberton's boss favored black furniture with silver accoutrements: a cavern of cold masculine modernity in a faux pueblo palace. The nameplate on his desk read ARTHUR CHICHESTER O'NAN. He held court with an attractive young blonde seated at the table next to his desk. He was pompous yet debonair in his own way. Pemberton wondered if he dyed his hair silver.

"Meet my new assistant." O'Nan's smile was so forced he looked like he was trying to cut wire with his teeth.

Pemberton eyeballed her Thunder badge—Melody—as he took a seat at the table. O'Nan's office was ten degrees cooler than the rest of the casino and smelled like an old-time barbershop.

"This is Pemberton," O'Nan said to Melody. "Hotshot creative type from L.A. You know the toothpaste commercial with the Asian chick that got smoked? That was Pemberton."

Melody nodded. She had no idea what O'Nan was talking about.

"He's mad at me," O'Nan continued, "because I hired him to write radio, and I haven't let him take a crack at it yet. Isn't that right?"

O'Nan's personality was so toxic Pemberton forgot how perceptive he could be, but he gave nothing away.

"Did you finish the copy?" O'Nan asked.

Pemberton slid the pages across the table. O'Nan flashed his gold Mont Blanc, filled with a cartridge of red ink. What kind of cocksucker put red ink in a Mont Blanc?

"Has this been proofread?"

Pemberton considered reminding O'Nan the proofreader he fired last week hadn't been replaced, but thought better of it. "No."

"Goddammit! How many times do I have to tell you? Never bring me copy that hasn't been proofread!"

When Pemberton first started working at Thunderclap, he believed O'Nan behaved this way to provoke him into standing up for himself, that this was O'Nan's way of letting Pemberton know he didn't take shit from anyone and expected his staff to follow his example. It was a curious kind of leadership, Pemberton mused, though in the dog-eat-dog world of Las Vegas casino marketing that spawned O'Nan, it must have made some kind of sense. It was sad and pathetic and so 1980s that Pemberton, a bit of a throwback himself, could almost relate.

But Pemberton was mistaken. O'Nan thought nothing of the sort. The first time Pemberton openly challenged O'Nan, he darkened a deep shade of red. The second time, O'Nan kicked everyone else out of the meeting and didn't wait for the door to close before declaring, "Congratulations, fuckhead. You just made my shit list!" Two months later, Pemberton was still on the list, a permanent fixture in the top slot.

"Pemberton's a good copywriter," O'Nan said to Melody with a wink, "but not as good as he thinks he is. But what do *you* think, Melody? Should I let him take a crack at a radio spot?"

Melody tugged on her skirt, straightening a wrinkle that wasn't there. When Pemberton's ex was having problems with her boss, she let him have it. After he got drunk and slapped her ass at a Christmas party, she laid into him in front of all the VPs and half the board. Debra was like that: ferocious in a confrontation. It was one of the things he loved about her: He always knew where he stood with her. Melody, though pretty, was nothing like Debra. His ex was comfortable in her own skin in ways that Melody would never be.

"I guess," Melody said.

"Excellent idea," O'Nan exclaimed before turning to Pemberton. "You heard the lady. What do you say?"

"I appreciate the opportunity," Pemberton answered.

"Don't thank me," O'Nan replied, his upper lip curling in disgust. "And you damn sure better not hug me. I know how you California fruits operate."

O'Nan rose from his chair and stood at the window to survey the Bingo Barn and the Yukemaya Reservation beyond. He fussed with his helmet of hair. A hawk wheeled across the sky, drifted between the distant mountains known as the Sisters—one lush with scrub, the other rocky and barren, unchanged for a thousand years. Pemberton imagined crawling in the brush, hunting game, gathering hawk feathers. He tried to pinpoint the source of a peculiar fishy odor when he realized it was coming from him.

Fish sticks. Pemberton's fingers smelled like fish sticks.

Fucking Kyle. Fucking Jasper.

"What are you doing?"

O'Nan had caught Pemberton sniffing his fingers, and not just a casual whiff, but a deep inhalation of the odor emanating from his hand. "Nothing," Pemberton said and tucked his fishy fingers under his legs.

"Melody and I have unfinished business to attend to. Don't we, darlin'?"

Melody nodded, but her eyes screamed, *Help me!* Pemberton scooped up the copy and left O'Nan's office, certain he wouldn't be asking for a raise after the status meeting later this morning.

ALICE SHIVERED IN HER SEAT. The darkness outside the Thunder shuttle's window was impenetrable, the cold relentless, and the combination depressed her. It was like she'd stepped into an alternate universe. Seizure World. When she started working graveyard, Alice's coworkers told her how hard it was but assured her it would give her plenty of time to think, to reflect on her life. These were the last things Alice wanted.

Just as she'd feared, Alice's urine analysis came back positive. She talked Dr. Marcus into writing a note explaining her situation, but in the end he refused to say he'd prescribed medical marijuana for her as it could get him into big trouble. "Besides," he'd protested, "it's not true." Alice rolled her eyes. Like that had anything to do with anything. In the end, he wrote a note explaining the combination of prescription drugs Alice was on could conceivably result in a false positive for illegal drugs she wasn't taking. This satisfied the gaming commission, but the casino put her on probation anyway, which included mandatory drug testing once a week and up to four additional screenings a month. A lady from HR warned her if she tested positive again, she'd be fired, and that was the good news.

"What's the bad news?" Alice asked.

"You're being transferred out of slots."

Alice should have seen it coming. They used the old "zero tolerance for anything that compromises the security of tribal assets" line, but what exactly was being compromised by her seizures? Customer satisfaction? *I was having a great time until that Indian chick started rolling on the floor.*

The shuttle stopped and Cindy, Alice's new supervisor in guest services, boarded the bus.

"Wake up, kid," she said as she settled in the seat beside her. Alice gave her a halfhearted smile.

"Uh-oh," Cindy said. "I know that look."

Alice hadn't known Cindy for very long, but she liked her. There were two kinds of people who worked at the casino, those who came from the beach cities to the west and those from the mountain and desert towns to the east. Alice liked the ones from the east, like Cindy. She'd told her all kinds of troubling stories from her past with neither shame nor regret. She held nothing back, a quality Alice admired. Cindy was far from old, but had aged badly from spending her days in the sun and her nights in bars. Cindy knew her way around horses and trailers and trucks. There was an ex-husband or two in the picture, but she seldom mentioned them or the adult son she'd lost custody of back when he was still a child. Cindy was fiercely protective of the people on her staff, even Alice, and she loved Cindy for this.

Alice hadn't had any incidents since the transfer, but she hated guest services. Absolutely hated it. A good host, Cindy had told her countless times, anticipated the guests' needs. Alice couldn't bring herself to even look them in the eye—a clear violation of the Steering Wheel Rule, which held that team members should make eye contact at ten feet and smile contact at two. Smile contact. Barfola. Alice was such a bad host that Cindy had already taken her off the floor and moved her to the Thunderclap Club Rewards kiosk until she got in the swing of things, which Alice hoped was never. Her interactions with guests were more predictable behind the desk ("I want to sign up for a card/I lost my card/My card doesn't work"), but it was *duller than dog shit* as her mother used to say.

"What's the matter? Feeling under the weather?"

Alice shook her head as the bus lurched around the corner and stopped at the team member entrance. They disembarked and made their way into the casino.

"I don't want to work at the kiosk anymore," Alice said.

"You think you're ready to go back to the floor?"

"I want to go back to slots."

"You know I can't help you with that."

"I think that sucks," Alice said, sulking because she could. Life was simpler in slots. With machines the problems were defined, and the solutions apparent: It worked or it didn't, you could fix it or you couldn't. They made sense. Guests were much harder to figure out.

"I know it does, sweetie. It does suck. But I've got no choice. To be honest with you, I'm surprised they've been so accommodating."

"It's because I'm Indian."

"Honey, that's not what I'm saying."

"It's all right. You can say it. It's true, isn't it? If I was some white boy in maintenance . . . "

"That's different. They operate machinery and heavy equipment. There are liability issues."

Alice sighed.

"All I'm saying is that someone is watching out for you."

"Bullcrap."

Alice clocked in, stashed her hat and coat in her locker, and made her way to the floor. It was Wednesday night and the place was dead. The Bingo Barn had emptied out hours ago and the tables were quiet. The graveyard crowd was different. They were younger and rougher looking. Shit-kickers, tweakers, out-of-work workingmen. People with no place to go. The kind of people you saw standing outside convenience stores in the middle of the night. Men who looked like they were on the losing side of the battle of life but would be happy to take on the next challenger. The women were even scarier. Whether it was the sun, cigarettes, chemicals, or a combination of all three, all that hard living took a toll on their femininity. Their strength had been sapped, their softness planed away.

Alice settled in behind the desk at the Thunderclap Club Rewards kiosk. Every fifteen or twenty minutes, someone approached with a question about the buffet or a problem with his or her account, which Alice typically fixed by showing them which end of their Thunderclap Club Rewards card to stick in which hole in the machine.

The alarm went off on her cell phone. Midnight. Time to take her meds. She fished a granola bar and a bottle of water from her bag. She wasn't hungry, but if she didn't eat, the medication would mess her up. She'd learned to follow the instructions as closely as possible or suffer the symptoms. Alice refused to call them "side effects," especially since the drugs were no good at stopping the seizures. If the drugs made her sick or sleepy or irritable, that was their prime function. Rashes and flashes. Constipation or extreme diarrhea. Sleeplessness, loss of appetite, and the complete erasure of her libido, which wasn't so terrible considering all the action she wasn't getting. The only man she talked to with any regularity was Dr. Marcus, and how pathetic was that?

Alice kept an online log of her medications and their effects, which she could access and update through her cell phone. It seemed like a waste of time at first, but she'd lurked on epilepsy forums long enough to understand the necessity of it, the danger in relying too heavily on Dr. Marcus's judgments. She was the one taking the medication, so she should be in control.

Control. Yeah, right.

Dr. Marcus was convinced the casino was the culprit, with its flashing lights, loud noises, and nonstop overstimulation. All that randomness. But, as Alice saw it, there was very little that was random about a slot machine. Everything about them was orderly and efficient, as predictable—in their own ways—as ATMs. The machines were what she liked best about the casino. It was the people who freaked her out. But how could she explain that to her shrink without sounding like a total weirdo?

For the last week, Alice had worked at the Thunderclap Club Rewards kiosk between the main entrance and Loot Caboose—the game that had gotten her banished to guest services. The machine was equipped with a plasma-screen display embedded in a superstructure that resembled the locomotive of a train. Every so often—she hadn't figured out the sequence yet—the screen lit up and the train trumpeted a long, wailing blast from its electronic whistle. If Alice thought she had a grudge against the game before, she definitely did now. After a week behind the desk, she'd come to loathe it.

At two o'clock, she put the sign with the clock face on the counter and set it for two-thirty. More than enough time to grab a bite to eat in the cafeteria. She pushed through the door marked TEAM MEMBERS ONLY! and the multicolored carpet gave way to beige tiles. The electronic squawks and squeals receded, replaced by the noisy rush of air circulating through the heating system. The walls were painted a dingy off-white that was a little bit lighter than the floor. The ceiling panels were painted the same shade of industrial depression. The fluorescent lights intensified the grime, like a soup kitchen under a spotlight.

An old Asian woman pushed a cart filled with beverages: pitchers of water, carafes of orange juice, giant urns of coffee. Alcohol was available in the restaurants. Beer only, no spirits. The treacherous road up the mountain made consuming alcohol a dicey proposition for both the drinkers driving home and the cars coming up to the casino. There were tons of accidents. Alice had heard of team members slaloming down the mountain, wagering with one another to see how far they could make it without touching their brakes. Madness.

The Asian lady didn't nod or acknowledge Alice's existence. Maybe she wasn't really there. Maybe she was a ghost, haunting her old routines.

In the break room, everyone looked exhausted. Team members sat slumped over tables, their bodies clinging to flimsy chairs. They poked disinterestedly at their food. Used newspapers littered the tables. The televisions were too loud and each one was tuned to a different station. Alice always felt like she was being watched in here and got goose bumps up and down her arms. It could be a symptom—her meds affected her in unusual ways—but she needed to get out of here as soon as possible.

The Thunderclap Trading Post used to be a store, but after the last round of layoffs, they took out the inventory and installed vending machines until the economy improved. The machines sold everything from cigarettes to soup, popcorn to postage stamps. Alice paid too much for a cup of yogurt and a brown banana and waited for them to tumble through the guts of the machinery. If she was hungry before, she wasn't anymore. She went back to the break room and picked at her food while updating the side effects log on her phone. When she was done, there was nothing more to do but go back to the desk, which she didn't want to do. It was moments like these when she felt sorriest for herself. When she readied herself for work, well rested and alert, it felt like she was doing the right thing, but in the middle of the night, when the silence echoed, the minutes dragged, and sleep became a concept, this faith deserted her entirely. What was it? A lapse in focus? A moment of clarity? Alice didn't know anymore, but tonight Thunderclap felt like the worst place in the world.

When her mother's tribe was granted permission to open a casino, it came as a surprise to the tribal elders. They'd expected a court battle, so when the government told them to proceed with their plans, they didn't have any plans to proceed with. They set up a bingo game under a circus tent and started taking in mountains of money. They quickly built a proper casino, but the structure was too small, and they had to expand. No one expected the casino to be successful, but it was—extravagantly so—and that's when the problems started. The tribe voted to pass a percentage of the profits on to tribal members. They brought in a genetics expert and tested everyone in the tribe. Those who met the criteria would get a monthly stipend, and those who didn't would be disenrolled.

Alice and her mother didn't qualify. They weren't the only ones. Entire families were stricken from the books. Her mother took it personally. She raged that the results were rigged to purge the rolls of the junkies and the drunks and the wild boys who stayed high for weeks at a time and engaged in running gun battles with the county sheriffs in the ultrarural outposts of the reservation. Alice's mother associated with bootleggers and drug dealers. She was a drunk who slept around. A terrible mother. A bad Indian.

Alice didn't understand what it all meant. For her, being an Indian was like being a girl, an indisputable fact of nature. All her life she'd been taught the many ways the white man had taken what was rightfully theirs. Then her own tribe did the same thing to her, but worse.

After Alice's mother died, there was no longer a reason to stay on the rez. There was nothing to keep her. So she left. She didn't grasp the enormity of what she'd lost until she came to Thunderclap and saw the kind of life the casino had bought for the Yukemaya, the kind of life that had been taken away from her.

She missed her reservation, the view from her bedroom, the way the sun came up over the hills in what amounted to her backyard. When she was very young, she became alarmed when she looked out the window during a rainstorm and couldn't see the familiar swells of the hills rising in the distance. Her mother told her the mounds of earth were actually elephants. Usually they were asleep, but from time to time they walked about, marching single file. That's why she couldn't see them, but they always came back to the same spot. Elephants were smart that way. They never forgot where they came from. And then her mother started to cry.

Alice never forgot the story. Even as a teenager, she recalled riding the bus to school and pressing her face to the glass to catch a glimpse of the elephants marching past, chained together trunk to tail. The light guided her eye, shaped the shapes, took her on a journey over the horizon and far away. She always knew she'd leave the rez to chase the elephants and now here she was, wishing she could go back.

Alice wandered into the Forest of Fortune, her favorite place in the casino. The fake trees rose to a ceiling decorated with images of densely foliated limbs. During the day, sunlight slanted through the atrium's beveled glass, but at night it was darker here than the rest of the casino. The lights from the slot machines cast a warm glow on the slack faces of the slot players, softening their features, so when they smiled, they were almost beautiful. A slow-moving creek meandered through the grove, and a footpath followed alongside. Animatronic creatures went about their business. She'd been told there were thirty of them in all, but Alice had only seen about a dozen.

The creek ended at a pool at the bottom of Thunderclap Falls, which ran twenty-four hours a day except when a maintenance crew turned it off to clean out all the coins that had been pitched into the pool. Not coins: tribal resources. At seven, eight, and nine o'clock at night, there was a laser light show. Because of the high ceilings and all the water cycling through the falls, something like a weather system had settled over this part of the casino, a mixture of mist and damp and fog that never really went away. For this reason, all the slot machines were moved away from the falls and replaced with blackjack tables, which were wiped down every night. Sometimes mold got into the felt. Once a table had to be scrapped after being colonized by snails, but that was before Alice's time and she wasn't sure if she believed the story.

On the footbridge that crossed the creek, Alice saw a filthy-looking woman dressed in rags, staring down at the water beneath her feet. There was a fake frog there, Alice knew, that croaked with the belligerence of a troll. The sound echoed off the underside of the bridge and startled passersby. But the woman wasn't looking for the frog. Her gaze was fixed on something beyond the bridge, the gurgling creek, the phony falls, and she glowed with a light that had nothing to do with the spotlights rigged along the path. It was like she was shrouded in a weird halo.

It was her, Alice realized. The woman from her seizure.

Her ghost.

She was younger than Alice thought. Her hair was fouled with clumps and knots, and her face was haggard. The woman looked up, smiled at Alice, and continued down the path.

An animatronic eagle perched on the rocks above spread its wings and shrieked, startling Alice. She needed to say something to the woman. This certainty assaulted her with dreamlike intensity. The eagle usually signaled the beginning of the laser show, but it was far too early in the morning for that. Something scurried in the understory, real or mechanized she couldn't say. The path was slick with condensation, and the railings on the viewing platform were spattered with water. The woman was now a blurry shape on the other side of the creek. Alice followed her before she slipped away.

Alice rushed to the end of the path, passing through a gap in the artificial boulders between the falls and the food court. The floor shined immaculately and stretched for what seemed like miles.

She was too late. The woman was gone. There was only a security officer and a wild-eyed weirdo, a vagrant whose heavy beard made him look older than he was. His pants were down around his ankles and his underwear was filthy.

"Sir," the guard said, "I'm going to have to ask you to put your pecker away."

Alice realized it was the same security guard who'd taken her to Surveillance. He didn't see her, and she slipped away to the Forest of Fortune before he did.

PEMBERTON MADE HIS WAY through the casino, taking comfort in the tinkling of unattended slot machines. A few souls drifted about the dim cavern of the main gallery. Elderly slot players, energized and alert to the possibility of an early jackpot, sat alongside youngsters pulling a chemically inspired all-nighter. Kooks and old folks trading their futures for the promise of here and now. Pemberton enjoyed walking the floor when there weren't many guests around, but this morning he was on a mission. O'Nan had sent him to study a slot machine that had captivated slot players and casino managers alike. It was called Loot Caboose, but in the management offices upstairs, it was known simply as "the Game."

The Game was neither new nor innovative: a simple five-reel video slot with the usual bells and whistles and an extremely catchy jackpot sequence, yet it was the most popular gaming device on the floor. Guests lined up and waited for hours to play, and when they got on the machine, they stayed on it. Although VIP players generally stayed away from the Game (they came to the casino to play, not wait in line) when ordinary guests got on the Loot Caboose, they played it like VIPs, and they kept playing until all their money was gone.

This was what had upper management in a tizzy. The hardest thing to do in the casino biz was to change a gambler's behavior. Even though this was ostensibly the point of all the marketing and data analysis they did at the casino, it was a pursuit with quasimystical undertones because when it worked no one knew why. That's exactly what the Game did: It changed the way players played. They might never figure out what made this game so special, but they sure as hell didn't want it to stop.

O'Nan believed the guests were playing because of the progressive jackpot, which grew and grew on the video display. But it wasn't the only progressive on the floor, nor was it the highest jackpot. Strange things kept happening that even O'Nan couldn't explain. Last week a man pissed himself while playing and had to be forcefully removed, chair and all, such was his reluctance to give up his seat. Reasonably healthy-looking people passed out during the bonus rounds. For team members, Loot Caboose had been nothing but bad luck. One of the maintenance men got his hand crushed when they were installing the machine, and a slot tech had some kind of seizure while she was working on it. Rumor had it the cameras picked up strange activity that no one could explain. There was even a story going around that before Loot Caboose came to Thunderclap, it paid out a million-dollar jackpot to a pair of sisters in the Dakotas. They'd been taking turns spinning the reels and got into an argument on the way home as to how the winnings should be split. They were both killed when their car went off the road.

"The Game is haunted," Cassi declared at the weekly status meeting.

"I don't care about all that hoodoo," O'Nan complained. "I'm interested in what makes people tick."

"You want me to play it?" Pemberton asked.

O'Nan glared at him like he had three heads and none of them were working right.

"You put money in that machine while you're on the clock, and we'll see how fast gaming pulls you off the floor."

"Right," Pemberton said.

"Go down and watch them play," O'Nan continued. "Don't be too obvious about it, but study them up, find out what's got them hooked."

Thankfully, there was hardly anyone on the floor to observe. The tweakers scattered when the suits showed up, and it was still too early for the housewives who usually didn't arrive until after their husbands had left for work and the children were deposited at school. The ubiquity of high-stakes poker tournaments on television reinforced the image of the gambler as an outlaw, a risk-taker, a figure on the fringe, but at Thunderclap, middle-aged women were the moneymakers, and *they* didn't seem to think the Game was haunted.

Pemberton didn't gamble. He considered himself fortunate not to have been wired that way. He found the machines relaxing, soothing even. Slot techs insisted video technology had revolutionized the gaming industry, but to Pemberton's eyes, the games looked the same: squat, stolid, monolithic. In an age when electronic equipment kept getting smaller and smaller, slot machines got bigger every year. Oversize calculators with bells and whistles to keep the suckers in their seats. Where the players saw symbols of fortune, Pemberton saw grossly inefficient random-number generators, outdated engines of chance, comforting in their predictability.

A disturbance near the front entrance caught Pemberton's attention. He could make out the flashing lights of an ambulance on the other side of the automatic doors and hurried to the scene. Sure enough, something had happened to someone playing the Game. Paramedics worked on an older white woman, gray-haired and big bellied, stretched out on the floor. A crowd gathered around her. The duty manager worked his phone. An elastic lanyard stretched from the woman's collar to her Thunderclap Club Rewards card inserted in the machine, creating the illusion that Loot Caboose was sucking the life out of her, like an umbilical cord in reverse. Pemberton withdrew the card from the machine and wrapped the cord around the woman's hands like a rosary. An elderly Chinese woman slipped into the vacated seat and began to play.

One of the paramedics wrote something down in a little notebook with a nub of pencil that didn't have an eraser. His associates brought in a stretcher and prepared to put the woman on it, but they were having trouble with its legs and they banged the contraption on the floor with some violence until it cooperated.

"Excuse me," one of the gawkers pleaded. "Can you help me?" A white woman in her late twenties or early thirties—it was hard to tell in the dim lighting—sidled up to Pemberton. She seemed anxious or distraught. Pemberton wondered if she was related to the old lady on the floor. She looked too young to be her daughter, too old to be her granddaughter. With some reluctance, Pemberton engaged her, though he didn't know what kind of assistance he could possibly offer.

"What can I do for you?"

"Oh, thank you!" The woman's gratitude was immense, inappropriately so. She clutched his forearm, latched on. Pemberton flinched and withdrew, but she wouldn't let go. Her hair was blonde on top and black underneath, and her eyeliner was thick and dark. Pemberton could feel her large, false nails press into his flesh through the fabric of his coat.

"I've lost the key to my hotel room," she said, flashing a smile. "And the woman at the front desk is useless. Can you help me?" Her jaw clenched, unclenched, and perhaps it was a trick of the light, but Pemberton swore her pupils flashed. She had to be on something.

"We don't have a hotel," Pemberton said.

The woman didn't miss a beat. "Would you like to help me find one?"

She wasn't asking for help; she was making an offer. Pemberton paused to consider the solicitation. He hadn't had sex since leaving L.A., but all he could think about were the cameras, the eyes in the sky. They saw everything, understood nothing. They had no grasp of context or nuance. They weren't watching him. They weren't watching her. They were watching *them*—for that's what Pemberton and this woman had become: a transaction. To the people who monitor the activity on the casino floor, *everything* was a transaction. In this case, they were right to think that way. He withdrew his arm and, without saying another word to the woman, fled. "Hey!" the woman called out, but Pemberton ignored her. He cruised past the falls, left the Forest of Fortune, and headed toward the team member break room. On the stairs, casino workers halfheartedly clapped their hands together. The halls stank of boiled beef, and the cafeteria was clogged with people. He tried not to freak out, but he had to get out of there. He needed fresh air, a place where the cameras couldn't find him.

Everyone Lupita knew was sick with the bug that had been going around. Yasmina and Elodia had it and then gave it to their mother. Now Denise seemed to have come down with it, too. They'd planned on going to Thunderclap in the afternoon, but when Lupita had called her last night to confirm, she'd sounded ambivalent, which wasn't like Denise at all. The woman loved playing video poker. It was more than entertainment for her. Mucho mas. It was her way of proving something to the world.

Lupita had met Denise three years before during an exclusive, invitation-only slot tournament for the casino's top Thunderclap Club Rewards members. The players with the five highest scores advanced to a second heat with a grand prize of $10,000. Lupita and Denise were seated side-by-side. Lupita was astonished by Denise's contempt for the women (and one gay man) on the events and promotions team, and the feeling seemed to be mutual.

"They love to hate me," Denise whispered to Lupita. She'd found a glitch in the Thunderclap Club Rewards program award structure. The way Denise explained it, a player like Lupita—a slots player who followed hunches and spent freely—was much more valuable to the casino than Denise. While Lupita might blow through a grand in a couple hours, Denise could battle all day long with the same hundred dollars. Because the system was set up to reward players based on the time they spent on the machines, Denise earned five times as many Thunderclap Club comps as Lupita, even though Lupita spent much more money and demanded far less attention from the casino staff. As a result, Denise was always in the running for the prizes the casino gave away to its most loyal members, because she earned so many entries with her play.

"How many?" Lupita asked.

"Shitloads."

What other people did at the casino was their own affair, no business of hers, but Lupita got a kick out of the way Denise tormented the events and promotions team, whose business was to care about such discrepancies, particularly when a certain, notoriously mean-spirited video poker player kept winning all the prizes. They had to at least pretend to be civil to Denise, who made no effort to temper her disdain toward them. Denise reminded Lupita of her mother, who dealt with people the way a machete sliced through fruit.

Neither Lupita nor Denise won the tournament that night, and afterward they had dinner together in the Chop House. In the weeks that followed, they carpooled to the casino, though Lupita always drove. Lupita asked Denise for advice when she bought her house after the money from Alejandro's insurance finally came through. If it weren't for Denise, she probably wouldn't have moved so far from San Diego, so close to the casino, but a good deal was a good deal. Once, Lupita asked Denise what her hobbies were, and the old woman laughed so hard Lupita thought she might collapse. Lupita considered Denise a friend, but ever since Denise started playing the Loot Caboose, she seemed different.

Lupita called Denise in the morning to follow up, and even though she didn't answer her phone or respond to her messages, Lupita took a chance and drove over to her house. Denise lived on the other side of the Sisters. Although their houses were minutes apart as the crow flew, it took fifteen minutes to drive around the mountain and up the hill to Denise's place. Her house overlooked the reservation and she had a beautiful view. It was spectacular when it was sunny, but today the skies were gray, and a strong wind blew across the desert and through the valley. The unpaved roads made driving feel like an adventure, even in her SUV. As Lupita labored up the grade, she wondered why some mountains here on the outskirts of the desert were jacketed in soil while others resembled piles of boulders stacked by a gigantic hand.

Not for the first time she wondered how two mountains could be the same height and shape, but so different. One covered in verdant scrub, the other rocky and barren. They sat side-by-side, inviting comparison. Similar but different, like Lupita and Mariana.

Lupita pulled into Denise's driveway, but the gate, which was usually open, was closed. She sat for a moment in her SUV, the ass-end sticking out in the road. She fumbled with her phone and her call to Denise went straight to voice mail. Lupita hung up and honked the horn six times.

I. Am. Here. Where. Are. You?

The front door opened and an old man dressed in a tattered bath-robe stepped out onto the patio. Although there was no glare, he shielded his eyes and squinted into the wind. Dios mío! It was Denise. Without her makeup and wig, she looked sickly and frail. Lupita pressed a button and waited for the window to lower.

"Ai, Denise! Como estás?"

Denise didn't acknowledge the greeting; instead, she turned and retreated inside the house. Lupita wondered what she should do. The iron gate shuddered and swung open. Lupita let her SUV roll down the drive. By the time she put it in park and killed the ignition, Denise was back on the front porch, looking bewildered and confused.

The wind blew harder up here in the mountains and the shrubs bent before its will, hugging the barren slopes. A gust caught the edge of Lupita's door and pushed it open with such force the handle slipped from her grasp. She let out a cry of alarm, then hopped out of the SUV, and wrestled the door closed.

"Lupita, is that you?" Denise clutched the edges of her robe to her bony chest. "I can't see a fucking thing without my contacts!"

"Sí, Denise," Lupita said, walking up the path. "I have come to take you to the casino!"

"The casino?"

"Yes, at three o'clock, remember?"

"Of course I remember. I'm not an idiot! I told you I'd call if I felt up to it."

"And here I am!"

"But I didn't call."

"Yes, I know," Lupita said. "That's why I called *you*!"

Denise shook her head. "Come inside. I don't want to argue with you in this weather."

Lupita followed her friend inside. It was a huge house with vaulted ceilings and marble floors. The curved staircase with a wrought-iron banister that matched the chandelier spiraled to the second floor. The lights were off. There was very little furniture, a couple of dark, ornate antiques here and there. The wind buffeting the house sounded louder inside than it did outside. Though she'd only seen them in travel magazines and jigsaw puzzles, Lupita had the impression of being in a lighthouse. It was an impressive waste of space. She wondered how Denise could afford it. There was so much about her friend that she didn't know.

"How are you feeling?" Lupita asked.

"Like shit," Denise said. "You?"

"A little cold."

"Yes, well, I'd offer you tea, but you probably shouldn't be staying. Germs and all." She said the word *germs* as if Lupita was the one who'd gotten her sick.

"No, no, no," Lupita said. "I should have brought you some pozole."

"Come again?"

"Soup."

"I don't want any soup."

"See, you really are sick."

"That's what I've been trying to tell you."

Lupita had a hard time believing this was really Denise and not some pinche imposter like on the telenovelas. She thought of the real Denise bound and gagged in a plush dungeon beneath her feet and almost smiled. This Denise would make a fantastic evil twin.

"Is there anything I can do?" Lupita asked.

"No. Nothing."

"Cook something for you? Water the plants?"

Denise laughed, and some of her old spirit came through. "Do you see any fucking plants here, Lupita?"

"No, of course not. I'll let you get back to bed."

Denise shuffled toward the door. In the big empty foyer, her slippers made a rasping sound like a carpenter sanding down a piece of lumber. Denise already had one hand on the door handle.

"Can I ask you something?" Lupita asked.

"Sure," Denise said, her tone flat, her eyes elsewhere.

"Are you lonely here?"

Denise shook with laughter, which convulsed into a spasm of wretched-sounding coughs, but the look on her face was full of glee.

"I'm sorry, Lupita, forgive me, but I thought you were going to ask me for money!" and off she went again, laughing and coughing.

Denise's confession shocked Lupita. Did Denise really think she would do such a thing? Was the value of their friendship priced as low as that?

Denise grabbed Lupita's arm just below the shoulder. Her grip was firm. Lupita tried to remember what her friend had used to kill her husband. Was it a gun, a knife, some kind of poison? The details escaped her.

"Are *you* lonely?"

"No," Lupita answered, her voice thickening with an emotion she could not control.

"Me either," Denise said and released her.

Lupita nodded and let herself out of the cavernous house. The wind had died down. Clouds gathered in the east. The sound of the door slamming shut with sudden violence startled her. The deadbolt slid home and a voice—loud and clear and strong—cackled with desperate laughter. Lupita ran to her SUV and locked herself inside. She turned the key, gunned the gas, and reversed out of the driveway before the iron gates swung shut.

"Hey, chief," Sam exclaimed as Pemberton came through the door. "Welcome home!"

Although it would have been cheaper for Pemberton to find a roommate and move into a trailer, he'd decided to stay in the tiny log cabin at the temporary resident rate as an incentive to get his act together and move back to L.A., but that wasn't working out so well.

"Who do we have tonight?" Pemberton gestured toward the flat-screen TV on the wall as he paid for his bourbon and cola.

"Miami Dolphins versus Buffalo Bills. Very good matchup," Sam said with great enthusiasm. He got so excited his oily comb-over fell out of place, and he rearranged it with delicate hands. Pemberton had learned that Sam was neither a gambler nor a fan of any particular team. Sam just really liked to watch football.

"What's the score?" Pemberton heard himself asking as he scanned the shelves. There was always something new: mousetraps, drain cleaner, jars of jalapeño-stuffed olives, scrapbook starter kits, a dusty bottle of Chadwick's Unadulterated Irish Whisky. None of the items on Sam's shelves were priced, and Pemberton suspected Sam did this out of loneliness, not laziness. If the customer didn't know the price, he had to engage Sam to find out how much the item cost, a service Sam was all too eager to provide. It saddened Pemberton how poorly Sam understood Americans.

"Ten to nothing in favor of the Buffalo Bills." Sam always used both the city and team name, never one without the other. Pemberton liked this about him, the needless specificity. It reminded him of something he would do.

"How much for the scrapbook kit?"

"Nine ninety-five. Very popular item."

Pemberton didn't doubt it. The impulse to preserve the past was strongest when the future was bleak. He pretended to follow the action on the screen.

"American football is the most complex game ever invented," Sam declared.

"More complex than chess?"

"Chess only takes two people. Football requires an army."

"What about cricket? I never understood that game," Pemberton confessed.

"It's just numbers," Sam said, with a dismissive wave of his hand. "Like baseball." Sam came around the counter with a folding chair. "You sit."

Pemberton declined the invitation and poured himself a drink from the bottle he'd just bought. Sam kept a bucket of ice and a stack of paper cups on the counter for "special customers." Pemberton made a bourbon and cherry coke that was nine parts of the former and one of the latter. After a few of these, his little house in the trailer park wouldn't feel so cheerless, his loneliness so acute.

Pemberton had tried drinking in Falls City's shabby saloons, but they were filled with laid-off casino workers who pegged him as a management type as soon as he walked through the door. He'd tried listening to their stories but it was no use; they always blamed Pemberton for their dismissal. *You think you're better than me, you son of a bitch?* they'd shout when he announced his preference for drinking alone. It was the same story everywhere he went, and eventually he ran out of places to drink. Pemberton dropped by the T.P. most nights on his way home from the casino, and he passed the time watching sports with Sam.

Tennis was the only sport Pemberton had ever truly cared about. He loved its rigid rules and odd scoring. He was a halfway-decent player with an accurate serve and a weak backhand. Once upon a time, he'd even belonged to a tennis club, which had amused Debra the night they met in a hotel bar. It was possible to believe you were someone else in a hotel bar, someone coming, someone going, someone on the move.

"I didn't know they still had those," she said.

"Tennis clubs?"

Debra plucked the cherry from his Manhattan and crushed it between her teeth. A dish of exotic nuts sat on the glass-topped table. A server filled the dish every few minutes. Pemberton liked this about hotel bars. The rigorous attention to detail.

"If you look hard enough, you can find anything you want in this town."

"Anything?" Debra asked, working the cherry stem with her tongue.

"Anything."

"Your serve."

They had a few more drinks, booked a room upstairs, and fucked like teenagers.

"I bet you do this all the time," she called out from the bathroom when they were finished. She used the toilet with the door open, which unnerved Pemberton.

"It's a pity my usual suite wasn't available," he replied, playing along. "The rooms up top are so much nicer."

Debra chucked a pillow at him as she charged out of the bathroom, and their clumsy wrestling gave way to more lovemaking, but when Pemberton woke the following morning, Debra was gone. This had never happened before. Usually, he was the one who slipped away. Debra's disappearance registered with a shock so devastating that after searching the bathroom and the hallway for her, Pemberton collapsed on the bed and wailed into his pillow. This brief yet intense moment of sorrow was followed by a knock at the door. It was Debra, of course, who'd gone to the lobby for coffees and the newspaper. Overcome with gratitude, Pemberton decided that he was going to latch on to Debra with everything he had and never let her go.

When they moved in together, Pemberton had plenty of occasions to reflect on the erratic events of that first morning. They had three or four arguments a year, usually over something minor: Debra's way of doing things versus Pemberton's. The War of the Tennis Club was their fiercest fight and lasted nearly a year. She couldn't understand Pemberton's stubbornness over his expensive membership to a stupid tennis club he seldom used. Pemberton had no argument for her. It was true, he didn't play tennis like he used to, was bored by it even. The things he liked about the club—the espresso bar, the French magazines in the lobby, the way the overstarched towels felt on his slack muscles after a spell in the sauna—were not going to win any arguments. He'd finally relented and given up his membership, but he couldn't shake the feeling that he'd lost something vital.

Pemberton never meant to stay at the T.P. long, but the time passed so quickly during the prerecorded games. Sam manipulated the remote so they were spared the pregame pageantry, in-game advertisements, and postgame blather. This speeded things up, but stripped the games of context, which was perfectly fine with Pemberton. He didn't check the scores or follow the standings. He was ignorant of the expectations the teams brought to the contest, oblivious as to what was at stake. The shameless truth was he was usually too drunk to comprehend what he was looking at.

The trailers all looked the same as he stumbled home, but there was only one log cabin, so he managed to avoid crashing into the wrong place. Walking by the open windows that all seemed to be blaring the same television show, he felt like the loneliest person on the planet. Pemberton knew self-pity was a weak crutch that would crumble if he put too much weight on it, but lately he couldn't go anywhere without it. Most days he blamed O'Nan; tonight he blamed the bourbon, finding the transition from *poor me* to *pour me another* way too easy. Pemberton stumbled into the cabin and said hello to Ramona. He crashed into his bed and buried his face in Debra's pillowcase. Its scent had all but disappeared, leaving an ache where a memory ought to have been.

LISA STUMBLED INTO ALICE'S ROOM with a "Hey, hey, hey, whaddya say?" She repeated it over and over again like a musical refrain until Alice lifted her head from her pillow.

"What's up?"

"You know what today is?"

"Monday?" Alice wasn't really sure.

"That's right, and you know what that means?"

Alice didn't. She located her cell phone on the nightstand and checked the time. Late afternoon. She'd been sleeping all day. Monday was Alice's day off. Now that she was working graveyard weekends, Monday was her Saturday. She wasn't sure what day it was for Lisa. Their schedules were out of sync, and Alice had hardly seen her roommate all week.

"We both have the night off. That means party time!" Lisa windmilled her right arm and strummed an invisible guitar. She looked tipsy, high, or both.

"Lisa—"

"I know, I know. You can't *party* party, but that doesn't mean we can't have some fun. Blow off a little steam, right?"

Alice cautiously agreed.

"Great! I invited some people over."

Alice sat up. Ever since she started seeing ghosts, she found comfort in the ordinariness of everyday things. Her hairbrush, her laptop, her meds. Lisa's party didn't qualify. Partying with Lisa was the opposite of ordinary.

"Who?" Alice asked.

"Oh, people." Lisa smiled. Alice wouldn't put up with this from anyone else, but coming from Lisa it was somehow beguiling. Earlier in the week, Alice dreamed she'd kissed Lisa, and the encounter had stayed with her so forcefully she wrote in her symptom diary "freaky dreams." It wasn't a kinky kiss. It was part of some kind of formal arrangement, but when the time came Alice was not unwilling. They held hands, closed their eyes, and went into the kiss open-mouthed. When she woke, Lisa was in bed with her, still dressed in her cocktail uniform. This happened from time to time. Lisa was one of those people who hated being alone. With the false memory of Lisa's tongue in her mouth still fresh, Alice understood why men got so crushed out over her. If she were a man, she would, too. But one thing Alice had learned since they'd been room-mates was that to know Lisa was to be let down by her.

Boom, boom, boom. Someone pounded on the trailer door.

"That's them!"

"That's who?"

"You'll see!"

"I have to get dressed!" Alice shouted, but Lisa was gone. All Alice wanted was to eat some yogurt, turn the heater up, and watch television. Was that too much to ask?

Apparently. Alice sighed and got out of bed. There was no point hiding out in her room when the noise from Lisa's party would keep her awake anyway. She looked for something to wear, and settled on dark jeans and a black turtleneck to match her mood. The front of the trailer was much colder than the back, especially with people coming in and out, and she didn't want to freeze.

Alice ate half of an energy bar while running a brush through her hair. She put on some makeup to cover the dark circles under her eyes and applied gloss to her lips, which she thought were too thin. Alice took her meds with the water she'd left on the nightstand and recorded them in her diary. She hadn't had any hallucinations since she saw the ghost by the falls, but she was mindful of the fact that it had happened after she took her meds. After two deep breaths, she was ready to face Lisa's idea of fun.

Loud music, a confusing mix of metal and hip-hop, like an argu-ment played out over buzz saws, blared from the living room. The music rose to an anxiety-inducing level, but Alice tried to push it out of her mind. She didn't want the first words out of her mouth to be *Turn that music down!*

"Alice!" Lisa wobbled over and pulled her into the living room.

Why, Alice wondered, was her roommate wearing heels with short shorts? At least she had the heater cranked up.

"I'd like everyone to meet my roommate, Alice!"

Two men nodded, said "Whassup?" A girl smiled and fidgeted with her expensive handbag as Lisa said their names: Lil' Smokey, Big Pipe, and Leila. Leila was a Yukemaya Indian dressed in hundred-dollar jeans, hoop earrings, and feathered hair like a chola. Ridiculous. Lil' Smokey and Big Pipe were also Indian, but definitely not Yukemaya. Lil' Smokey wore his hair in cornrows and looked like he had white blood in him. Big Pipe weighed at least three hundred pounds and his T-shirt was big enough for Alice and Lisa both. The two boys, Lisa excitedly explained, made up the rap group Red Dawn.

"We're kind of a hip-hop/rage-metal hybrid," Lil' Smokey clarified.

"So that explains the strange noises coming from my stereo," Alice said.

Lil' Smokey laughed. It was a mischievous chuckle, and he flashed a smile to go with it. Alice decided he was charming but untrustworthy. Another rowdy boy from the rez.

The party got under way. Lisa poured everyone cranberry juice with too much vodka. Alice stuck with water. Leila was quiet, starstruck even. She kept picking up Red Dawn's CD case, *No Justice on Stolen Land*, to read the lyrics. Lil' Smokey told her she could keep it. "Seriously?" she asked as she stuffed it in her purse. Big Pipe said, "Yeah, yeah, yeah" which he added to just about everything Lil' Smokey said. It was the only thing the big dude seemed to know how to say, except when his phone rang, which he answered, "Yo, yo, yo."

Lisa was definitely interested in Lil' Smokey. She was into the music, angry songs about life on the rez, the sovereign ghetto, and all the addiction and abuse and sorrow that went on there. Though she grew up poor, Lisa couldn't possibly relate. Neither could Leila with her monthly stipend from the casino. But Alice understood, and she bobbed her head to the beat. She supposed it wasn't *too* terrible.

Lisa poured herself another drink. Her eyes were glassy. She seemed to be waiting for something to happen. Alice never knew how to act at parties. She considered going back to her room when Lil' Smokey set his sights on her.

"You're not Yukemaya," he said, almost like an accusation.

"Neither are you," she replied.

"No, or else I wouldn't be driving that rez rocket parked out front."

Alice didn't want to talk about where she was from with Lil' Smokey. "I like your music," she said.

"Thanks. Do you work at the casino?"

"Yeah, graveyard."

"That sucks."

"It's not too bad. I used to be a slot tech. Now I work in guest services."

"I work in transpo," he said.

"Oh, yeah?"

"Valet. I just started."

"That's cool."

"Not really. But graveyard? I couldn't do that. I like my sleep too much." He wore a gold chain with the Washington Redskins logo stamped into an oversize medallion.

"What's this about?" she asked. She took the medallion in her hand. She couldn't believe how forward she was being.

"I want to do for *redskin* what gangster rap done did for *nigger*. Some people think it's offensive. Some people don't think it's offensive enough. Red Dawn is all about owning the slur. It's more than the color of our skin, it's a way of life—for some of us, a very fucked-up way of life. That's our legacy. We didn't make it, but we have to turn it around, like the Yukemaya did. To better ourselves. I'm proud of my red skin, but it's not just my skin that's red. I ain't no apple. The redness goes down to the bone." His voice went singsong; he turned his screed into a song. *"I'm red from my toes to the ceil-ing. It's a gift from my ancestors I'm feel-ing!"*

And that's where Lil' Smokey started to lose Alice, not because she didn't understand. Rather, Lil' Smokey seemed to have shifted away from her, even though she was still fingering the bling, shiny and studded with what she assumed were fake diamonds, but the chain felt like a leash and Lil' Smokey's voice came from a distant part of the room. She was having a seizure, a slow-motion seizure that stretched things out and distorted them. She was having, she realized with the clarity of an epiphany, an Alice in Wonderland experience.

"Can I ask you something?" Lil' Smokey said from across the room. The other sounds in the apartment—Red Dawn raging against the government, Lisa and Leila chatting about wine coolers, Big Pipe yo-yo-yoing into his cell phone—were muddled and indistinct, but Lil' Smokey's voice cut through the noise like a bell.

"Sure," Alice said.

"Do you want to smoke out?"

Alice wanted things to go back to normal, but that wasn't going to happen. She had to figure this out on her own. What would Wonderland Alice do? She'd probably get high. When the signs said *Eat me* and *Drink me*, Alice obeyed, but it wasn't what that other Alice *did* she wanted to know, but how she dealt with the bad craziness swirling in her head.

"I have to go," Alice said, and headed down the hallway to her bedroom. The corridor stretched to an impossible length and curved like the hull of boat. She held out her arms to steady herself and her palms whispered along the thin trailer walls until she reached her room and tumbled into bed. She rolled over and watched the ceiling breathe, then rise, and float out of sight. Alice closed her eyes and told herself everything was going to be all right. She used to tell her mother the same thing when she came into Alice's bedroom on hangover mornings, stinking of booze, whimpering for forgiveness, mumbling promises that she'd make it up to Alice someday until her mother finally passed out, and then Alice, too, would drift off to sleep, wondering if that day would ever come or if she was a fool for allowing herself to hope.

Lupita stood in the Thunderclap Gift Emporium transfixed by a massive picture of a full moon over the Sisters. A smudge of cloud streaked across the top half of the moon, so that it looked like a giant eye against a blue-black sky. She couldn't tell if it was a painting or a photograph, but the image so strongly resembled the view from Denise's house Lupita was convinced it must have inspired the scene. This revelation spoke to her with the urgency of a prophecy: She must buy it for her friend. It cost a small fortune, but Lupita could afford it. She'd had a good day at the casino. Her system had worked to perfection, and she'd hit a small jackpot. It took her longer than she would have liked, and she had to call her sister at the last minute to tell her she wasn't going to be able to attend Elodia's recital, but she'd make it up to her with a lovely dinner, just the two of them. Mariana wasn't happy—was she ever?—but it didn't matter what Mariana thought. Six hours wasn't *that* long, almost like a job, but what job paid $2,000 a day?

The woman behind the counter wheeled the work of art around on a dolly. She told Lupita that she'd covered the glass with foam and then wrapped the whole thing in brown paper to keep it safe during the ride home. It was even bigger than it seemed on the gift shop wall, and would look lovely in Denise's gloomy house. If only she could figure out how to get the pinche thing into her car . . .

"Can I help you with that, ma'am?"

Lupita turned, and one of the valets, a handsome young mixteca with cornrows in his hair, was there to help.

"Why, thank you," Lupita said, more flattered than grateful.

The valet lifted the package off the cart and carried it out of the emporium with ease. Lupita followed him outside. He was skinny, but his shoulders were broad, and his arms were powerful. Her SUV awaited, washed and waxed compliments of Thunderclap.

"This you?" he asked.

"Sí."

"Nice." He said it as if he were admiring a beautiful woman. Lupita blushed as she climbed into her SUV to open the hatch, and the boy slid the package into the back.

"Come here," she said through the open window.

"Yes, ma'am?"

"My name's Lupita, not ma'am."

"Is that short for Guadalupe?"

"Sí."

"A beautiful name."

Again, she blushed. She was at least ten years older than him, but still . . .

"Thank you for your help." She offered him a hundred-dollar bill.

"I couldn't."

"Take it."

"Yes, ma—Lupita."

He smiled and took the money, just like she knew he would.

"Maybe I could—"

"Help me hang it?"

"Sí," he said.

"Perhaps you could help me admire it."

He flashed that beautiful smile again. "Of course."

He gave her his phone number. She made him repeat it so she could put the number she would never use in her cell phone. Lupita drove off, pleased with herself. Life was easy when she let it be.

The feeling lasted all of five-and-a-half miles. Lupita sat in her driveway, wondering how she was going to get the moonscape into her house. Maybe she should have accepted his offer after all. She got out of the SUV, punched her code into the keypad for the garage door, waited for it to creep open. She rummaged around in the dark until she found what she was looking for: a handcart concealed under a drop cloth she'd left there the previous summer. She dragged the thing out, startling a mouse. The sudden flash of fur nearly gave her a heart attack. She wasn't the kind of woman to get spooked by such things, but the creature's sudden appearance (and just as sudden disappearance) unnerved her. Lupita got back in the SUV and turned it around so the hatch was facing the garage and clumsily maneuvered the package onto the cart and into the house. She removed the brown paper and foam to make sure the glass hadn't cracked and left the picture propped up against the fireplace she never used. She took a step back and was struck by how different it looked—not nearly as dramatic as it seemed in the gallery with all the fancy lighting. She was certain Denise wouldn't like it. She could already hear her: *Why do I need a picture when I can look out my own window?*

Throughout the evening and into the night, Lupita found herself standing in the living room, staring at the scene. There was something about it. At first she thought it was the size of the thing. There was so much to look at. The clouds humanized the moon by making it look like an eye peering back at her. Then there was the wind, which she hadn't noticed before, but now she could see how it pressed down on the scrub in the foreground—just as it had the other day at Denise's house. As the light changed and her house darkened, she thought she could see a face shrouded in the clouds. It was only there for a second, and then it was gone. Her eyes were tired from looking at Golden Gizmos all day. She felt a chill and was struck by an odd notion: The picture was making her cold.

It was nonsense, of course, but her heat had been cutting out lately. Sometimes it stopped and wouldn't kick on again. Just imagining all that wind blowing was enough to send Lupita scurrying up to her bedroom for her slippers and robe. Once there, she buried herself under the covers and succumbed to a deep and dreamless sleep.

ALICE SKIMMED THE PRINTOUTS of her symptoms journal while waiting for Dr. Marcus. *Monday: Irritable, exhausted, freaky dreams. Tuesday: No appetite, unfocused, borderline depressed. Wednesday: Same as Monday. Thursday: Same as Wednesday only worse.* Not a day passed without something strange happening to her: a rubbery feeling in her arm, loss of feeling in her feet, those odd moments when her perspective became distorted and unreliable. The lost time was the worst. She'd be sitting at the Thunderclap Club Rewards kiosk or watching television at home and just kind of zone out. Nothing fancy or dramatic. She didn't even realize it was happening. When she snapped out of it, she'd find chunks of time had gone missing. Five minutes, ten minutes, half a television program. Gone. This terrified her. Where did the time go? Or was *she* the one disappearing down the rabbit hole? Whatever it was, she told Dr. Marcus to make it stop.

"I can't."

"What do you mean?" she asked. No doctor she'd ever seen had admitted there was something he couldn't do.

"Well, first of all, they're not side effects."

"Excuse me?"

"They're seizures."

"Come on," Alice said, "I know what a seizure feels like. It's got to be a side effect of the medication, right?"

"I'm afraid not." Dr. Marcus adjusted his glasses. "After a major episode, it's not unusual to experience a series of minor ones. Like the aftershocks that follow an earthquake. It works the other way, too. Sometimes smaller ones come before a full-blown seizure."

"So what are you trying to tell me? The big one's coming?"

"That's what we're working to prevent. With the right treatment, you may never experience another grand mal. That's the goal, and we shouldn't lose sight of it. Of course, by proper treatment, I mean getting you in to see a neurologist."

Alice had no intention of going to see anyone other than Dr. Marcus, but she understood it was prudent to play along. "So do I just ignore these miniseizures or whatever they are?"

"Record them, keep doing what you're doing, but we have to keep our eye on the prize."

Alice flushed with anger. "Basically, I'm fucked. Is that what you're saying?" She rolled up the printouts and slapped them against her leg.

Dr. Marcus drew his palms down his face, smoothing out his beard like it was wrinkled. "I understand you're upset, and you should be. This is upsetting stuff. It scares the hell out of everyone who has to deal with it."

"It's not fair," Alice sniffled. The worst thing about her condition was that it had turned her into a sniveling buffoon. What would Lisa's word for it be? A twat. A complete and total twat.

"No, you're right, it's not." Dr. Marcus got up from behind his desk to pluck a box of tissues from a table at the other end of the sofa. He set the box down and though she hoped he'd sit beside her, he returned to his chair behind the desk, his fortress of platitudes.

"Then what am I supposed to do?"

"In order to prevent these seizures, we need a better understanding of what's causing them."

"The triggers," she said dejectedly.

"Exactly. Now, I know it's not what you want to hear, but it's possible that you've been having these miniseizures for some time, all your life even, but their expression was so minor you didn't notice them."

Alice shook her head. "I don't think so." But what about when her mother died? In the days following her death, the time passed so quickly. A blur. They were days of waiting, and yet they flew by. It started when they told her she would have to identify the body and how difficult it would be because the body wasn't a body but a collection of parts. Actually, identifying her mother had proved to be not so hard, she told people afterward, but now she couldn't remember a thing about it. She'd met so many people. Doctors, cops, and all their aides and assistants, but she couldn't remember any of their names, what they looked like. Was her mother on a table or a gurney? Did they let her walk up on her or did they do the ta-da thing with the white sheet? She had no idea. Was it the seizures that made this so? Was her mind inventing ways to deal with what had happened? If she chose to ignore it, would her brain keep devouring chunks of time until there wasn't any left? Would that really be so terrible?

"Is there anything that might be causing you stress?"

Alice laughed. "You mean aside from the fact that I'm losing my mind?"

"Yes, well, there are plenty of studies, documentation that suggests—"

"Dr. Marcus?"

He looked up, adjusted his glasses.

"I was joking."

Dr. Marcus smiled. He was kinda sorta good-looking when he wanted to be.

"And the stress?" he asked.

"Yes, there's definitely some stress." Loads of it, actually. Though she was finally getting used to life in guest services, she was dying a slow death sitting behind a desk all night. When she was a slot tech she was always on the go, moving from job to job, machine to machine. And then there was the camaraderie of the crew, which she missed more than she thought she would. This was something of a surprise since she kept to herself, but it had been nice to know there was always someone in the shop to hang out with if she needed to.

Last week she finally caved and called Cindy to see if she could get back on the floor, but Cindy didn't pick up the phone. Alice knew what she'd say. The only available shifts were during the day, and they were hard to get. She was stuck.

Toward the end of her shift, Cindy came to see her, appearing out of nowhere like a fairy godmother, but she didn't bring the good news Alice had been hoping for. Instead, Cindy explained that the gaming commission was monitoring her situation closely, and it wasn't because they were worried about her well-being.

"They're waiting for an excuse to fire me," Alice said.

"You may not like hearing it, but you're just going to have to get through this."

"So I'm stuck here," she said. The Loot Caboose echoed what Alice was feeling with a long, low blast of its electronically simulated train whistle.

"Just until you get better, sweetie."

"And if I don't?"

"Don't think like that. Of course you will."

Alice appreciated Cindy's optimism, but it was a pill she couldn't bring herself to swallow. Alice wasn't a perky person. Not on her best day.

"Look on the bright side," Cindy said as she checked her messages and pocketed the phone. "You could be working a maintenance crew!"

For the rest of her shift, Alice watched the sweepers, trash collectors, and restroom cleaners as they crept past the booth. They pushed their carts and quietly went about their work. *That didn't seem so bad,* she thought. *Where do I sign?*

"Are we back?" Dr. Marcus asked.

"Huh?"

"Just now, when you were spaced out?"

"Yeah," Alice said, reluctant to agree.

"That was a seizure."

"No way!"

"Oh, yes."

"I don't believe it."

"What's the last thing you remember?"

"We were talking about my triggers."

"We were about to. That's when you went away. You stopped and tilted your head like this . . ." Dr. Marcus sat up and leaned forward in his chair as if listening to something on a frequency that only he could hear. "Textbook petit mal."

"That's bullshit." Alice felt compelled to argue. "How long was I . . . ?"

"Not long. More than a minute, less than two."

"Weird."

Dr. Marcus shrugged.

"You don't think so?"

"It's a very mild expression."

"You say it like it's no big deal."

"On the contrary. It's a very big deal. There's a lot we can learn from it."

"Such as?"

"That your epilepsy doesn't always manifest in dangerous ways, which gives me hope that we can manage it."

Alice rolled her eyes.

"I'm going to insist we go deeper into your childhood," Dr. Marcus said. "Explore some of the unresolved issues that are causing you so much pain."

The tissue in her fist was wadded up into a ball, a cocoon of worry. Alice pulled another one from the box and blew her nose. Dr. Marcus was right, she knew that, but if managing her epilepsy meant telling him about the rez, she didn't know if she could do it. Dr. Marcus wanted to know what her triggers were; Alice would like to know what wasn't: coming home in the morning and finding Lisa and Lil' Smokey chopping up white lines on the kitchen counter; drifting off to sleep at the Thunderclap Club Rewards kiosk and hearing her name called only to open her eyes and find no one there; the memories of her mother that came and went like the ghost in the casino. Fuck yeah, she was afraid.

Dr. Marcus would be, too, if he'd been raised in a home where he never knew if his mother would be drunk or sober, with a new boyfriend or alone, violent or depressed. All those days Alice would come home from school to find a party in her trailer and have to lock herself in her room all evening without any dinner for fear of what might happen, what she might see. Every morning a guessing game: How bad was it going to be this time and how long before she got her mother back? Alice knew she couldn't continue like this, telling Dr. Marcus half the story. Before long, she was going to have to give up her secrets. That day may not be far off, but it sure as hell wasn't going to be today.

"I'm sorry," Alice said as the tears started to flow again.

"You have nothing to be sorry about. You're doing the right thing. You're taking care of the problem. There's still so much for us to figure out and work over. But we will, Alice. We will."

In that moment, Alice could have kissed Dr. Marcus on his big beardy lips. She was so full of gratitude she felt it swell up inside her until she was ready to burst, and the mental image this conjured up made her giggle. Now she was laughing and crying at the same time when she seldom did either. Alice got up from her chair so fast it tipped over, but she didn't stop to set it straight. She just barreled through the door and out of the office. Halfway to the bus stop, Alice realized she'd left her jacket inside. There were no options to weigh, only what needed to be done versus what she wanted to do. Why weren't they ever the same? Why wasn't anything ever easy?

Alice returned to Dr. Marcus's office to retrieve her jacket and found him standing at the sideboard, sipping a measure of whisky from a crystal tumbler he kept stashed inside a cabinet.

"I left my jacket." Alice said and then surprised herself by walking right up to Dr. Marcus. She put one hand on his forearm and, clutching his lapel with the other, lifted herself onto her toes as if he were a set of monkey bars she intended to climb, and kissed him on the lips.

WHILE WAITING FOR THE WATER in the tea kettle to boil, Lupita reminded herself to call her sister, but by lunchtime she'd forgotten. She took her Thunderclap mug into the living room, because it got the most sunlight and was close to the switch for the heater. She'd gotten it into her head that she was going to catch the damn thing in the act of shutting off. She drank her tea and returned again to the moonlit scene in her living room. The more she looked at it, the more she found to admire. She supposed this was true of most things, but it had never really occurred to Lupita before. Aside from gambling, she had few interests, none of which she could say she felt particularly passionate about.

Cheered by the warmth of a bright, sunny day, Lupita resolved to start with a good breakfast, a hot shower, and a thorough cleaning of her kitchen. Then she'd return some phone calls and arrange to see her nieces. She was about to embark on these plans when she realized with a jolt that the picture had changed again. It seemed darker, wilder. She put bread in the toaster and eggs in the skillet and was in the middle of flipping an omelet when she thought she'd figured out what had disturbed her and rushed into the living room to look. In the foreground, coming up the mountain slope, hidden in the chaparral, was the partial snout and single gleaming eye of a wolf.

Dios mío.

An alarm sounded and she shrieked with surprise, but it was only the smoke detector in the kitchen—her eggs were burning. She opened the sliding glass door and threw the omelet into the backyard and immediately regretted it; it would only encourage her four-legged visitor to return.

She traded her slippers for shoes and went out to collect the waste and put it in the trash bin. The toast was cold by the time she got back to the kitchen, and she didn't bother buttering it, just pitched the blackened bread into the sink. She was more tired than hungry and returned to the living room to lie down on the couch and close her eyes for a few minutes. When she woke, it felt like a different day: dark skies castled with clouds. The bright sunlight of an hour ago irrevocably gone. She headed toward the kitchen to put the kettle on the stove when something flashed past the glass door.

Was the beast back? Had he come for her?

Lupita ran to the door to check the locks. Her niece Yasmina was playing in the backyard, walking along a fallen tree limb, perilously close to the edge of the canyon. What was she doing here? She shouldn't be out there! Lupita put all of her strength into pulling the door open.

"Mija!" she shouted. "Come quickly!"

Yasmina stood perfectly still, happily confused. She started to run toward Lupita, but as she approached the patio she veered away toward the shadow of the canyon.

"Yasmina, no!"

"Lupita!" Mariana shouted. "What's the matter with you?"

Lupita pulled herself together. How long had her sister been standing there? "Mariana."

A look of dark uncertainty crossed her sister's features. "We came to check on you. It's Yasmina's birthday."

"I know. I stopped by but you weren't home."

"You came to our house?"

"You weren't home, so I went to the panadería. Do you remember the panadería?" As if anyone could forget.

"We were home all morning," Mariana replied.

"Not today. It was Thursday."

"Last week? Did you call?"

"Why don't you answer your phone, Tia?" Yasmina asked, her little chest rising and falling.

"It's not holding a charge," Lupita lied. "Pinche phone!"

Yasmina laughed. A golden bubbly sound that did wonders for Lupita's spirits.

"Do you see these two mountains over there? The ones that look a little bit the same, a little bit different?"

"I see them!"

"Do you know what they call them?"

Yasmina shook her head.

"They call them the Sisters," Lupita said. "Just like you and Elodia."

"Because we're a little bit the same and a little bit different?"

"Right! They even have names."

"What are their names?" Yasmina asked.

"Ramona is the rocky one and the other one is called Ysabella. They watch over the casino and the rest of the reservation. Just like your mother and I watch over you." Lupita waited for her sister to say something sharp and cutting. She didn't have to wait long.

"You spend a lot of time at the casino, don't you?" Mariana asked.

Lupita didn't know how to answer the question. What was a lot? It wasn't like she was some pinche bingera with nothing better to do with her time. Lupita led a simple life, much simpler than Mariana's, that's for sure.

"Come, let's go inside."

She took them through the kitchen and into the living room and saw the place through Mariana's eyes: dirty and cluttered with teacups and empty wine bottles. The packaging from the picture was strewn about the floor. She wanted Mariana to look at the moonscape, really look at it and comment on its strangeness, but she didn't even seem to notice it.

"Let's go out to lunch," Lupita said.

"You mean dinner," Yasmina said.

"I mean linner," she responded, trying to coax another laugh out of her niece by combining the words, only this time the laughter didn't come.

Mariana looked warily about, like she couldn't wait to get out of there.

"It will only take me a moment to get ready." Lupita shuffled down the hallway and up the stairs to her bedroom, she heard Yasmina ask her mother, "Why is Tía's casa so cold?"

"I don't know, mija," her sister answered. "I don't know."

PEMBERTON CLAIMED HIS NAME TAG at the registration desk at the Gamboa Beach Hilton and filled his plate with miniature muffins—not so much out of hunger but as a hedge against the very real possibility he'd feel the need to flee before lunch. The seminar was called "Radical Radio" and he fully expected it to suck.

Nevertheless, Pemberton was grateful to be off the reservation and away from the casino. It was his first trip down Thunderclap mountain since his arrival, and it was shaping up to be a gorgeous spring morning. The salt air felt like a miracle in his lungs. Before he got back on the bus and returned to Falls City, he resolved to walk down to the beach and bury his feet in the sand.

The San Diego Ad Society sponsored the seminar, and the hotel was packed with its members. Pemberton knew their roles by the way they were dressed. The stiffs in upper management wore golf shirts tucked into pressed khakis with belts that didn't match their shoes. The account executives compensated for their low standing in the food chain with tight-fitting clothes, spray-on tans, and bleached teeth.

Pemberton could spot the creatives right away. They were dressed in a style he thought of as premeditated casual: an ensemble of expensive sneakers and jeans with a loud, button-down shirt, sleeves rolled up. The creatives wanted you to think they were so preoccupied with game-changing, needle-moving ideas they could barely be bothered to dress in the morning. In truth, each item of clothing had been scrupulously selected. The getup reminded Pemberton of the sad defeatism of a fourteen-year-old boy who desperately needed to be thought of as "cool" while out on a date with a girl he knew would soon be, if she wasn't already, miles out of his league. Pemberton's own style of dress was both formal and plain: a black ensemble that he'd wear until the cuffs frayed, the buttons loosened, and the threads stuck out. It was a look of shabby gentility he modeled after reporters and piano players from old black-and-white films.

The parade went by and Pemberton took it all in with considerable amusement. Ad execs scanned name tags and pressed the flesh, convinced this was how the game was played. Every once in a while one of them would put a card in Pemberton's hand and start their spiel, but he refused to hold up his end of the conversation. They didn't know what to make of this, but the words *Thunderclap Casino* on his name tag meant they had to be nice to him because of the boatloads of money O'Nan spent on advertising.

Pemberton had no idea what his boss hoped to gain by sending him to a seminar to learn how to do something he already knew how to do. Maybe O'Nan was taunting him because being here was like pressing up against the window of his former life: Pemberton could look all he wanted, but he couldn't quite grasp what he once had.

Pemberton took a seat in the back of the conference room and prepared to be bored silly. The first speaker was the president of a data analysis company. He was a balding, heavyset pitch man in a dark suit, a fast-talker who used crude slides and terms like *activation* and *effective reach* to demonstrate "what my company can do to improve your business." It was a sales pitch disguised as an essential component to understanding "Radical Radio." One-hundred-percent hooey.

The speaker had a nervous habit of stroking his upper lip, and whenever his hand cupped the microphone, the volume ramped up and his amplified voice acquired a booming, cavernous quality like the voice of God. The radio-station flacks and ad-agency hacks worked their smartphones with frantic intensity.

Pemberton bolted for the door at the first tremor of applause and made his way to the empty bar. He ordered a double bourbon from a girl who looked too young to be serving alcohol.

Fortified, Pemberton returned to the seminar in time for the second presentation: a demonstration from a national advocacy group about the power of radio. More propaganda. Pat Hamilton, the tranny chaser, declared himself "an icon of radio" and introduced the next speaker. Pemberton hadn't seen someone this much in love with himself since he left L.A. He wished he'd lingered longer at the bar, but O'Nan expected a full report.

After the presentation, Pemberton went for reinforcements. He wove through the slow-moving herd and ordered another double. The girl remembered him and poured a triple. Or maybe she didn't know what a double was. He was still the only customer.

"Do you like working here?" Pemberton asked as she set the drink in front of him.

"Not really." She resumed slicing limes with a knife that was too big for the job. "Do you like what you do?"

"No."

The girl smiled. "I can tell."

On the flat-screen mounted on the wall behind the bar, a basketball player acrobatically laid the ball in the basket. Pemberton knew it was a highlight of some sort, but from last night or last year he couldn't say. He asked the bartender if there was a football game on.

"Isn't football over?" she replied.

"Over?"

"The Super Bowl was, like, last month or something," the bartender said, running her fingers through her hair.

"Yes, of course." The first bloom of intoxication shielded him from feeling embarrassed, but he took this misstep as a cue to finish up, overtip, and move on. With twenty minutes to go before the next session, Pemberton stepped outside and dialed Debra. For the first time in weeks, she took the call.

"Pemberton," she said, "what a surprise."

She didn't say it was a pleasant surprise, but it was a start. He told Debra about the seminar. Pemberton had always hated having to go to these kinds of things, and he wanted her to be amused that he was at one now.

"You're working?"

"At an Indian casino."

"What are you, a blackjack dealer?"

"No," he said, forcing a chuckle.

"I'm glad things are going so swimmingly for you. Really. I am. But I've got some bad news."

"Oh?" Pemberton asked.

"You got a letter from the courts. Failure to appear. There's a warrant for your arrest."

"I'm taking care of it," Pemberton lied.

"I'm sure you are. I just wanted to make sure you knew. It's the only reason I took your call."

"Right, thanks."

Pemberton marveled at how quickly they had fallen into their old roles, their tired patterns of communication.

"Fine then, ciao!"

"Debra, wait!" Pemberton shouted, but she had already ended the call. He looked at the phone to make sure it was over, that she was really gone.

It was over. She was really gone. For Pemberton, the obvious truths were the most elusive.

Back in the conference room, Pemberton barged in on a conversation between two women who professed to be excited about the keynote speaker.

"Oh," one of them said as she eyed Pemberton's name tag, "you're from Thunderclap."

They were from a casino elsewhere in the county. "The competition," Pemberton said with uncharacteristic cheerfulness. The women smiled and fidgeted. He professed great admiration for their latest campaign, but halfway through his overeffusive assessment of its merits, it became clear that he'd confused their casino with one that was located north of L.A.

Awkward.

He wasn't drunk but felt flushed with alcohol. He took out his phone and there was Debra's name in his dialed calls. He pressed a button. *Would you like to send a message to this contact?*

Yes.

Apropos of nothing, you're still my everything.

Send.

There, that was over with. His phone buzzed with Debra's reply.

INAPPROPRIATE!

OK, but I still love you.

Send.

Incoming.

RU sober?

Sadly.

Send.

Incoming.

1 more & UR blocked 4ever!!!

Pemberton sighed. It wasn't so much the message but its inelegant composition, the awful abbreviations and hideous elisions. Mercifully, the host approached the lectern and adjusted the microphone.

"I'm sorry to announce we have a change in schedule. Our speaker was unable to make his flight last night due to the weather in Chicago, but we are fortunate to have another legend of radio with us today."

Pemberton perked up, curious as to what the weather in Chicago might be, and was startled to see a familiar figure mount the stage.

"Ladies and gentlemen, please welcome the creative director for GB&H, Peter Metro!"

Peter Motherfucking Metro.

Peter Metro was a junior copywriter who started working at Pemberton's old agency a few months after Pemberton had signed on. He was a decent writer with an inflated view of his own talent. He wrote quickly but sloppily and didn't choose his battles well. He challenged every change, fought for every word. Someone must have told him the key to success was to spend part of every day networking, and

Pemberton had had to endure his loud, chortling conversations with former colleagues. *I can't believe you fucked her! Harf harf harf!* Peter Metro was a lousy listener and had an annoying habit of talking over people, even when they were answering his questions. In spite of his douchebag name, or perhaps because of it, he was a slovenly dresser and had the personal hygiene of a video-game addict. He also had the memorably annoying habit of using the same expression for every segue, only he used it incorrectly. *At the same token this. At the same token that. That* was Peter Metro.

There was a time when Pemberton would have given his left nut to work at GB&H, and now Peter Metro was running the creative shop. He was dressed in a dark, no-nonsense suit with a white dress shirt and black shoes. In other words, Peter Metro was dressed exactly like Pemberton.

"Motherfucker," Pemberton whispered. The women from the casino scooted their chairs farther away.

"It's a pleasure to be with you here today," Peter Metro began. "I'm here to talk about radio. First let me say, I love radio. Why do I love radio? Well, let me count the ways."

Peter Metro paused for the cheap applause, got it, and laughed. *Harf harf harf!*

"First, a bit about my background." Peter Metro told anecdotes about big-boy advertising in L.A., shamelessly dropping names of clients and campaigns. "Work that has done more than win awards, it penetrated the zeitgeist."

Puh-lease.

Pemberton remembered the afternoon he and Peter Metro spent "brainstorming" poolside at a Beverly Hills hotel for no other reason than they could. Neither one of them felt particularly inspired. They couldn't find the idea to get them started, put them on the path to better ideas, concepts with enough legs to sustain months of scrutiny and strong enough to survive being barnacled with the client's bad ideas. They were stuck.

Pemberton drank too much. Peter Metro gawked at the women and got stupidly excited about one of Pemberton's underdeveloped ideas. Peter Metro asked Pemberton for his notes so he could have them typed up in the morning. Pemberton, who was fighting off a sledgehammer of a hangover, handed over his notebook. The following day, he learned Peter Metro had taken his idea and pitched it as his own. Pemberton had forgotten all about the ugly episode. Until now.

"At the same token," Peter Metro continued, drawing out the pause for effect, "it doesn't always go your way."

"It's *by*," Pemberton said.

"Excuse me?" Peter Metro asked, momentarily thrown off his game. "Is there someone who has something to add?"

Pemberton gripped the edge of his chair, prepared to stand, but didn't quite make it out of his seat. "It's *by* the same token," he exclaimed. "Not *at* the same token. You've been saying it wrong for years, you assclown!"

A confused look crossed Peter Metro's face while he struggled to locate the source of the insult. Peter Metro finally saw him, and his inner douchebag asserted itself.

"Pemberton," he said. "What are *you* doing here?"

"Leaving," Pemberton replied as he stood up, knocking over his chair and causing much more of a scene than he'd intended. He moved into the aisle and out of the conference room, a trail of whispers in his wake.

"I apologize for my former colleague's behavior," he heard Peter Metro say and the rest was drowned out in laughter. *Harf harf harf!*

By the time he made it outside the hotel, he was already regretting the pointlessness of his outburst. The world was full of assholes. The world tolerated them because they were mostly harmless. Pointing out Peter Metro's shortcomings only made Pemberton look like an even bigger asshole. The whole affair left a sour taste in his mouth, and he could think of only one way to wash it out.

ONE LOOK INSIDE the Hole in the Wall Saloon and Pemberton knew he'd found what he'd been looking for: a decrepit saloon, a dive that even the hipsters shunned, an old-man bar. Pemberton figured if he couldn't drown his sorrows here, he'd at least give them a thorough soaking. He took the only empty seat at the bar and ordered a double bourbon from the bartender, a tiny Filipina with big hair.

"No whisky," she said.

"No whisky?"

"No gin either. You look like a gin drinker to me. Plenty of rum though."

"Dark or light?" he asked.

"Does it matter?" While the bartender built his drink, a dim figure addressed him from the corner of the bar.

"Pencil dick."

Pemberton peered into the gloom and immediately wished he hadn't. A biker, big and ornery looking, glared at him. Pemberton looked away and then back again, which was all the brute needed to get off his stool and come lumbering toward him. Pemberton stood to meet what he presumed would be quick trip to the dark side of consciousness when he realized he knew this man, though he couldn't quite place him.

"You should have seen your dick door hanging open," the biker roared. "You were about to shit your pants!"

Pemberton offered his hand, and the biker wrapped his arms around him. He smelled like old sweat and motor oil. For a moment, Pemberton thought the man was affiliated with the casino somehow, an off-duty tribal security officer that Pemberton had failed to recognize out of uniform. But then it came to him: it was the bouncer from one of his old haunts back in L.A.

"D.D.?"

"The one and only. What are *you* doing down here?"

"I ought to ask you the same question."

"This is my home now, homie. Welcome to Gamboa Beach, where the syphilis meets the sand."

"Nice place."

"What are you really doing down here? Your old lady kick you out?"

Pemberton tried to hide his surprise, but gave up the ruse. He used to buy cocaine from D.D. "You know about that?"

"I'm just messing with you. That's what happened to me. Old lady ran me off."

Pemberton wasn't sure he bought it. D.D. was many things: a giant of a man, a towering six foot six in his boots, a rarity for a Mexican American with indigenous features; a high school football star in East L.A.; a wrestler on the amateur lucha libre circuit; and a member of a seminotorious Latino motorcycle gang. He worked on numerous films, boasted of uncredited cameos, partied with the stars, and screwed a few of them, too. He once confessed to having killed someone in a rug seller's shop in Egypt and bragged about the year he spent in Japan training to become a sumo wrestler. In other words, D.D. was a bullshit artist, which was a charming thing to be for a man capable of extraordinary violence. In all the years Pemberton had known D.D., he'd never seen him get physical with a customer.

Pemberton expressed his condolences.

"No worries, I'm chasing the pussy away with a stick. How about you? You doing all right, homie?"

Pemberton had never been anyone's homie—not in this life—but D.D. didn't discriminate when it came to laying on the charm.

"Not so good."

"Everything okay? You working?"

"Yeah, at a casino."

"Which one?"

"Thunderclap."

"No shit? What are you, a blackjack dealer?"

"No, I'm still in advertising."

"That doesn't sound so bad," D.D. said. "My homeboy Miguel works up there. Real good with security systems. Maybe you know him?"

"I'm afraid not."

"Things will turn around and you'll forget all about what's-her-name."

"One day."

"That ain't no kind of attitude. Here, I've got something for you." D.D. reached into his pocket and held out his fist like a rich uncle dispensing treats. "This'll change the way you feel."

"I shouldn't."

"No one should. We're just taking up the slack for those who can't."

"Really, I—"

"What if I told you it was primo shit. Best I've had all year. Would that make a difference?"

"I kinda promised I wouldn't."

"Who? Your old lady?"

"Yeah," Pemberton admitted.

"And how's that working out for you?"

Pemberton glanced at his phone and set it down on the bar. "It isn't."

"To thine own self be true. Now giddy up."

Pemberton took the baggie and walked down the carpeted passageway to the men's room. He pushed through the door to the miniature vestibule and then into the restroom. Slipping into the oversize stall designated for the handicapped, Pemberton secured the door with the flimsy latch. He felt badly about using the handicapped stall, but in ninety seconds he'd be handicapped, too.

Pemberton used the key to his cabin to spoon the blow out of the bag and onto a Thunderclap Club Rewards card. He twisted the baggie shut and set it on the toilet paper dispenser. He arranged the cocaine in neat, parallel lines. He balanced the card on his thigh and rolled up the bill. The restroom stall was bright and quiet, suffused with an electric hum. The drug radiated a chemical smell, a marvelous potency.

This was his favorite part.

He inserted one end of the rolled-up bill into his right nostril and vacuumed up the first line. He switched nostrils and obliterated the second. He didn't snort the cocaine so much as breathe it in, deeply and with great satisfaction. He wiped the card clean with his index finger, rubbed the residue into his gums, and put the card in his wallet and the baggie in his shirt pocket. He flushed the toilet with his elbow and exited the stall.

Pemberton washed his hands, pushed his wet fingers into his nostrils and gently inhaled to keep his sinuses lubricated. His gums were already starting to feel numb. He scrutinized the mirror for tells: cellophane peeking out of his pocket, a white clump lodged in a nostril, coke dust on his collar. Everything checked out okay. His heart and brain felt synchronized, and the possibilities this unification of purpose might yield were dizzying.

The tequila shots were lined up on the bar. D.D. and Pemberton clinked their glasses and took their medicine. D.D. settled into a story about his old lady that concerned her reluctance to have sex with one of his buddies while D.D. filmed it with his iPhone. The story lasted ten minutes or an hour. Pemberton's judgment had become hopelessly skewed, like it had been taken apart and put back together wrong, and that was just fine with him.

"Mas tequila?" D.D. asked.

"A bird never flew on one wing."

D.D. laughed. "You are a seriously ate-up individual. Ever been to jail?"

"Sure," Pemberton said.

"What for?" If D.D. was surprised by Pemberton's reply, he didn't let on.

"Field trip. Seventh grade."

D.D. started rambling about one of his favorite subjects: life in the hoosegow. As near as Pemberton could tell, D.D. had spent a considerable amount of time incarcerated because of a murder charge he couldn't beat. It was a story full of bad breaks and bum raps, and Pemberton had trouble following all the twists and turns. The legalese and police jargon reminded him of his DUI, which he hadn't done anything about and the longer D.D.'s story went on, the worse Pemberton felt about it.

"I'm sorry," he declared.

"Don't be," D.D. said. "I totally did it."

"Oh."

"Let's go someplace we can get serious with this bag."

"Okay." He wondered why he found D.D. so easy to be honest with, yet so difficult to say no to. They stumbled out of the bar into the dark street. Nighttime already? When did that happen? Pemberton wondered if the universe was playing a trick on him. He closed his eyes; when he opened them again, he expected the sun to be shining, but it was still dark.

D.D. steered them toward a Carter-administration Thunderbird parked outside the drugstore across the street. D.D. climbed inside and reached across to open the passenger door.

"Why'd you park all the way over here?"

"Don't worry about it."

D.D. dumped the bag on the dashboard and cut up the lines with a razor. When he finished, there were four thick rails, each about two inches long.

"Jesus," Pemberton said.

"Do your worst."

Pemberton rolled up a dollar and hoovered up half the cocaine, switching nostrils as he went. Then D.D. did the same.

"You good?" D.D. asked.

Pemberton was better than good. His nose tingled, his lips were numb, and his chest buzzed like a beehive. The white lines separated him from the events at the conference, as if they'd happened to a different person: Pemberton the meek. That dude was long gone. Pemberton the bold was ready for business.

"Don't forget to breathe."

Pemberton's phone pulsed in his pocket and he fumbled with it while D.D. finished up the coke. It was a text from Debra, which gave Pemberton a very bad feeling.

WTF???!!!

Pemberton scrolled through his sent messages to see what prompted Debra's text, and when he found the exchange, his spirits went into a nose dive.

GFY.

???

Go fuck yourself.

Pemberton had no recollection of sending, typing, or even thinking these messages. His bafflement was total, his confusion complete. Did his inner O'Nan send Debra these texts? He was still wearing the name tag from the seminar, only Pemberton had been crossed out, and now it said: *LIKE YOU CARE.* He didn't remember doing that either.

"Hey, homie. We got company."

A black man holding a bag of groceries peered at them through the windshield, like a visitor at the zoo examining a curious specimen.

"Let's go." D.D. gave the dashboard a quick wipe.

"What?"

"This isn't my vehicle," D.D. announced as he jumped out of the car. Pemberton followed. The man with the groceries just stood there, frozen with fury or fear.

"Sorry about that, old-timer," D.D. said. "Wrong car."

The man didn't move. He clutched a week's worth of eggs, bread, and cans of soup to his chest.

"Just keep walking," D.D. said as he led Pemberton across a parking lot patchy with fog. Like his past. Like his future. When they reached the street and rounded the corner, D.D. howled with laughter, but Pemberton didn't see the humor. He'd made a fool of himself in front of his peers, wrecked any chance of reconciling with Debra, and risked incarceration or worse by ingesting gross quantities of cocaine in a stranger's car.

"Now what the hell do we do?" Pemberton asked.

"We find another bar."

"And then?"

"We get another bag."

"I don't think so."

D.D.'s ferocious beard made it hard to read his expression, but his eyes were fixed in a murderous squint.

"Did you make death tremble today?"

Pemberton shook his head.

"Then the day's not over yet."

Pemberton had heard this from D.D. before, on a night like this one, and he remembered not remembering that things didn't turn out so well.

"You sure about this?"

Alice nodded, distracted by Cindy's shiny blue lighter with the Thunderclap logo.

"Absolutely positive?"

"Yes," Alice answered, though she was neither positive nor absolute.

Cindy shook her head, spun the lighter on her desk. Cindy's tiny alcove of an office behind the gift shop wasn't much bigger than a broom closet. Alice didn't even know it was there until she started working in guest services.

"I hate to lose you, kiddo, so what I'm about to say comes from the heart, okay?"

Alice nodded. She wished Cindy wouldn't make this so hard.

"I understand your situation. At least I think I do. But you need to know that no one's ever done this before and, to be perfectly frank, it makes me look bad."

"I'm really sorry, but . . ."

Alice couldn't find the words to express what she was feeling. If she spent another week at the Thunderclap Club Rewards kiosk, she was going to lose it. The last few nights had been tolerable only because she had made up her mind to request a transfer to maintenance. She felt better as soon as she made the decision, like she'd been given a reprieve. But if she'd had any doubts about leaving guest services, last night had sealed the deal.

A female guest had gotten belligerent with her when Alice told her she couldn't enroll her in Thunderclap Club Rewards without a valid ID. The woman had no purse, no wallet, no teeth, and from the way she kept fidgeting with the pack of cigarettes tucked into the waistband of her sweatpants, no underwear. She had once been a pretty brunette, but now she had the leathery, used-up look of a desert tweaker, and she didn't like being talked down to by some *uppity Pocahontas bitch.*

"Did she really say that?" Cindy asked.

Alice nodded.

"Everyone in guest services has a story like that."

Did everyone in guest services have a ghost? Alice saw her between two banks of machines, neither moving nor completely still, floating above the carpet, as quiet as a dream. Draped in dirty furs and filthy pelts, she looked feral and strange, like a creature that had wandered out of its lair. Alice froze when she saw her. The tweaker turned to see what Alice was looking at, and when she saw the ghost, she dropped to her knees and started screaming. She begged Alice to make it go away. Alice knew that look. She'd seen in it in her mother's face when Alice roused her after a bad night of drinking and drugging. Her face convulsed with fright, ripped from one world and into another, crazed with fear.

Tribal security was on the poor woman before Alice could think the word. They had to summon an ambulance to get her off the floor. It took four security officers to strap her to a stretcher. Alice took one last look at her as they rolled her away. Her mother had once told her a story about a cousin from a faraway place with lakes and rivers and forests and snow in the winters. The woman had been drinking with her husband and passed out, and when she came to, her husband was on the floor with his throat slashed to ribbons. He'd killed himself with a razor. A lightning storm rolled over their cabin, and she sat with the body all night until the storm passed. Every time the lightning flashed, the body appeared to move, jerking this way and that. When it was over, the woman's hair had gone gray. That's what the tweaker looked like: a woman who'd seen a corpse walk.

"Are you all right?" Cindy asked.

"Huh?" Alice looked around Cindy's claustrophobic office, tried to remember what she was doing here, what she came here for.

"I thought maybe you'd gone off on one of your—"

Alice didn't let her finish the thought. "I'm good."

Cindy didn't look so sure. "Have you thought about what you're getting into? I mean *really* thought about it. The work isn't easy, and with your condition . . ."

"I'll be fine."

"You know what kind of people work in maintenance, right?"

"I guess." Alice shrugged.

"Minorities. Mexicans mostly."

"Why don't you just say *brown people*?"

"That's not fair," Cindy protested. "That's not what I meant, and you know it. What I'm trying to say is you get a lot of people who don't speak English so good, and they stick together."

Alice had seen them in the break room. Little clans of Mexicans, Filipinos, and Vietnamese sharing meals brought from home, community bowls of rice and stacks of freshly made tortillas. She envied their camaraderie, a distant recollection from her earliest memories on the rez. Now look at her: no family, no tribe, no nothing. All she had was Lisa, Dr. Marcus, and Cindy.

And her ghost.

"It can get awfully lonely."

"Lonelier than a graveyard desk shift?" Alice answered.

"Okay, you got me there, but if that doesn't get your attention, maybe this will. When gaming transferred you out of slots, they kept your hourly rate the same. But if you go through with this, you need to understand it's a voluntary transfer, so you'll be taking a substantial pay cut."

"I'm prepared to make the sacrifice."

"You really got your head set on this, don't you?"

Alice nodded. She didn't trust herself to speak. If she opened her mouth she might change her mind, chicken out, cry. She hadn't counted on a pay cut. She didn't make a lot of money, but she didn't spend much either. Her expenses were minimal, and she had a little bit put away in the bank. She was thinking of moving into a trailer on her own, but that would have to wait. She stared at the lighter until Cindy pushed it aside and slid the form across the desk.

"I hope you know what you're getting into."

Alice pressed her signature into the paper.

THE THUNDERCLAPPERS WERE LOOKING GRUESOME this morning. The midmorning bus had brought a legion of cadaverous gamblers to the casino, EDPs and LCDs of every persuasion. Most of them were female and nearly all were handicapped: women with walkers, ladies in wheelchairs, old crones dragging oxygen tanks. Middle-aged divorcées packed the twenty-one tables, their asses hanging out of their tight, low-slung jeans while they flirted with the dealers. Young, strung-out hustlers clustered around the ticket-redemption machines, desert tweakers with faces etched by the sun, transmitting signals from a place beyond the realm of sleep. Diabetics stuffed their faces with nachos at ten in the morning. The oldest woman Pemberton had ever seen devoured a chicken wing with a rack of brown teeth and a skeletal claw while propped up in a rig that was more gurney than wheelchair. To top the morning off, a Korean dwarf came running through Slotville waving a fistful of dollars, broadcasting her good fortune. Yes, it was going to be a glorious day, and Pemberton felt something akin to love for these misfits with money to burn.

His phone rang and the display read Jasper, which meant it was probably Kyle.

"Dude, where are you?"

"I'm on the floor."

"What are you doing down there?"

"Why do you want to know?" Pemberton asked. The best way to frustrate his coworkers' schemes was to never, ever give them a straight answer.

"You better get up here," Kyle (or Jasper) said.

"Why's that?"

"O'Nan's on the warpath."

"I'll be right up."

Pemberton considered the possibility he was being set up. It wouldn't be the first time. For the last few days Jasper and Kyle had been cruising past his cubicle, snapping photographs. Pemberton would be typing away at his computer, someone would call his name, and when he turned to look, he'd be blinded by a camera's flash as Jasper (or Kyle) slipped away.

"Where's the Loot Caboose?" demanded an ornery-looking lady with hair the color of a tangerine.

"It's right over there." Pemberton pointed toward the main entrance. As the woman turned to look, he heard the echo of a train whistle. "Did you hear that? That's it."

The woman nodded, her face breaking into a smile. "Yes! Thank you ever so much!" Other players heard it, too. Some looked searchingly toward the sound, while others spun their chairs like heliotropes turning toward the sun, somehow managing not to take their eyes off the machines they were playing. As the woman shuffled off, Pemberton marveled at the transformation of her mood. All because of the Game. That's when it clicked: It was the *sound* that hooked them.

Pemberton had been tasked with finding a way to replicate "the Loot Caboose experience" with other games. Loot Caboose was the loudest, most obnoxious gaming device on the floor. The answer wasn't to crank up the volume on the other games. That would drive guests away. But what would happen if they synchronized the sound system? What would a clap of thunder sound like if it came through every speaker at once?

He imagined howling winds, rumbling thunder, an approaching storm, emanating from each machine . . . What if it was all tied to a promotion? *When you hear the storm, Thunder Cash is coming!*

Pemberton experienced a tingling sensation, a prick of creative curiosity, a *what do we have here?* feeling that came when he knew he was on to something. It wasn't all that different from the rush he got from doing a fat line of coke.

Like the one he did this morning. He'd been spending his week-ends on D.D.'s couch down in Gamboa Beach. Not that he did much sleeping there. Lately, he'd been bringing a baggie back to Falls City to help straighten out after the weekend's excesses, and this morning he took a toot before boarding the Thunder shuttle. Pemberton was no stranger to being coked out on the job. He was, after all, a dedi-cated advertising professional. Although the drug swirling through his bloodstream was efficacious for cranking out ad copy, it left him inca-pable of dealing with O'Nan.

When O'Nan arrived from Las Vegas, it was a relatively simple thing to bring a bush-league gambling hall up to the standards of a big-time casino. Now the economy was tanking, the casino's numbers were going south, and O'Nan's antics had worn down the marketing staff. Cassi spent her days holed up in her office having panic attacks and Amy's allergies had cranked up. Even Bacteria Barbara was rumored to have filed a report with Human Resources for O'Nan's inappropriate conduct. All out of tricks, O'Nan needed a big idea, and Pemberton had it.

On his way up the stairs to the management offices, Pemberton nearly crashed into O'Nan.

"There you are," he snapped.

"Loot Caboose," Pemberton said. "I know why it's so popular . . . I've got an idea for the summer promotion that . . ."

O'Nan cut him off. "Way ahead of you, pal. We're giving away a Porsche."

"A Porsche?"

A wolfish smile peeked through O'Nan's inflamed cheeks. He was so pleased with himself his garrulousness momentarily slipped away. "I got a buddy in Vegas who owns a dealership. An absolute cocksucker—you'd like him—but he owes me a favor. Now what was your idea?"

Pemberton tried to tell him about Thunder Cash. How they could use a sequence of synchronized sounds to attract the guests. He took a step back down the stairs so that he'd be eye level with O'Nan, but every time Pemberton moved back O'Nan stepped up to claim the dominant position. It was like a dance, but Pemberton had always been a clumsy dancer, and his explanation suffered for it. His great new idea suddenly seemed not so new, not so great.

"I'll take it under consideration, but let's go with the Porsche for now. I want to see something by the end of the day." O'Nan stormed off, leaving behind a whiff of hair oil and flatulence.

A Porsche. A Porsche wasn't a car. It was a $50,000 penis extension. For the majority of Thunderclap's guests—the people from the desert, the people from the mountains—a Porsche was a grossly impractical way to get around. The clearance was too low, the trunk too small, and the taxes were more than most could afford. A car like that had zero appeal in a place like this. They could give away a pickup truck or a year's supply of gasoline for a fraction of the cost and generate twice the response. O'Nan's promotion was destined to flop. While walking back to his cubicle, it occurred to Pemberton that maybe that wouldn't be such a bad thing.

Pemberton spent the afternoon working on the Porsche promotion for the April newsletter. Every spread featured a Thunderclap Fun Fact: seasonal tidbits and historical ephemera of the "Did You Know?" variety. Pemberton found the information on the Internet. He doubted the veracity of many of the "facts" he uncovered online, but he never knowingly manipulated the information—until today.

First, he credited the invention of bingo to the Navajos. Then he asserted the Apaches had trained a certain breed of chicken to run in excess of one hundred miles a day. For the finale, he posed the following question: *Did you know "Porsche" is the Yukemaya word for "runs like the wind"?* The last one was probably pushing it too far, a suspicion that was borne out when O'Nan summoned him to his office later that afternoon.

"Where did you get these Fun Facts?" O'Nan asked, stabbing his finger at the copy attributing the name of a German automobile manufacturer to a tribe of Southwest American Indians. "Because I've never heard of this before, *and I own a Porsche.*"

"I made it up."

"You. . . made . . . it . . . up?" O'Nan looked like he might actually choke on his words.

Pemberton nodded.

"Explain."

"It's a joke. You know, for April Fools' Day."

"Are you calling me a fool?"

"No," Pemberton quickly protested. "I was simply—"

"What's Cassi's extension?"

Pemberton recited his supervisor's number. O'Nan dialed. O'Nan summoned. Pemberton shifted uncomfortably while they waited for Cassi to arrive.

"You wanted to see me?" Cassi asked from the doorway, reluctant to enter.

"Take a seat," O'Nan pointed at a chair. Cassi looked harried and terrified, which was precisely how O'Nan liked his women.

"Did you approve this?" he asked.

Cassi shot a furtive glance Pemberton's way.

"Yes."

"Including these Fun Facts?"

"Including everything," Cassi said. "Is something wrong?"

"These Fun Facts suck."

"Yes, but—"

"You're fired."

"What?"

Cassi looked more confused than upset, like she couldn't quite process what was happening. Pemberton waited for O'Nan to shout "April fools!" but the moment passed. When it became clear that O'Nan had nothing more to say to her, she started to cry and fled the office.

"That should be you."

"You're not really going to fi—"

"I'm gonna do whatever the fuck I wanna do!" O'Nan exploded.

Pemberton was as shocked by his anger as he was by his poor diction.

"You like making a fool out of me? Well, this is what you get. April-fucking-fools! Now get out of my fucking office. And if you don't get my fucking newsletter fixed by the end of the day, you'll be looking for work, too!" His chest heaved like a boat in boiling water, his eyes portholes into insanity.

O'Nan's phone rang. He picked it up without looking to see who was calling.

"Hey, baby, what do you say?" he asked with more warmth than Pemberton would have imagined possible. O'Nan gave him the jerk-off gesture. Pemberton got up and left. A tired-looking cleaning lady dusted off the decorative axes in the hallway. Pemberton considered walking out and never coming back, saving everyone a good bit of trouble. But sparing O'Nan trouble wasn't what he signed on for, and he went looking for Cassi instead. The cubicle farm was empty, the conference rooms strangely barren. Pemberton found his supervisor sitting at the bottom of a stairwell, hunched over her cell phone, her thin shoulders shaking as she wept.

Pemberton tried to conjure up some words to console her and failed, which was unacceptable. Words were Pemberton's forte. But this wasn't a pitch or a concept, but a human being, a person in distress. He should be able to reassure her somehow, to find the words that would put her mind at ease, but all he could think about was the line of cocaine he would reward himself with when he got back to his cabin. Pemberton backed out of the stairwell and quietly snuck away.

AFTER HER MOTHER DIED, Alice worked as a cleaning lady in one of the hundreds of Northern Arizona motels that boasted of being the gateway to the Grand Canyon. It was the only thing she could find. Why not? She'd been cleaning up after her mother her whole life. How much harder could it be?

At the motel, they gave her two checklists: one for the room, and one for her cart. She liked the orderly progression of it. Room to room, bed to bed, toilet to toilet. The motel only had sixty beds, and even though her manager rotated the cleaning staff from the top floor to the bottom, east wing to west, Alice learned her way around the rooms so well she could pick out the things that made them distinct, A loose tile in the bathroom, a burn mark on the nightstand, a mirror with a warped frame that made her look superskinny. She seldom had to talk to anyone other than her manager, and she didn't have to answer any questions about her mother because for the first time in her life no one knew who she was.

As much as she enjoyed the work, Alice resented the guests. She had a particular contempt for those who didn't check out when they were supposed to. She hated having to deal with them, especially the men with their greasy eyeballs and hairy paunches, springing out of bed naked or barely clothed when she walked into the room, pretending to be surprised when the whole thing was carefully orchestrated so he could waggle across the room with his junk hanging out. She thought about getting a knife or something, but she remembered the time her mother went after one of her boyfriends. Alice thought her mother would kill him, but the man just laughed and knocked the knife out of her hands and slapped her to the floor. Alice didn't stick around to see how it went after they made up.

She liked it when the curtains were open and she could look inside the room before opening the door. She hated surprises. The other maids told her stories of junkies shooting up in the bathroom or people tied to the bed. Alice was convinced she was going to stumble upon something horrible. She promised herself she'd be calm, that she wouldn't freak out. She imagined finding a young woman in bed all pilled-up and dead, her face as blue as the disinfectant Alice put in the toilet. If the note the woman left was mean or desperate or cruel, Alice would rewrite it, make things right. She played this fantasy in her head so often that sometimes when she opened the door to an empty room she almost felt disappointed.

Once, someone left a cat in the room, and she'd screamed as it darted past. She'd spent her lunch break looking for it, trying to coax it out of its hiding place with a bowl of milk. This had spooked her for the rest of the day, and she'd broken two water glasses. Another time she found a magazine with pictures of naked couples having sex, the men and women equally beautiful, and there was nothing strange or weird about what they were doing to one another. It was different from the ones she usually found. Alice didn't know there were magazines like that. After she changed the sheets, she lay down in the cool clean bed and tried to get herself off but froze every time she heard footsteps in the passageway.

What Alice hated the most were the looks she got from other Indians. They didn't know her, but Alice knew what they saw: another poor Indian girl trying to make it in the white world. All it took was a sidelong glance from an old Indian woman or young mother as they opened the door to their room, a room she'd cleaned, a look that said, *You turned your back on your people for this?*

It was so unfair. Everything Alice tried to leave behind came rushing back until it was like she'd never left. She'd sit in the studio apartment she shared with two other ladies who worked at the motel. There were no hills outside her windows, just a freeway that kept her awake at night, so she watched television. Her window to the world.

Working on the maintenance staff at Thunderclap was easier than cleaning hotels. A lot easier. On her first day on the job, Alice's new supervisor, Ruby, a Mexican lady who spoke heavily accented English, told her not to push herself too much.

"The people come here to have a good time. They don't want to see you working so hard. They don't want to see you at all. Be like a ghost," Ruby said with a wink.

No problem.

Alice worked on the casino floor, picking up trash, wiping down machines, vacuuming the endless carpets. She had two checklists: one for the casino, another for the cart. She had all night to get her work done, and she could do it in any order she liked. The only thing she had to do according to schedule was clean the restrooms four times a shift and sign her name on the chart posted on the wall. Otherwise she could roam about as she pleased. Not being seen, going unnoticed, appealed to her immensely. She loved exploring all the hidden places she didn't know about. Her first week was like a dream.

Alice wasn't sure if her supervisor was aware of her seizures or if there was someone else Ruby reported to who kept tabs on those sorts of things. Alice assumed everyone knew everything. While far from gruff, Ruby displayed none of the sisterly affection that made working for Cindy so pleasant, which was fine with Alice. She didn't want to be best friends with her supervisor. When she worked in slots, she hardly ever talked to her boss—he didn't even work the same shift. Those were happy days.

Sometimes when she trundled past the Thunderclap Club Rewards kiosk, she'd see her replacement, a puzzled-looking white girl. Though Cindy was right about the maintenance workers being cliquish and remote, getting out of guest services was the best thing Alice had done for herself since she started seeing Dr. Marcus.

She hadn't had any major seizures since she transferred, but she'd had plenty of minor episodes. Alice didn't know if they were increasing in frequency or if she was simply more aware of them. She still hadn't figured out the triggers, but she recognized how they made her feel. If she sensed one coming, she'd stop what she was doing and push her cart away from the crowd. Sometimes she zoned out. Sometimes she hallucinated, and the spatial relationships inside the casino went a little haywire. Sometimes she heard a woman's voice calling out to her underneath the noise of the slot machines, but she could never quite make out what she was saying. The important thing was to not freak out.

The best place for her during these episodes was the waterfall in the Forest of Fortune. The sound of the falls calmed her down until she snapped out of it. She could stand there for as long as she needed to, and no one would say a word. Everyone was distracted in the Forest of Fortune, if not by the slot machines, then by the creatures or the laser show. Alice liked to watch the animals do their thing. The bear growled, the wolf howled, and the eagle . . . cried? What was it that eagles did exactly?

And then there was Mike who started working the graveyard shift full-time a few weeks after she'd transferred to maintenance. Whenever he saw Alice pushing her cart, his eyes got big, and he broke into a goofy smile. She never saw him while she was in guest services, because she wasn't allowed to leave her desk. Now when they ran into each other on the floor, Mike walked with her. He was a big, athletic man with broad shoulders and a thick neck, and legs that were almost skinny. Unlike the other people on the security detail, he wasn't always down in the chow hall stuffing his face. She wondered what he'd look like without a mustache. He was always offering to go and get her a cup of coffee or something to eat from the vending machines. She refused because she could get these things herself, and she didn't want him to get the wrong idea, but she was intrigued by the possibilities.

She did get lonely. Alice tried to talk Lisa into taking her old job at the kiosk. She'd make better money, something Lisa was always bitching about, though with her long red hair she'd be a freak magnet. She'd have all the party people from here to Gamboa Beach lining up for a

Thunderclap Club Rewards card. Lisa didn't want to give up her tips, which in a good week more than made up the difference between what she made as a cocktail waitress and what she could earn in guest services, but lately there had been more bad weeks than good.

"What about the future?" Alice asked. "Do you want to be slinging cocktails all your life?"

"You sound like my dad," Lisa scoffed. The future wasn't something the citizens of Falls City spent a lot of time thinking about. The future was for other people. Lisa lived for the heavy immensity of *now*.

Lisa had been spending all her free time with Lil' Smokey, staying up late, losing time in her own way. Alice didn't know what went on in their trailer when she was at work and she didn't want to know. Sometimes she didn't see Lisa for days and days. Alice had noticed more of Lil' Smokey's stuff around: T-shirts in the laundry hamper, hair product in the bathroom. On their days off, Lisa went with Lil' Smokey to Red Dawn performances on Indian reservations around the state. She helped him sell CDs and God knew what else out of the trunk of her car.

When Alice caught up with Lisa, she was always going on and on about the big break that was just around the corner. The A&R guy who came to one of Lil' Smokey's shows, the hip-hop artist making noise about bringing Red Dawn on tour, the television executive who wanted to use one of their tracks on a pilot he was filming. She was full of talk. But fortune had eluded Red Dawn. No record deals, no name in lights, and no money.

Alice found the end of her shift the most depressing part of her day. She had to return her cart, clock out, ride the bus to Falls City, and walk the last few blocks to her trailer. If she was lucky, it only took half an hour, but it could take longer if she was late and missed the bus. The minutes she spent waiting at the bus stop were the slowest. Every minute felt like ten. This morning it took longer than usual to get home, and she was feeling pretty beat. She changed out of her uniform and poured a bowl of cereal. As she sat down to eat, Lisa's boyfriend walked out of the bathroom with a towel wrapped around his waist. One of *her* towels.

"I didn't know you were here," Lil' Smokey said, not seeming at all surprised to see her.

"Well, I am," Alice snapped.

"Is there a problem?"

"I wish you'd ask before using my towels."

"You want it back?" he asked. Alice knew if she said yes, he'd drop the towel.

"Where's Lisa?"

"She went out."

"Out?" Alice couldn't believe it. Now Lisa was letting him stay in the trailer while she was out? Definitely not cool.

"What's the big deal?"

Alice speed-dialed her roommate. Lisa picked up after the first ring.

"Hey, Alice."

"Can you tell me why your half-breed boyfriend is hitting on me?"

"What?" Lisa shouted into the phone.

"He's standing here in the kitchen without any clothes on," Alice said.

"Let me talk to him."

"Lisa, why aren't you here?" Alice turned away from Lil' Smokey.

"I'm running errands."

"At seven in the morning?"

"I'm sorry, Alice. This is bullshit. It won't happen again. I promise."

Alice ended the call. She didn't want to hear promises. She wanted Lil' Smokey out of her kitchen.

"Half-breed?"

"Well, aren't you?"

"I see how you are. You're no different than these stuck-up Yuke-maya bitches."

"You will never know how different I am."

"You got that right." Lil' Smokey stomped down the hallway to Lisa's bedroom and slammed the flimsy door.

Alice dropped the spoon in her cereal and took it to the sink. She let the tap run and thrust her hands in the scalding water for as long as she could take it. Why did she call him that? Alice dried her hands with a dirty dishtowel and hid in her bedroom. Alice wanted to take a shower and go to bed, but couldn't do either until Lisa came home. Lil' Smokey's phone rang, and his muffled explanation in the next room sounded more indignant than apologetic. Alice tried to fall asleep, but tossed and turned for the better part of an hour, alert to every sound in the trailer. She finally drifted off, but snapped awake when Lisa came home and started arguing with Lil' Smokey. Lisa would stay mad at him for a few days, and then her anger would inevitably turn toward Alice. It was just like being back on the rez, her mother sleeping with some man she didn't really know, his wife or girlfriend coming into the picture, and then the whole rez turning against them. As Alice tumbled into sleep, she wondered if her life was just a messy dream of what it would be like to run away from home. What if she woke up tomorrow back on the rez, her mother sleeping one off in the next room?

No thanks. Even if it meant seeing her mother again, Alice didn't want to go back. Those days were over, and she wanted them to stay that way.

SUMMER

THEY SPIRITED US AWAY *to the mountains, costumed in the skins of animals. They powdered our flesh until we resembled the ghosts we were fated to become. The men were savage, the women cruel. Their ways were not our ways. I understood before Ysabella there was no going back to the life we knew before. The pain we'd endured at the orphanage was nothing compared to this. Each night we prayed for our rescue, and every day our suffering continued. We were captives, trophies of war.*

The women hated us. Our skin was fairer than theirs, our features more delicate. They wanted to tear out our hair and batter our bodies. They gave us spoiled food and foul water. They worked us like slaves, punished us for no reason. At the end of a long day's march, they tied us to trees and left us there for hours. The shadows crept across the ground, devouring sunlight, cloaking us in cold. Hawks circled and the crows watched over us, their cries drowning out our pitiful whimpering. When they released us, we could barely stand much less walk, but I tied strips of lace to the trees for Gamboa to find. The natives kept running, moving us from mountain to mountain, camp to camp. How could one catch what never stopped moving?

Finally, we came to a canyon, a shadowy box at the base of a peak higher than the rest. Water fell from its bald crown and tumbled into a deep pool and began its long voyage to the sea. The canyon was strewn with great rocks. There was one near the falls that rested flat like a strange red table. There were many such rocks, but only one was stained red.

Our first night in the canyon, two savages came for us. They took us to the red rock. A boy who had worked at one of the ranchos conversed with us in our own tongue. He told us it was to be a celebration. The men laughed and offered us food and drink. I accepted the former and refused the latter. Ysabella didn't show the same restraint. She became raucous and loud, full of musical laughter that carried across the camp. Before long the men were drunk and prodded her into a dance I found grotesque, her shadows rising and falling on the canyon walls.

After the dance, I kept her close to me, told her it was time for sleep. Gamboa will come and right this wrong, *I whispered in my sister's ear.* Gamboa will save us! *This was my answer to everything. The Indian Killer, my husband-to-be, our savior.*

We were returned to the women. The wives and mothers and concubines. They were furious with us. They believed we had slept with their men. There was nothing we could do to persuade them of our innocence. Ysabella's drunkenness told them everything they needed to know.

They took us into the canyon and tied us to some trees beside the falls, their bark slick with spray. The crashing of the falls filled my ears, but I could still hear my sister's cries. All through the night I listened to her wailing. Then the women came for us.

I heard them before I saw them. I was so thirsty. I wanted to cry out for a drink of water but knew I mustn't. Ysabella didn't hold back. She shouted at them, and their answer was a whirring in the trees. An invisible rustling. Some kind of spell that made the stones fly up the hill and back into the mountain.

The women were stoning us. The stones came in great numbers, senseless and fierce. They crashed at my feet, screamed past my ears, shook the trees. I only saw flashes of the women. Their naked arms, their wild hair. The missiles were everywhere, but I was barely touched. I turned to my sister and saw her bent double over the ropes that bound her to the tree, her pale face broken like a doll's.

The air was filled with the shrieking of the women. It drowned out the falls, and as darkness fell, their jubilant cries harried me in my sleep. When I finally succumbed, I dreamed of my one true mother, the mother I never knew. She was old and wrinkled. Her actions were kind; her eyes were not. She fed me milk from a breast not her own. Why did you leave me? *I asked her. Her voice was soft, her language strange. I couldn't understand what she was trying to tell me. I opened my eyes and looked into those of a wolf. She opened her powerful jaws and I prepared to be devoured, but she chewed through the rope that held me to the tree and I fell to the damp earth. When I looked up, the wolf was gone.*

I could hear my sister moaning. I thought it was more mischief from the falls, my ears playing tricks on me. Though Ysabella's eyes were closed, she was still breathing, still alive. I untied her knots, loosened her ropes, and carried her to a pool beside the falls. On the red rock, I gave her water, cradled her to my bosom. She wasn't my blood sister, but blood united us now.

High atop the canyon, a man astride a wild-looking horse appeared on an outcropping of rock. Gamboa! My husband-to-be had finally come! I wanted to shout, to warn him of the savages hiding in the trees, but I dared not betray his presence. He looked down at me, regarded me with a look of regret that haunts me still, turned his mount around, and disappeared into the forest forever.

I cried out for him to come back, not to abandon me in this weird place. Ysabella's eyes opened. Something like a smile fluttered across her lips. Ramona, *she whispered as an arrow fastened to her throat.*

Lupita waited for the wolf to return. The light from the clock radio on the bedside table cast an orange glow. She wondered if there was a way to turn the light down. Her feet tingled, an unscratchable itch. She'd worried loose a button on her duvet cover, and it had slipped between the comforter and the covering. The thought of it rattling around in there like a coin in a slot machine drove her mad.

On the nightstand rested a pair of binoculars. They'd been a godsend, but they were useless at night. Her newly purchased Lil' Sure Shot air rifle sat propped up against the wall near the window with a clear view of the backyard. She had a vision of herself crouched at her bedroom window, dressed all in black, scanning the canyon until she had the wolf in her sights.

She wanted to order a pair of night-vision goggles, but they were so expensive. Every time she was ready to make a purchase, she had second thoughts. She didn't want to buy just any old pair; the online reviews were all over the place and most of them were fake anyway. Who could trust them?

Denise would call it a failure of nerve. Alejandro would call it something worse.

Lupita didn't know the first thing about shooting a rifle other than what the man in the store told her, an older gentleman whose name tag read Jorge. She wanted to buy a shotgun, but he assured her it was too much for what she needed, and then there was the matter of the waiting period.

"I can't wait," Lupita explained. "I need it now."

Jorge showed her how the air rifle worked, and she found herself coming around. It didn't *look* like a toy. He demonstrated how easy it was to control, how she could scare off any creature that crept into her yard.

She wasn't completely sold until he put the rifle in her hands, and she felt a charge go through her. She'd always been afraid of guns, but this was *sexy*.

There it was again. The sound she'd been hearing all night but couldn't pin down. The *scritch* of a loose rock skittering across the dirt. The squeal of her rusted gate. The strangled cry of the wind. It could have been *anything*.

She didn't think she'd have to worry about wild animals after she left North Dakota, the last place she and Alejandro had lived together. She'd stood by his side for nine years, moving from base to base, town to town. Arizona wasn't so bad. Texas was awful. But nothing could have prepared her for North Dakota. Something bad happened every time Alejandro went away, but North Dakota was the worst. The men were awful, the wives worse. Bored bitches with nothing better to do than spread lies. When Alejandro came home, he was full of jealous rage over all the things they'd said she'd done. He'd get drunk and start fights—with her, his friends, strangers in bars. He got in trouble with the air force every time. The MPs would lock him up and knock him down in rank, undoing all the good work he'd done while he was overseas.

On the night before Alejandro's third deployment to Iraq, they got in a terrible fight that left her with bruised ribs and a black eye. Lupita resolved to leave him for good. Those last weeks in North Dakota, getting her affairs in order, saving what money she could, were the loneliest of her life. She stayed in their house on the outskirts of town and watched raccoons, deer, creatures she couldn't identify wander through her yard. She could no longer remember the names of the streets of all the shitty houses and apartments she'd lived in over the years, both on and off base, but she'd never lived in a place so remote. Alejandro had wanted her to get a gun for when he was gone, but the way they fought, it would have been a terrible mistake.

On the morning she got the news that Alejandro had been killed by friendly fire at a military checkpoint, a hawk alighted on the picnic table in her backyard, a jackrabbit twitching in its talons. Lupita watched in horror as the hawk tore the thing to pieces. To be in love is to be tormented: You're either the rabbit or the hawk. She moved back to San Diego the next week.

She missed him. Especially on nights like this, when she was sure the creature that scavenged her trash and marked its territory in her kitchen was out there waiting for her. But he would never have put up with her obsession with Denise's picture. It got so bad she'd wrestled it onto the handcart and wheeled it out to her SUV. She listened to the weather reports on the way to Denise's house and wondered if Denise owned a gun. Maybe they could go shooting together . . .

As Lupita drove up the road that overlooked the Sisters and the reservation beyond, she saw the FOR SALE sign planted in Denise's yard. She slowed to a crawl. There wasn't a car in the driveway, and the gate was secured with a chain. There weren't any curtains in the windows, and she could see all the way through the house and into the backyard. It was empty. Denise had moved away without telling her. Her friend was gone. As Lupita's bafflement gave way to understanding, she pounded the steering wheel with her fist.

"Why does this keep happening to me?"

When she got home, Lupita dragged Denise's picture up the driveway, the gilt frame scraping the paving stones, and left it in the garage. All day long she kept going outside to check on it, to see if the wolf had crept any closer. Her eyes were drawn to the place where the scrub and chaparral were draped in shadow, a place where anything could be hiding. But nothing had changed. She stood in the garage, gently rubbing the heel of her tender palm, cursing her stupidity.

Then, two nights ago, she'd awoken to the sound of heavy breathing, a restless panting, so loud it felt like it was in the room with her. The beast had come back. She could smell its rank odor, feel its hot breath on her body until she vibrated in anticipation of jaws closing around her throat. She expected a pair of eyes to peer at her from the dark, but, of course, there was nothing there.

It's all in your head, you stupid woman. That's what Alejandro would say. He was always knocking her down, making her feel dumb so that she would second-guess the most obvious things.

The sound of the trashcan toppling over on the back patio reverberated up to her bedroom window. *What noise?* Alejandro would say and then he'd go back to sleep. But Alejandro wasn't here.

Lupita put on a robe she kept draped across the foot of the bed. She crept into the hallway and down the stairs, the air rifle in her sweaty hands. A real gun was what she needed, the kind her father used to shoot the big black birds that invaded his garden. She remembered how they looked when they dropped out of the sky and tumbled like umbrellas in the wind. Her father would make a clicking sound in his throat, pick the bird up by the wings, and unfold it like a map of the world, its black heart weeping blood.

Lupita slipped into the kitchen and checked the sliding glass door. It was closed and locked. She flicked on the patio light she couldn't remember turning off, but there was no creature, no carnage, no refuse scattered about the yard. The trashcans were where they were supposed to be, tidy and unmolested. The patio was swept clean. The wind buffeted the house—she could hear it on the other side of the glass—but that was all. For a second she thought she saw something, a woman, Denise maybe, running for the canyon, but it was only the ghost of her own reflection looking back into the house, her eyes hollowed out with fear.

ONE MOP . . . TWO BROOMS . . . four kinds of cleanser . . . Alice went through her checklist, fussing with her gear. The spray bottles sat in a rack like bottles of booze. They were all from an Indian-owned outfit called Hippetonka Cleaning Supply. Whenever possible, the casino used products from Indian-owned enterprises. From the bulbs in the light fixtures to the horrible carpeting on the floor, Thunderclap supported the red economy. The spray bottles were stamped with a logo featuring an Indian who looked like a cross between Hiawatha and the Virgin of Guadalupe, straight out of the Noble Savage school of Indian art. Alice found it strangely comforting.

Her cart sat half-in and half-out of the utility closet on the backside of Thunderclap Mountain. Over the muffled rush of the falls, Alice didn't hear Mike come up behind her, and she jumped when he said hello. A pile of rags resting on the edge of her cart tumbled to the ground. Only Alice could make a mess out of cleaning supplies.

"I'm sorry," Mike said as he stooped to pick them up.

"Let me do that." Alice knelt next to Mike. "I don't want you to get in trouble."

"No chance of that. No cameras over here."

"Really? I would have thought they'd have one aimed at the closet. Tribal resources and all that."

"They do, but it's a fixed-angle job," Mike said, eager to show off what he knew. "If something turns up missing, they can check to see who went into the closet without seeing the closet itself."

"You seem to know an awful lot about this."

"It's my job."

"Then you must be very good at it."

"I figure it will pay off someday."

Alice watched with amazement as Mike blushed—the last thing she expected from the broad-shouldered, square-headed tribal security officer. She wasn't crazy about the mustache, but it made his military haircut seem even shorter and she wanted to run her hands through it.

"Are there many places like this?" she asked to get the conversation back on track.

"You'd be surprised. There are dead spots all over the casino. Like right here." Nice Mike thumped the backside of Thunderclap Mountain. It gave a hollow-sounding report.

"What else is in there?"

"They control Thunderclap Falls from in here. There's an auxiliary control panel for the lights and some of the animatronics, although those are mostly preprogrammed."

Alice gazed up at the three-story mountain with a new appreciation. "Which animals?"

"I'm not sure . . ."

"The bear's my favorite. What's yours?"

"I wouldn't know. That's really not my area."

"Come on," Alice taunted, but there was no edge to it, the opposite of an edge really. A softness that caught them both by surprise. "You can tell me . . ."

"There's, um, a bunny rabbit at the edge of the forest, tucked under some ferns."

"A bunny rabbit?"

"Yeah, not a lot of people see it, but it's really cute."

No, Alice thought, you're *really cute*.

"But the bear's good, too," he said. Nice Mike slapped the side of the mountain again, and the whole thing shuddered. "There's a platform up top. Great view of the Forest of Fortune. Do you want to see it?"

It was the most interest he'd shown in her since she'd signed on with maintenance. "Okay," she answered, "but on one condition."

"I'm afraid to ask."

"You have to make the bear dance for me."

"I'm not sure if . . ."

"Then I'm not going."

"Come on."

Mike's reversal took Alice by surprise. She wiped her damp hands on her uniform. The door handle painted to resemble the rest of the rock disappeared in Mike's palm, and the hidden entrance swung open. She felt nervous, but not in a bad way. She liked this feeling, wanted it to last, though it seldom did and then never for long.

"They don't keep it locked?" Alice asked.

"They're supposed to, but they don't."

Mike held the door open, and Alice went inside. It was muggy and damp and surprisingly loud. She expected it to feel like a cave, but it was more like an unfinished basement. Tools were scattered about. A white grease-stained bag from the food court was wadded up in a corner. Alice picked it up and put it in her apron pocket. A puddle of water slowly spread under a leaky pipe.

"This place needs a good cleaning." If there was a control panel in here, she didn't see it.

"Over here." Mike called from the foot of a steep, rickety set of stairs that was more ladder than staircase.

"You first," Alice said.

Mike climbed, quickly and confidently. Alice tried not to poison the moment by wondering if he'd taken other girls up here.

At the top of the landing, a small platform extended over the falls. Various props, including a row of sturdy-looking Yukemaya war axes, hung from pegs. Mike fussed with a box mounted to the wall.

"Is that it?" Alice asked.

"Is that what?"

"You know, the controls."

Mike turned away from the box, and suddenly they were very close. Close enough to kiss. She tilted her head back to make sure he knew it, but was glad when he didn't make a move. She liked it when boys asked for permission.

"Turn something on," Alice said. "I came here to see a show."

Mike made up his mind about something. "Come here," he said, motioning her toward the edge of the platform.

With each step she took on the platform, the sound of the falls grew louder and louder.

"Don't go too far out," Mike cautioned. "You don't want anyone to see you up here."

Coming here was a huge risk, a violation of who-knows-how-many rules. It would be so easy for him to . . . Stop. She hated this anxious, fearful part of herself. This was how the seizures started, which she didn't want to even think about . . .

"Look out at the casino. Tell me what you see."

From the platform Alice could see the entire Forest of Fortune. It was all so astonishingly ugly. Everywhere she looked she saw wires and trestles and supports for signage. The slot machines were big, garish boxes, their candles protruding like nipples and caked with grime. How disappointing it was to see things as they really were.

"Do you see the bear?" Nice Mike asked.

Alice found him perched atop a fake boulder on the other side of the forest. "I see him!"

"Watch this . . ."

Mike fiddled with the controls and the bear came to life. It shuddered and in a burst of motion Alice wouldn't have believed possible rose up on its hind legs and let out a roar. A few of the Thunderclappers looked up, wondering at the sound, and then went back to their games.

"Now make it dance," she said.

"I'm on it."

The bear bounced forward and back, shaking its massive backside.

"What is that, some kind of line dance?" Alice asked.

"That would be the hokey pokey."

Alice laughed and withdrew into the hollow mountain. She trembled with something between gratitude and fear.

"Pretty cool, huh?"

"Yeah," Alice answered.

"It's even cooler when the laser beams shoot out of its eyes."

"I didn't really come up here for the view." Alice grabbed Mike by his stiff shirt and before he could use his sweet, dumb mouth to say another word, she pulled him in for a kiss.

"You know the difference between a dick and an asshole?"

"No," Pemberton answered, though he ought to know better by now than to indulge D.D. like this.

"You wouldn't," he sneered. D.D.'s voice was thick, his eyes at half-mast. They'd been at the Hole in the Wall since it opened at six. It was the kind of bar that was busiest the hour before it closed and the hour after it opened. It was nearly noon and they had the place to themselves. Even though the hands on the clock were pointed up, Pemberton suspected things were about to go south.

"So are you gonna tell me?" Pemberton asked.

"A dick chooses to be a dick; an asshole can't help but be an asshole. That's why you're a dick, and I'm an asshole." D.D. cackled at his own cleverness.

This revelation—if that's what it was—stung. "You really think I'm a dick?"

"Sure you are. It's like a point of pride with you. I mean look at the way you're dressed."

"What's wrong with the way I'm dressed?"

"You dress for a day at the beach the same way you dress for work."

"So, I'm consistent."

"Don't feel bad, amigo. Anyone can be an asshole, but being a dick takes commitment."

D.D. collapsed with laughter, and the Filipina bartender joined in. She poured D.D. a shot. Even though Pemberton spent most weekends here at the beach with D.D., the bartenders at the Hole in the Wall hadn't warmed up to him. This bothered Pemberton more than it should. After all, none of the other patrons traveled all the way from Falls City to come here. The bus ride to Gamboa Beach

was excruciatingly long, its conduciveness to ingesting drugs less than
desirable, the camaraderie among the EDPs and LCDs that constituted
his fellow coachmen nonexistent. Each time he boarded the bus, he felt
a little of his old self slip away. He stared out the window, watching
the mountains soften as they rolled through the canyons and into the
suburbs east of San Diego. Pemberton doctored a liter of orange juice
with a half-pint of vodka and sipped it as the bus crawled to Gamboa
Beach. He'd made the switch to vodka after D.D., of all people, complained about the odor.

"It's the whisky," Pemberton answered.

"No shit. It's seeping out of your pores!"

D.D.'s warning gave Pemberton pause. If D.D. could smell him,
so could O'Nan.

"If you're gonna go pro, you need to switch to vodka," D.D. said,
seemingly reading his thoughts, his knack was uncanny. "Every professional alkie I ever knew was on the junkie juice."

"But I'm not an alcoholic."

"And I'm not wanted in five states."

D.D. was always bragging about his bench warrants. He was a
two-striker in California, wanted on drug possession charges in Arizona and New Mexico, and faced gun charges in Utah and Colorado.
Or maybe it was the other way around. Pemberton could never keep
it all straight.

The beach was socked in with a bad case of May Gray. Tourists
clogged the surf and tramped the strand in inappropriate footwear,
gawking at nothing in particular while the locals played it safe in the
bars. Pemberton belonged to neither tribe. He was some other species
of visitor.

"I wonder if O'Nan is a dick or an asshole," Pemberton mused.

"Definitely an asshole."

Pemberton had spent so much time complaining about his boss,
cataloging O'Nan's transgressions against fair play and human decency
that D.D. knew O'Nan as well as Pemberton did.

"I think O'Nan might be an all-world dick," Pemberton said.

D.D. disagreed. "It all comes down to self-awareness. Sure, he's a dick on purpose, but I'd be willing to bet he thinks he's a pretty cool guy, that these stunts he pulls are what good managers do to get the job done. You know what I'm saying?"

Pemberton nodded.

"It all adds up to a guy who's pretty much in love with himself. Your classic narcissist with anger management issues, and it don't get much more assholish than that, amigo. Because the bottom line is the man can't help but be anything other than who he is, and that's an asshole. There ain't no recovery program for people like that."

"How'd you get to be such an expect?" Pemberton asked.

"Clean living. Another cocktail?"

"Sure."

The bartender changed the channel on the television behind the bar to a baseball game. Even though the volume was low, Pemberton watched the commercials out of habit. There was a girl in a beer commercial who reminded him of Jenny and she wasn't even Asian. When their drinks arrived, D.D. swiveled on his stool and lowered his voice.

"Listen to me."

"Okay."

"I gotta leave town."

"Oh?"

"There's some drama getting ready to go down, so I'm gonna head out, visit my old lady in St. Louis."

Pemberton didn't know D.D. had an old lady in St. Louis.

"I hope everything's okay . . ." Pemberton said.

"Everything's copasetic, but it won't be if I stick around, so . . ."

D.D. reached into Pemberton's coat and stuffed something into his breast pocket. "That's a quarter key," D.D. said. "Do whatever you want with it, sell it, snort it, save it for a rainy day. Only you didn't get it from me. On second thought, you haven't seen me down here period. Not since the bad old days up in L.A., okay?"

Pemberton nodded.

"Speaking of which. You still in touch with that chick? What's her name? Debbie?"

"Debra and no."

"What happened there? I thought she had you on a pretty tight leash."

"I kinda sorta got in a threesome."

"A ménage à trois?"

"Yeah."

"You and your old lady?"

"No, uh, someone else."

D.D. pounded the bar, making glasses, cell phones, and car keys rattle with the force radiating from his gargantuan fist. Pemberton decided not to mention that one leg of the threesome was a dude.

"That's what I like about you," D.D. said, wiping his eyes. "You're full of surprises. And here I am thinking I played a role in the dissolution of your long-distance relationship."

"You?" Pemberton asked.

"Those text messages I sent?"

"What?" And then Pemberton finally understood. D.D. had sent the *GFY* messages to Debra the night he'd first bumped into him here at the Hole.

"That was you?"

"Yeah. Are you mad?" D.D. asked.

Pemberton shook his head, but he wasn't really focusing on what D.D. was saying.

"When are you leaving? Maybe we could take a trip to L.A. for old time's sake."

"Negatory, amigo. I gotta split and don't know when I'll be back. But if you want my advice, let bygones be bygones."

"You're not going to prison, are you?"

D.D. laughed. "St. Louis is a shithole, but it ain't that bad. I'll tell you all about it when I get back, but you're a smart guy. You'll figure it out."

"Okay," Pemberton said. "Let me buy you a drink?"

"Shit, homie, you're picking up the tab!"

On the television screen, somebody in blue hit a home run off somebody in red. The camera panned over thousands of cheering fans and Pemberton wondered what it would feel like to care about something, anything that would make him stand up and shout like that.

Lᴜᴘɪᴛᴀ ᴡᴀꜱ ᴏꜰꜰɪᴄɪᴀʟʟʏ ᴏɴ ᴀ ʀᴏʟʟ. The feeling she might be on to something big came after she hit two quick jackpots on Golden Gizmos. But she wasn't greedy. She moved along to the next game, Donkey Stompers, and hit triple haystacks, which was good for a mega bonus. That's when she knew. She shouted with excitement as the money rolled in. Ladies at the other machines scowled at her. They'd been scowling at her all her life. Mind your own business, you pinche bitches!

There was no better feeling than playing on a hot streak. The way the reels spun and the jackpots lined up on the pay line with a *ka-thunk* . . . It was as primal as sex, only better. The bonus treasure sequence in Golden Gizmos. The braying of the Donkey Stompers. The sound of the counter ticking off the credits. Sex couldn't compete with that.

Lupita let herself be taken. This wasn't the kind of roll that heated up a machine for a while and moved on. This was different. The games had nothing to do with it: *She* was the one who was hot. It was all about her, not the machine.

Lupita knew exactly what this felt like because it had happened before, though not in a long time and not like this. She was feeling so good she turned off her phone, which had been vibrating nonstop. She didn't want to talk to anyone. She didn't want to eat. She didn't want to stop playing. All she wanted was one more score.

The Loot Caboose had thirty pay lines and a progressive bonus, yet was deceptively simple. The goal was to line up an Engine, three Cash Cars, and a Loot Caboose to trigger the progressive that no one had hit since they installed the damn thing late last year. Slot players took a look at the sum—it hit the half-million mark last month—and lost their freaking minds. Even experienced players like Denise. The

Loot Caboose taunted them with blasts from its steam whistle. *Wooo-wooooooo! Catch me if you can, suckers!*

Lupita was up for the challenge. With the size of the stake she had to work with and the zone she was in, she was ready to go after it. It was a change-your-life jackpot. If she hit it, she'd never think about gambling again.

But just like that, her luck changed. She could feel the machine go cold almost as soon as she sat down. It was stupidly obvious, like trying to seduce a man when his heart wasn't in it. It simply wasn't going to happen. She knew she should stop. She knew she couldn't turn her luck around just because she wanted to. But she pressed on anyway. The sick feeling in her stomach grew and grew as her winnings evaporated. She thought of the things she could have bought for her nieces with the money she had left over if she stopped right now. But she didn't stop. She kept playing. Not because she wanted to, but because she had to: The cold streak was like a ride she couldn't get off. She could make it stop, she knew, but to bail out would have been bullshit. There was no shame in losing, so long as she didn't let the game beat her. What did she care about a few thousand dollars? A couple grand never changed anyone's life. The credit meter got smaller and smaller, and went all the way down to double digits. It would be over soon, she realized with a hopeful surge of relief, this ride she'd never intended to take. It didn't matter. Win or lose, she never played with regret, even though she could pinpoint the moment she knew it was going to end badly. That's when the hole opened up inside, and she had no idea how to fill it.

Lupita took her Thunderclap Club Rewards card and sat down in the Hong Kong Kafé for a cup of tea. A chill had come over her, and she wanted it out before she set off for her lonely house at the edge of the dark canyon where strange things lurked. She thought about Denise and wondered where she was. Part of Lupita felt responsible for driving her friend away, which was ridiculous. Denise let the Loot Caboose beat her. The game got under her skin and messed with her system. Toward the end, she stopped playing video poker and gave all her money to the game. It dragged her down into the darkness, and when she had nothing more to give, she left town. Unforgivable.

But hadn't Lupita done the same thing as an air force wife? In every duty station she'd made friends with women on the base, but whenever Alejandro got orders to move she'd pack up and leave without saying goodbye. Same thing with the men she met in the bars and nightclubs. Her husband would come home from deployment, and they'd never hear from her again. She swept all that out of her mind. It had been a hell of a ride, but now it was over. Why was that so hard for her to accept?

Her tea had gotten cold so she asked for another and when the waitress asked, "Will that be all?" Lupita didn't even bother to answer.

ALICE THOUGHT SHE WAS DONE with the Loot Caboose when she quit guest services, but the game was more popular than ever and the crowds left messes for her to clean up. Thank goodness she got away from the Thunderclap Club Rewards kiosk when she did because now the players lined up for the Loot Caboose around the clock. They insisted it paid out more than the other games, but a slot rep told Alice it had one of the highest holds of all the machines on the floor.

The blasting of the train whistle still got on her nerves. More shriek than whistle, it was like a banshee. The sequence was programmed to sound at random intervals, making it impossible to predict. If Alice hadn't heard it in a while, the suspense of waiting for it made her anxious. It was like turning the handle on a jack-in-the-box: knowing that it was coming didn't lessen the jolt of surprise when the little freak popped out. Just being *near* the machine made her feel like a lab rat waiting for an electric shock. Even when she was working on the other side of the casino, she could hear it over the other games. She'd be cleaning up a spill and hear it howling away.

While heading for the Forest of Fortune, Alice absentmindedly knocked a bottle of window cleaner into her empty trash barrel. She leaned in, but she couldn't quite grasp the bottle, its trigger just out of reach. The last time this happened she used her scooper to fish the bottle out, but she'd left it in the maintenance closet all the way on the other side of Thunderclap Mountain. Alice wedged her cart against some rocks in one of the dead spots upriver from the falls. An animatronic wolf perched on the rocks above blocked the camera's view. Whatever the wolf could see, the camera could not. If it were up to Alice, she'd rig all the creatures of the Forest of Fortune with cameras. She told Mike her idea when he showed her the dead spot, and he laughed and laughed and laughed.

Alice didn't know what she was going to do about Mike. She thought about him all the time. It had been ages since she'd felt this way, and never about a white boy. Her "thing" with Mike, as Lisa called it the last time they'd argued, was complicated. For one thing, there was no "thing," just a moment of passion the one and only time they'd kissed. Alice wanted more than a moment. She wanted, well, she wasn't sure. But there was no denying the intensity of their make-out session last week with the falls crashing down around them. She couldn't stop thinking about it.

She definitely wasn't going to tell Dr. Marcus about him. Dr. Marcus wouldn't approve. Dr. Marcus would give her some gobbledygook about how it wasn't Mike she was falling for, but the security he represented. That was the thing about Dr. Marcus that drove her bonkers. He read meaning into everything she said. *Everything is a symbol.* Except when it wasn't. Even so, what was wrong with wanting to feel protected? Especially after all the times she'd woken up in the middle of the night and found whatever stranger her mother had brought home stumbling into her room, her mother passed out or unconscious or indifferent to her screams as she fought the fucker off. The ones who shacked up with her mother were the worst. All those nights she'd spent waiting for the gray fog of dawn to creep through the curtains that didn't quite cover her window, listening for the sound of booted feet stopping at her door, the persistent rattling of her bedroom doorknob as her mother's new boyfriend tested the lock, the slivers of nervous light that shot across her ceiling as they came to her room again and again and again. Wasn't she entitled to a little security?

It wasn't like she and Mike had exchanged numbers or traded texts. They hadn't even spent time together outside the casino. But whenever they did see each other, Mike was all smiles and asked a million questions about her day. *I didn't have a seizure today,* she would like to tell him. What would he say to that?

He was *too* nice. That was the problem. Too nice for Alice at least. Every time it occurred to Alice that she might enjoy a "thing" with Mike, she thought about telling him about where she was from, what she'd gone through. He couldn't possibly understand the things she'd experienced. He'd never lived in a house where liquor was more important than food or heat or running water. Or love. He'd never come home to find his mother pissing in a pot because the water had been turned off and the toilet was clogged with filth. He'd never had to pick his unconscious mother up at some stranger's house, burn marks on her body, her clothes soiled with piss. And he'd certainly never dated anyone who jerked around on the floor with her eyes rolled back in her head. If he knew half the things she'd been through, he'd turn and run.

No, it wasn't a matter of Mike being too nice, but of Alice not being nice at all. She was a freak, and nice guys didn't date freaks. That was the truth that stared up at her as starkly as the white bottle of cleaning supplies at the bottom of the trashcan. Might as well come to terms with it now rather than be all *woe is me* when Mike stopped being nice to her. If only she could stop thinking about him.

Alice made sure her cart was secure and reached into the barrel, leaning over the edge, farther and farther until—*shit!*—she lost her balance and tumbled inside. The trash barrel seemed much larger from the inside, and it took a while to hit bottom. She landed in a pile of paper towels and Styrofoam cups. Alice brushed herself off and searched for the spray bottle. When she found it, the bottle seemed enchanted somehow, the figure in the logo glowing with luminous intensity. The top of the trashcan felt a long way off. It was like being at the bottom of a hole.

Or a grave.

But Alice wasn't afraid, because she could see the wolf watching over her. The wolf didn't belong here. Who ever heard of a wolf in San Diego? But she was grateful for its presence. Wolves were watchers from the spirit world, symbols of protection. Put that in your notebook, Dr. Marcus!

Then something curious happened: the trash receptacle deepened. Alice didn't know how to make sense of this. The spray bottle was still a spray bottle. The trash can was still a trash can, but the lip felt far away, out of reach. If she didn't know better, she'd think she was looking up at the mouth of a tunnel, a tunnel that was getting longer and longer.

No reason to be alarmed, she told herself. *You're having a hallucination.* The realization calmed her, but it didn't make things right. She was still sitting in the bottom of a trash barrel.

It's okay, Alice.

"I'm fine," she said, but there was no one there. She didn't know who was speaking, but it felt like it was coming from a place deep inside her. Not thoughts exactly, but something else.

You have finally come.

Come where? To the bottom of a trashcan?

I have been waiting for you for so long.

Wait, was the voice talking back to her? Alice laughed, or at least she meant to, but tears rolled down her cheeks.

You must be patient.

You're not my mother.

No.

Who are you?

Who do you think I am?

A hallucination. A side effect from my antiseizure medication.

Does it help you to think this way?

No, hallucinations don't talk back.

Very good.

What are you?

A child, lost in the wilderness, like you.

I'm not lost. This isn't real.

Look at me, Alice.

Alice opened her eyes. The ghost floated in the center of her confusion, a crackling corona of dark energy. Her savage smile an eruption of light on a face streaked with filth. Blood-crusted pelts draped her shoulders and arms. Her hair was bound with strips of hide. Her words were kind, but she was a horror to look at.

Soon your suffering will come to an end, and you can reclaim your place among your people.

I don't have any people.

That's not true.

How can you say that?

I can only speak the truth.

Am I losing my mind?

No, you are having what your doctor would call a seizure. A good medicine woman would call it something else.

The ghost went deeper into the black. They were out on the ledge atop Thunderclap Mountain and the falls were roaring. Alice began to panic.

Is this really happening? Do you even have a name?

Ramona, but it's not the name my mother gave me.

I'm so frightened.

Don't be.

What am I supposed to do?

Save yourself.

You're leaving me?

Yes.

Ramona stepped off the platform and disappeared into the roaring curtain of water.

"No!"

Alice lunged after her but the ghost was gone. She wasn't on the platform or in the falls or anywhere in the casino. Down below, the Thunderclappers stopped playing to gawk at Alice. Some pointed. Others clapped. Some asshole called out to her to jump. Alice pulled back from the ledge before the cameras spotted her if they hadn't already.

Why did Ramona bring her here? Why did her ghost leave?

Easy: She didn't. Her ghost didn't "go" anywhere because she was never there in the first place. None of it was real; but if this was all in her head, Alice wondered as she headed down the stairs, what was she doing inside Thunderclap Mountain?

IT HAD BEEN YEARS since Pemberton prayed, but he uttered a silent plea to heaven and held on to the Porsche's door handle as O'Nan navigated the hairpin turns down Thunderclap Mountain at pants-crapping speeds. Pemberton fancied himself a fairly unflappable fellow, but with each turn he fought off the urge to scream. He couldn't decide if he felt this way because he'd had too much coke or not enough alcohol. When O'Nan told him they were heading to San Diego to produce the radio spot that Pemberton had written he was thrilled, but that feeling was fading fast.

Ever since the April Fools' fiasco, Pemberton had tried to cut back on his coke consumption, but it was his birthday and he overdid it this morning, chopping up a D.D.-size rail for breakfast. In the past, Pemberton was conservative with his drugs. A toot here, a toot there. Just to add a little something to his day. He could make a bag last a couple weeks this way. He was nothing like D.D. who would dump the whole thing on the table, snort everything he had in one go, and then face the world like a Viking on a rampage. He even looked like one: a Latino, motorcycle-riding, moon-howling Viking. But thanks to the mother lode D.D. laid on him, Pemberton's days of take-a-toot-and-scoot were a thing of the past.

Clouds convoyed across a sky so clear and blue that—for a split second anyway—Pemberton could see all the way to the ocean before the Porsche whipped around a wall of rock and dropped into a canyon. Pemberton consoled himself with the notion that when the car flew off the road and exploded in a fiery conflagration those who knew him would be able to say he died on a beautiful day.

O'Nan didn't speak during the death ride down the mountain. Any thought of relaxing when they got on the interstate disappeared when

O'Nan pushed the Porsche up to ninety and wove around the semis and SUVs. O'Nan drove with one hand on the wheel, the other gripping his cell phone, into which he screamed obscenities as he tried to reach his attorney. From what Pemberton could gather, O'Nan's lawyer wasn't taking his calls, and he demanded an explanation. He abused the attorney's assistant, called her a *mouthy little yap cunt,* which didn't strike Pemberton as an efficacious way of getting what he wanted. But what would Pemberton know about that?

O'Nan took the now-familiar Gamboa Beach exit and navigated the surface streets like a predator searching for something to kill. The commercial buildings and warehouses clustered around the freeway off-ramp gave way to subsidized housing complexes and low-end condos. Tired-looking people congregated in the street, leaning on railings, draped over cars. It was nearly noon, and the LCDs looked like they wanted nothing to do with the day. Pemberton could relate.

The studio sat at the end of a block of mom-and-pop shops, across the street from a vacant lot dominated by an enormous palm tree. They weren't far from D.D.'s apartment. The realization hit Pemberton with a jolt that initiated the ghost of a plan: Once the recording session got underway, he'd slip away to the restroom and straighten out.

"Let's go over the ground rules," O'Nan said as he slid into a space and engaged the parking brake.

"We're here?" Pemberton played dumb.

O'Nan nodded impatiently. "I want you to back me up in there. If I ask you for your opinion, it's not because I'm interested in what you think. It's because I want you to agree with me. It's not that I don't respect your opinion—because, let's be honest, I don't—but in a deal like this, the engineer's going to want to put his two cents in every chance he gets. And then the talent will start with their suggestions and script changes. I don't work like that. When I produce a spot, I'm in charge. You hear me?"

"Yes, sir."

"All right then. Let's make some radio."

O'Nan's phone chirped angrily. "Where the fuck have you been?" he shouted.

O'Nan's attorney, Pemberton presumed.

"Go on in," O'Nan said to Pemberton, "and get the show rolling."

The recording studio was a dark little shoebox with an office in the front and two sound booths separated by a tiny space packed with equipment. Sound-eating insulation cushioned the walls. Cords snaked across the carpet. Half-empty coffee cups sat perched on top of expensive equipment. Pemberton had logged weeks in places just like it, and they were all pretty much the same, but Paradox Productions was a decidedly no-frills affair.

The engineer was as bland-looking as his studio: a heavyset Lebanese fellow named Stuart who made a name for himself in the 1980s as the jingle king of some faraway Midwestern city. Now the only instrument he picked up was the remote control on his television, and he got other people to do the shuck and jive for him. His current specialty was Spanish-language ads for car dealerships but the only Spanish Stuart spoke was when he was ordering carne asada fries at the taquería down the street.

Pemberton offered a weak handshake and explained the situation. Stuart introduced Pemberton to the talent: Bob, Kaitlin, and Juan. Pemberton immediately forgot their names and addressed them by their roles in the script: the Boss, the Secretary, and the Suck-Up.

Pemberton distributed the scripts and explained the purpose of the spot, how he wanted it to play out. The gist of the script went like this: The Boss was a short-tempered, largely incompetent casino manager. His Secretary trumpeted the news of Thunderclap's great new promotion. The Suck-Up had some hare-brained scheme the boss shot down but eventually put forth as his own. As soon as the Boss turned his back, the Secretary and the Suck-Up skedaddled to Thunderclap.

Pemberton wasn't crazy about the script. The set-up was dated, the characters were flat, and the gags were all O'Nan's. He'd given Pemberton the situation and told him to take a crack at it. O'Nan revised a dozen different drafts with his red Mont Blanc. The last draft didn't look all that different from the first. O'Nan took masochistic glee in making the boss a hotheaded buffoon, like he was daring Pemberton to make the connection, but it was a game he refused to play. If O'Nan was the Boss, what did that make Pemberton?

The session went well. The actors were much more talented than Pemberton expected. Somehow they managed to make O'Nan's script somewhat compelling, almost interesting, and after just a few takes Stuart had enough to piece together the sixty-second spot. He was just about to play it back when O'Nan entered the studio with a scowl on his face.

"I thought I told you to get started."

"We're done," Stuart announced, a bit too pleased with himself.

"Done?" O'Nan shouted.

"We haven't mixed anything yet," Pemberton said. "It's just a rough cut—"

"Play it for me."

Stuart fiddled with his board, manipulated his mouse. The spot played. O'Nan listened to about ten seconds before he ordered the actors back into the booths. He wanted everyone in the room to know two things: He was in charge, and he knew what he was doing, but in doing so, he made it clear there could be just one boss, ergo no one else knew what he or she was doing.

"To be a good producer," O'Nan said to Pemberton, "you have to be a little bit of an asshole."

Then you must be one of the greats, Pemberton wished he had the balls to say.

After an hour, O'Nan still wasn't satisfied. The Boss wasn't ornery enough, the Secretary was too shrill, and while the Suck-Up was just fine, O'Nan had taken an instant dislike to the actor, and he made him do his lines over and over again just because he could. Then O'Nan started tinkering with the copy, going back to many of Pemberton's gags that O'Nan had revised out of the script. To Pemberton's way of thinking, this went against the cardinal rule of radio: Never rewrite in the studio. The pressure of writing while the actors waited for their lines could lead to mistakes, and it was expensive as hell.

Another hour passed.

Pemberton was considering going to the restroom to do a rail when O'Nan pushed the revised script into Pemberton's hands and went back to his car to make more phone calls. The actors went back to the mics and Pemberton tried to make sense of the changes. The copy was now much too long. Pemberton massaged it into shape and distributed the changes to the actors. They got it down after a couple of takes. They did two more versions to stay busy: one mild and one wild. Finally, the actors filed out of the sound booths browbeaten and discouraged.

"Will we be done soon?" the Suck-Up asked.

Pemberton shrugged.

O'Nan returned, but he seemed distracted. Pemberton asked him if he wanted to hear the new cuts. O'Nan nodded. After the track played everyone looked to O'Nan for a reaction, but he was barely there. He must not have liked the news his lawyer had given him.

"That's the keeper," he said at length. "What do you think, Pemberton?"

"It's good," Pemberton agreed.

"Don't just say it to say it," O'Nan said. "Tell me what you *really* think."

Pemberton thought the spot sucked. The concept was tired, the promotion was watered down, and the jokes were borderline offensive. The only thing that saved it was the talent, but there was no way he could tell O'Nan that.

"I like it," Pemberton said.

O'Nan shook his head. "Jesus, you really are a suck-up."

THE HANDICAPPED STALL in the men's room at the Hole in the Wall Saloon had become something of a sanctum sanctorum for Pemberton. He was intimate with its appointments and cherished its familiarity. He'd spent so much time in there that the smell of beach mold and disinfectant sent a signal to his brain that meant: *party time!* But he was in a hurry and there was no time for ritual and decorum. He arranged a line on the toilet tank and ripped it up. *Ahhhh. Happy birthday.* Now he was ready to deal with the disaster unfolding at the bar.

O'Nan sat slouched on his stool, fumbling with a smartphone Pemberton was certain he didn't know how to operate. The bartender brought another round of cocktails. A couple of summer tourists sized up the place at the door. A man in a wheelchair shot pool by himself.

Pemberton had lost track of how many martinis O'Nan had had, and the drinks were starting to pile up at the bar. He was ready to leave, to ditch O'Nan here in Gamboa Beach, but he had no idea how he would get back to Thunderclap. Normally, he'd stay at D.D.'s, but D.D. was gone. He'd been asking himself what he should do since they'd left Paradox Productions. O'Nan had complained what a shitty anniversary he was having and Pemberton had made the mistake of telling him it was his birthday.

"Is that right?" O'Nan had asked, suddenly interested.

"Um, yeah," Pemberton said, regretting he'd opened his mouth.

"Aren't we a couple of sorry sacks of shit. We should be out raising hell."

Run, Pemberton told himself. *Run like an Apache chicken.* But Pemberton didn't run. He thought about his empty, cheerless cabin in Falls City, and decided that even O'Nan's company was preferable to spending his birthday drinking alone while Ramona scowled at him from the wall.

"I know a place," Pemberton said.

"Do you now?" O'Nan started the car and pressed down hard on the accelerator, revving the engine as if it were a toy.

When they pushed into the Hole in the Wall, the bartender, a gruff old guy named Steve who reeked of Aqua Velva and alimony, took one look at O'Nan and hooked an eyebrow at Pemberton as if to say, Why are you bringing this asshole into my bar? "I'd like to buy my boss a beer," Pemberton declared, and Steve got the message.

"Beer? Only rednecks and welfare cases drink beer!" O'Nan shouted. A dozen regulars shot scowls their way.

"What'll it be then?" Steve asked.

"It's his birthday!" O'Nan exclaimed.

"Fresh out of cupcakes. No candles either."

O'Nan laughed—so he did have a sense of humor—and ordered two martinis up with olives. He blabbed about his plans for the casino's thirteenth-anniversary celebration, which was fast approaching.

That had been hours ago. The skies had darkened and the marine layer had crept up the beach like a thief. The carpet smelled of vomit. The bar stools were torn and sprouted stuffing and foam. O'Nan was hopelessly drunk and Pemberton had no idea what to do.

"There you are," O'Nan slurred when Pemberton returned to his seat.

"I went to the restroom."

"I don't want to know your business, you fruitcake." O'Nan sipped his drink and sloshed half his martini down his shirtfront when his phone chirped.

"What does this say?" O'Nan asked, holding the phone up to Pemberton's face. "I can't read it without my glasses."

"Um, happy anniversary?" Pemberton lied.

"The hell it does. Tell me what it really says."

"Fuck you," Pemberton blurted, louder than he intended. Heads turned down the length of the bar. Pemberton could feel their eyeballs sliding over them, sizing up the situation.

"Very nice," O'Nan said. "This is what I get on my anniversary. From my second ex-wife no less."

On the television behind the bar, its non-high-definition screen gunked with smoke, there was a news story about a statewide sting that resulted in the arrest of more than two dozen members of a notorious Southland motorcycle gang involved in a narcotics ring. Pemberton thought about it for a second. So *this* was why D.D. had left town.

"I'll show her." O'Nan fumbled with the tiny keypad. "Go to hell, you cum-guzzling cooze. That'll teach her, right?"

"Teach her what?" Pemberton had adopted the strategy of answering O'Nan's questions with more questions. Their conversations were a game of verbal Ping-Pong, but O'Nan hadn't caught on yet.

"Ah, fuck that twat," O'Nan said. Down went another martini, and with it, the last of O'Nan's restraint.

"Excuse me," a voice called out. "Would you two watch the profanity? There's a lady present." A middle-aged man wearing deck shoes and a yachting cap called out from the other side of the bar.

The man's wife, a skinny woman buried in hairspray and cheap jewelry, fixed them with a frosty glare. Pemberton tried to think of something that would distract O'Nan, but the feisty old bulldog was already off his stool and jabbing his finger at the tourist.

"You call that cooze a lady?" O'Nan shouted.

The tourists stared at O'Nan in horror. Although the man was six inches taller and ten years younger than O'Nan, he didn't get up to confront him.

"That dried-up cunt has seen more action than a catcher's mitt," O'Nan continued, "and probably looks like one, too."

The woman didn't wait for an encore. She snatched her purse from the bar and blew through the door. Pemberton envied her decisiveness.

The tourist fumbled with his wallet, clearly shaken. "You're despicable."

"Tell your story walking, Ahab."

The tourist did just that and scurried out the door. A few of the regulars laughed. O'Nan, the conquering hero, returned to his stool at the bar. The man in the wheelchair rolled over from the pool tables. "You showed those assholes!" he said over and over again.

"Fuck off, scooter. Nobody's talking to you."

"Let me buy you fellas a drank!"

"Roll your gimp ass somewhere else!"

"That ain't right," the man said and pushed off. The bar went silent. Whatever good will O'Nan had generated with his dismissal of the tourists dissipated in the soggy air.

O'Nan climbed onto his stool and nearly knocked over his drink. He looked worn-out, like the confrontation had sapped his strength. Incredibly, he started to sniffle.

"Uh, you all right?" Pemberton felt obliged to ask.

"You know what happened to me today?"

Pemberton was afraid to ask.

"My wife, my soon-to-be *third ex-wife*, served me with divorce papers! Can you believe that shit? On our fucking *anniversary*."

Pemberton could believe it.

O'Nan put his head down on the bar. Steve jerked his thumb at the door. Pemberton nodded, whispered in O'Nan's ear.

"We have to leave."

"Why, why, why?" O'Nan moaned.

"Because it's getting late."

Pemberton's future was clear: He was going to have to drive O'Nan's Porsche to the harbor where he kept his boat and then take a cab to the bus station and hope he made it in time to catch the last express to Falls City. He was reasonably sober, reasonably alert, reasonably fit to drive, but if he was going to have to put up with O'Nan for the next hour, he was going to need a straightener.

"I'm going to use the head and then we'll go."

"Whatever," O'Nan wailed.

Pemberton ran to the restroom and slipped into the handicapped stall. He started cutting up the coke when someone banged on the door.

"Open up! I know what you're doing in there!"

It didn't sound like Steve and it definitely wasn't O'Nan. Pemberton stuffed his gear in his pocket and peered over the stall's flimsy door. The man in the wheelchair looked up at him. His dark face was round with bloat and stubbled with gray whiskers. Behind military-issue glasses burned a pair of angry, red eyes that had EDP written all over them.

"Let me in!" he shouted.

"Be right out," Pemberton said.

"You're a friend of D.D.'s, right?"

"Um, D.D. isn't here."

"I know that! D.D. is a friend of mine. Always real good to Reggie. He ever talk about me?"

"I don't think so . . ."

"I just told you, motherfucker! D.D.'s my boy!" Reggie's eyes went glassy and he had a hard time keeping his tongue in his mouth. His chair was an old-school rig and his hands white-knuckled the wheels.

"I have to go." Pemberton lifted the latch. Reggie barged in and blocked the door.

"Going? This party's just getting started!"

"Well, you see," Pemberton said, trying to find a way to move past Reggie without having to touch him.

"Come on now. Motherfucking-Steve won't cash my check, and I need something to get me through the night. You know what I'm saying?"

Pemberton knew exactly what he was saying, but he wasn't buying what Reggie was selling. He lunged to the left and attempted to escape by vaulting over his wheelchair.

"Motherfucker!" Reggie hollered. He tripped Pemberton up, pulled him down onto his lap, and held him tight. Reggie's legs were spindly and weak, but his arms were powerfully strong. Pemberton felt like he was trapped in the pincers of a terrible insect. Filled with revulsion, he thrashed until the chair tipped over and crashed to the floor. While Reggie pleaded with Pemberton to help a goddamn veteran, Pemberton extracted himself from the tangle of metal rods and useless legs and bumped his head on the underside of the sink as he leaped to his feet and fled the restroom.

The bar was mostly empty. O'Nan was gone.

"Your friend left," Steve said.

"He's not my friend," Pemberton said.

"You got that right. He stiffed you with the bill."

A wailing sound emerged from the restroom. It was both a curse and a cry for help, the end of anger and the beginning of fear. It was the sound, Pemberton realized with a shudder, of death trembling.

AFTER AN ALL-NIGHTER AT THE CASINO, Lupita stopped at the Trading Post in Falls City to get some orange juice and a plastic-wrapped conchita. She waited in line behind a gaunt-looking güero who reeked of booze, while the brown-skinned man behind the counter bagged his purchases. Lupita turned on her phone and waited for the messages to arrive. Mariana didn't like to talk on the telephone, and she never told Lupita why she was calling when she left her a voice mail. Her messages were always the same. *It's me*, followed by a vaguely accusatory question: *Where are you? Are you at the casino again? The girls are fine in case you were wondering.* This made Lupita more than a little crazy. When she called someone, it was for a reason, and when she left a message, she told the person why she was calling. It was called communication. It's the reason these pinche devices were invented. Good luck explaining *that* to her bitchy little sister.

But sixteen messages? Alarm bells went off in Lupita's head once she started to process it. All but one of the messages were from Mariana and they all had come through in the last few hours. The first messages were frantic. Little bursts of panic that accelerated Lupita's heart rate, but told her nothing. The middle messages were more like the ones Mariana liked to leave: short, abrasive, seething with spite. Lupita deleted these, two, three seconds into the recording. The last messages were different. Much different. Mariana pleaded with Lupita to call her back. The nervousness Lupita had been able to push aside came creeping back, a tingling feeling that told her something was seriously wrong. Not here-we-are-in-the-emergency-room-again wrong but the-universe-as-we-knew-it-has-been-changed-forever wrong.

The next message: Weeping that went on for too long.

The one after that heralded a return of the accusatory voice.

Then, panic.

Okay, Lupita, now I'm really scared. I . . . I . . . can't believe something terrible has happened. I won't believe it. I can't lose you. Not now.

Lupita was many things, but lost wasn't one of them. She knew the way. But what if something had happened to one of the girls?

The man in front of her finished. As he withdrew his hand from his pocket, something fluttered to the ground.

"Excuse me," Lupita called to the man as he began to leave. "You dropped this!"

The man was halfway through the door before he realized Lupita was talking to him. He stopped and turned. Lupita picked up the money. A twenty-dollar bill that was curled up like a cigarette. Lupita knew what *that* was all about, and offered it to the tired-looking boracho with a forced smile, but the man's eyes were glazed over, his face vague, his sadness eternal.

Lupita paid for her conchita and juice and returned to her car. She immediately called her sister and Mariana picked up on the first ring. Lupita could hear one of the girls crying in the background.

"Thank God," Mariana gasped and dissolved into sobs, and it took considerable effort, some serious freaking communication, before Lupita was able to coax the news out of her.

"Yasmina is sick."

"What's the matter with her?"

"What's the matter? Didn't you listen to my messages?"

"No, there's something wrong with my ph—"

"She's in the hospital, hermana! Where have you been?"

Lupita adjusted the rearview mirror and ran her fingers through her hair. The ends were dry and needed to be cut. And she hadn't had a manicure in ages. There was a time in her life when she got her nails done every week without fail, and it didn't matter if Alejandro was home or away. Those days were long gone. What had happened to that person?

"I'm sorry." What else was there to say when a lie would be too obvious, and the truth just wouldn't do?

Lupita didn't know how much more of this she could take. It was warm in the hospital waiting room. Yasmina had been admitted after coming down with a potentially life-threatening virus. Lupita had read in the paper about the seriousness of the superflu, especially in the very young and the very old, and she couldn't help but think of Denise. Maybe she'd caught it, too. Maybe that was why she'd left.

Mariana was decent at first. Kind even. When Lupita arrived, Mariana expressed enormous gratitude—"Thank goodness you're all right"—but her relief gave way to exasperation—"Where have you been?"—and then anger—"What's wrong with you? How could you be so selfish?"

Lupita held her tongue—for her niece's sake. Could she help it if the cell phone service in the casino was shitty? They probably rigged it that way on purpose, jammed the signals so no one could get through and tell the gamblers to come home. Mariana told Lupita about the fever that nearly took Yasmina, saying it like she was out of the woods, a thing of the past. But if this were true, she wouldn't be in the hospital.

Mariana surrounded herself with her bitchy friends, who glared at Lupita like she was some kind of pariah. When she'd had enough, Lupita went to the hospital chapel. It was a tiny little place bathed in the warm tones of flickering votive candles. So quiet. She could stay here all day. She prayed for her niece's health and her sister's sanity. She prayed for the strength to make the changes she knew she must make. She resolved to open up her home to her family, spend more time with her nieces, and be a better sister. But before she did all that, she needed to get help, to talk to someone about why she felt best when she felt nothing, why the impulse to be alone was always the strongest. She needed to talk about Alejandro, the violence and the infidelity. And though she wasn't addicted or broke, she needed to stop going to the casino so much.

Or at least cut back. It shouldn't take up so much space in her life. Hold such sway over her decisions. There were mornings when she got out of bed with every intention of going to the post office and grocery store, but by noon she still hadn't managed to dress or feed herself. And when her appetite returned, swiftly and suddenly, there was nothing in the fridge and no time to throw a meal together, so she caved and went to the casino because she could eat for free with her comps.

Madness. Or a species of it anyway.

If she was really going to change, she needed to get the gambling out of her system. There was only one way to do that. One last trip. A final purge. It would be like a cleansing. Nobody needed to know. When they were finished here at the hospital, Lupita would go back to her sister's house and help prepare dinner and then, when the kitchen was clean and the plates were put away and her sister finally succumbed to sleep, Lupita would leave and go to the casino. No one would miss her.

Lupita headed back to the waiting room. Empty coffee cups scarred with lipstick cluttered the end tables. A single scarf dangled over the armrest of a worn sofa. Mariana and her friends were nowhere to be found. The duty nurse told Lupita that visiting hours were over, and they'd all gone home. Lupita hustled back to the elevator and caught up with Mariana in the parking garage.

"Are you leaving, hermanita?"

Her sister whirled on her. Tears spilled down her cheeks, but her face was wrenched with fury. "What difference does it make to you?"

"Que?" Lupita asked, startled by Mariana's tone.

"You know, when Alejandro left you—"

"Alejandro didn't leave me. He was killed." Her words carried in the low-ceiling garage. Lupita looked past her sister at her gaggle of friends and shouted, "This is no business of yours, you pinche bitches!" The women scattered, embarrassed and incensed.

Mariana gathered herself. She breathed through her nose. "When you came back to San Diego, I thought you'd changed. My husband warned me that you hadn't, but with Alejandro gone I thought you'd finally gotten the message. But there's nothing to get. You haven't changed. You're not like me or Mom or anyone in this family. You never were and never will be. That's just the way it is."

Watching Mariana reign in her emotions made Lupita lose control of hers. "You think you know what's best for me?"

Mariana ignored her sister's outburst.

"Alejandro told his father all about your behavior."

"Lies!"

"I didn't want to believe it, but looking at you now, I can see it. And though it saddens me, it doesn't surprise me. You never wanted to be a big sister to me. You never wanted to be an aunt to my daughters. You never wanted anything to do with our family. You just ran off with Alejandro and look what you did to him!"

"So that's what this is about. Me leaving? You're still upset about *that*?"

The expression on Mariana's face changed from disappointment to grim amusement, but there was no joy in her laughter.

"You still don't get it. You're still so donkey-headed after all these years. So unbelievably stubborn, choosing to believe what you want to believe."

Lupita felt the anger rising within her, the way it would during her fights with Alejandro. She'd pound and kick and claw at him, whether he was ready for it or not.

"But I came back!" Lupita shouted, and she didn't care who heard her or how big a scene she made. Mariana looked away, fixed her eyes on the cars in the garage.

"No, Lupita, you were never here. You are like a ghost to this family. I'm done with you."

Confusion closed in on Lupita. The anger she'd felt just a moment ago deserted her. Gone, too, was the righteousness she thought she had on her side.

"I've finally come to accept that you never wanted to be a part of this family," Mariana continued. "Now you are free to do whatever you want with your life, just so long as you stay out of ours." Mariana turned and headed down the ramp to her car.

"Wait!" Lupita cried. "Come back!" But her sister who was no longer her sister got in her car and drove away.

PEMBERTON SPENT THE DAY AFTER his debauch in the grip of a grue-some hangover, drifting in and out of sleep. In his dreams, he was confined to a wheelchair and shunned by old friends and former col-leagues. Everyone was there except Debra, and what did that say when the woman of your dreams no longer showed up in them?

That night he sat in a chair by the open window and drank hot black tea and ate a package of crackers. On Sunday he read two novels by different authors with identical plots—a man moves to a foreign city where he begins a new life under an assumed identity. Both books ended badly for the protagonist, yet Pemberton was suffused with ridiculous envy.

When he'd first moved to L.A., he'd worked as a proofreader at a publishing company that specialized in science fiction. To prevent him from getting invested in the narratives, his supervisor had split the manuscripts down the middle so he never got more than half the book. Pemberton had hated this, yet he'd stayed with the company for years. Eventually he composed his own beginnings and endings. He told himself the stories he came up with were better than those on the page, but he had no real way of knowing if this was true. It was something he chose to accept the way he accepted everything, and if it hadn't been for Debra's prodding, he might never have found the cour-age to leave the company. He was aware of his propensity for staying in bad situations too long, but who was going to get him out of the mess he was in now?

Monday morning, the need asserted itself anew, and he chopped up two lines on the mirror he kept on the coffee table and snorted them through a hard plastic straw that was cruddy with residue. The effect was instantaneous. He felt a thousand times better, a feeling he endeavored to expand by dumping the last of the vodka into some orange juice and gulping it down. Much, much better. So much better he spun a record on the turntable and danced around the cabin in his shorts and socks until he peeked out the window and saw the Thunder shuttle rumble by.

Crap.

He had nearly thirty minutes to kill before the next bus, but he didn't trust himself with the cocaine, so he left the cabin and waited at the bus stop. It was already blazing hot. By the time the shuttle arrived, Pemberton was soaked with sweat, and his jacket, as rumpled on the outside as he felt on the inside, smelled like a train-car seat cushion.

As the bus lurched up the switchbacks, Pemberton imagined going directly to Human Resources and lodging a complaint against O'Nan, as so many of his coworkers had done. But when the bell rang, and the recorded voice announced through shitty speakers—*Welcome to Thunderclap Casino! Please display your Thunder badge at all times*—he pushed the thought out of his head. What could Human Resources possibly do to someone as inhuman as O'Nan?

The marketing department's air conditioning was going like gangbusters. It sounded like an airplane engine in distress. The vents were open and blew straight down on his desk. This was delicious for the first ten or fifteen minutes and then turned into a kind of torture. At the very least, it was good cover for why he seemed to be sniffling *all the time* these days.

"Dude," Jasper said, his voice arriving somehow before the rest of him appeared in his cube, "do you know anything about an event downstairs you were supposed to write something for?"

The casino anniversary. Lucky thirteen. Pemberton had forgotten all about it. Shit.

"You better get down there!"

"Okay, I'm on it."

Pemberton searched for his sunglasses until he realized he was still wearing them.

"Hey, bro?"

"What?" Pemberton asked, starting to get a little annoyed.

"You got a little something . . ." Jasper pointed to his nostril.

Pemberton wiped his nose and dislodged a white clump.

"Uh, thanks, Jasper," Pemberton said, forcing a smile that Jasper didn't return.

"It's Kyle, but whatever."

Pemberton hustled down the stairs to the casino. All of Thunderclap's animatronic creatures were out—some that Pemberton had never seen before—gnawing on fake logs with fake teeth, spreading their fake wings in a fake breeze, roaring their recorded roars. Those who'd come to witness the anniversary spectacle were players with a nose for free cake. All the regulars knew that whenever the tribal elders showed up on the casino floor, there was going to be free cake, the ancient ceremonial food of the Yukemaya.

Pemberton had missed the dedication, and the only people left were tribal members, upper-management suck-ups, and the life-size foam board cutouts of revelers the graphic team installed on the fringes of the Forest of Fortune to create the illusion of a crowd. O'Nan was nowhere to be found. Pemberton checked his phone. No missed calls.

The animatronic animals screeched, chattered, and cawed as a green mist from the falls, underlit by a filtered glow, descended over the forest with a malevolence Pemberton hoped he was only imagining. At the periphery of the celebration—and he couldn't believe he didn't see this sooner—stood Pemberton. It wasn't him, of course, but a foam-board replica. His face had been transferred onto the body of a guy wearing a silk shirt. Pemberton above the neck; douchebag below. And not just one, but dozens of replicas were scattered around the forest, all dressed in different getups. The Pembertons were everywhere.

Fucking Jasper. Fucking Kyle.

"Just the man I wanted to see." Chairman Cloudshadow stepped off the dais and put his arm around Pemberton.

Uh oh, Pemberton nearly said aloud. The Chairman was big and moist and gave off a slightly yeasty smell like fresh dough. He was nearly as tall as D.D. and had to be pushing three bills or more. Galled by the unwanted contact, Pemberton forced a smile while the Chairman wiped his forehead with a silk handkerchief.

"I've been looking for you," he said.

"I'm sorry," Pemberton answered. "I was indisposed."

"Very important event we have here today."

"Yes, sir."

"Of course, you know the story of Thunderclap Falls . . ."

The question-that-wasn't-a-question caught Pemberton off-guard. He tried not to show it—"Um, yeah, sure"—and failed. Big-time.

"Lay it on me."

"Well, it goes back a couple hundred, uh, thousand years when the Yukemaya roamed the land. Then, um, the white man came."

"Actually, it was the Spaniards."

"Right, the Spaniards. They came, and the Yukemaya fought them so that your people could be, uh, free."

The Chairman hauled out his silk handkerchief again, and as he lifted it to his face, something fell to the patterned carpet. Pemberton instinctively stooped to pick it up and immediately wished he hadn't. Sitting in the center of a psychedelic swirl that resembled a purple sticky bun was a small baggie of white powder. Pemberton closed his fist around it. He straightened, slowly, unsure of what he should do about the bag of cocaine that had fallen out of the Chairman's pocket.

"I, um, found some contraband . . ."

"Why don't you put that in your pocket, and you and me go for a ride."

The Chairman placed an enormous hand on Pemberton's shoulder and steered him away from the celebration. Pemberton could hear his heart chugging in his chest. He imagined coughing up the muscle and spitting it out on the casino floor. Probably wouldn't faze the Thunderclappers. Nothing they hadn't seen before . . .

"Hold on a second. I want you to *experience* something."

The Chairman paused at the Thunderclap Club Rewards kiosk near the main entrance. He glanced at his watch and looked around as if he was waiting for something to happen. Pemberton nervously studied the expressions of the guests thronging around the Loot Caboose. Their faces were tense with a restless expectancy that Pemberton had come to know well: It was the face that greeted him in the mirror each morning.

The house lights flickered as the speakers came to life with the sound of wind blowing. A peal of thunder rumbled through the casino. Pemberton could hear it moving through the Forest of Fortune, like a distant echo.

"Do you hear that?" a husky female voice that Pemberton immediately recognized as belonging to Kaitlin, the voice actress who played the Secretary at Paradox Productions, boomed over the public address system. The guests stared up at the ceiling, marveling at the sound. *"Hold on to your seats, Thunder Cash is coming!"* And then, a lightning strike, a clap of thunder, and someone shouted, "I won! I won!"

Fucking O'Nan.

"What do you think of that?" the Chairman asked.

"It's, um, great?"

"We'll see what the response is. The numbers don't lie. But the creativity is excellent." The Chairman smiled and guided Pemberton through the main entrance. He couldn't believe O'Nan jacked his Thunder Cash idea. Actually, he could believe it. He should have seen it coming. When was he going to learn? He slipped on his sunglasses and took a deep breath as they approached the Chairman's brand-new black Hummer parked in a spot reserved exclusively for his use.

"Nice ride," Pemberton said.

"It's not exactly eco-friendly," the Chairman replied, "but I got a great deal. The dealership brought the cars to the reservation. No sales tax on sovereign land." And there was that smile again.

Pemberton climbed into the crisp-smelling vehicle. The Chairman steered out of the casino parking lot and through a gate marked YUKE-MAYA INDIAN RESERVATION that the buses and shuttles never used. The grade here was much gentler, and the Yukemaya reservation stretched from one end of the valley to the other. To the east, houses dotted the hills that rolled down from the Sisters. Cows grazed and wild horses roamed the pastures, which gave way to sparse scrubland stippled with desert mesquite and green-barked chinaberry. There was a cluster of larger buildings in the middle of the valley where the Tribal Education Center and the Thunderclap Fire Station were located. As they passed a stand of cottonwoods and cleared a rise, Pemberton spied an Indian graveyard replete with statuary and falling-down slabs of weather-beaten rock, the epitaphs devoured by the sun.

"Cool, huh?"

"It's amazing," Pemberton said.

"This is my favorite spot on the whole rez. My cousins and I used to come out here when we were teenagers. Get wasted, shoot at each other." He said it like he was talking about the past, distant and remote, but Pemberton guessed it was no more than ten years ago. He had trouble putting the pieces together. He couldn't match what he saw with the words coming out of the Chairman's mouth. Pemberton's thoughts kept drifting to the baggie in his pocket.

"Have you ever been?"

"No." As they made their approach, Pemberton saw that the grave-yard was actually a paintball course, which possessed a Wild West theme, complete with a general store, a hotel, and a saloon with bat-wing doors. A sign that read DODGE 'EM CITY hung above the corral. The graveyard was laid out in a circular pattern, like a replica of the Sad Hill Cemetery from *The Good, the Bad and the Ugly.*

"I've, um, never been . . . paintballing."

"Didn't think so," the Chairman continued. "You don't seem like the type." The Chairman brought the Hummer to a halt and gave Pemberton his full attention. "Now, about that medicine . . . ?"

It took Pemberton a moment to catch his drift, but when he did, he wasted no time removing the plastic bag from his pocket and handing it to the Chairman, who had already produced a mirror and a razor from a compartment in the armrest. While he cut up some lines, the Chairman expanded on his intention to renovate the paintball facility and turn Dodge 'Em City into a "camel jockey's compound in the Middle East."

Pemberton couldn't concentrate on what the Chairman was telling him. He was fixated on the cocaine. His body tensed as he tried to figure out if the Chairman was cutting up a line for him, and if so how big. Did he want it? Yes. Should he take it? No, he should not. Or should he? Maybe the Chairman was a regular guy, a guy who liked his blow. Nothing wrong with that, but what if it was a test? A trap to lure him in . . . Pemberton began to sweat.

"Here." The Chairman offered the mirror. Two healthy lines. Not long, but not skinny either. One for each of them.

"I . . . "

"Just do it."

Pemberton accepted the Chairman's mirror and rolled-up one-hundred-dollar bill. The anticipation was over. The moment had arrived. There was no better feeling than this, and the truth of it made Pemberton go splotchy with shame as he snorted his line.

"That's more like it," the Chairman said.

"*Ahhhh,*" Pemberton said, exaggerating the satisfaction he'd taken in what had been a disappointingly dinky line. *More, more, more,* Pemberton thought. He disguised his disappointment when the Chairman stowed the works—baggie, mirror, and razor—in the armrest and dragged a knuckle across his nose. "I suppose I ought to take you back."

"Yeah," Pemberton said with a sigh. "O'Nan's probably looking for me."

"O'Nan? That's a good one."

"What do you mean?"

The Chairman studied Pemberton with an air of deepening mirth. "You don't know, do you?"

"Know what?"

"O'Nan got the ax. He no longer works for Thunderclap Enterprises."

Pemberton felt something give way inside him. A fluttery, jittery feeling. "I . . . I don't know what to say."

"You don't have to take up for him. I know what an asshole he was, especially to you. Everyone did. It's just that these things take a while."

The Chairman turned the key, started the truck. "In case you're wondering, we're not going to bring anyone else in to fill his position—not yet anyway."

"I wasn't wondering," Pemberton answered.

"Everyone wonders," the Chairman said with a wink. "We know Thunder Cash was your idea. If it does well, it could be very good for you."

"Thank you."

"Do you know the Yukemaya story of the gambler?"

"I don't think so."

"It's one of our oldest stories," the Chairman continued. "A man celebrates a big hunt by gambling his share of the game."

"Does he win?"

"No. He gambles his war ax, and when he loses that, he gambles away the rest of his possessions. He goes home angry and upset, but not as angry and upset as his wife, who tells him to go back and get his shit, or don't bother coming home. So he goes back, but the game is over. Everyone has gone home, except for an old, old woman he's never seen before. The woman offers him a chance to win it all back if he wagers his land. The man doesn't want to lose his land, but he's certain his luck will change."

"Does it?"

"No," the Chairman said somewhat wearily. "He loses his land, his family's land, and the Yukemaya's land from the ocean to the mountains. All of it. Gone and lost forever."

Interesting, Pemberton thought, *but how about some more cocaine?*

"You know the moral of the story?" the Chairman asked.

"It's pretty obvious isn't it? You have to . . ."

"Know when to walk away."

"Know when to run," Pemberton finished.

"See," the Chairman said as he put the truck in gear, "you do know the story."

FIRE

I GAVE MYSELF TO MY CAPTORS, *accepted my fate as a slave, but they didn't need me anymore. They came down from the mountains, dressed in their heathen finery, and sold me to a foreigner, a dirty Englishman who had been made to believe I was an Indian girl from across the desert. He put me in ridiculous costumes, a white man's idea of what a native girl ought to look like. He befouled me night and day. My protests persuaded him of my savage nature. One day he showed me off to some soldiers who stopped to water their horses in his stream. They recognized me for what I was, and told the fellow I was no more native than he was. This so enraged the Englishman that after the soldiers left he dragged me out of his filthy shack and across his barren fields to the chopping block where he threw me down, tore the clothes from my body, and opened me with an ax. I watched the clouds go by. The sun beat down on my entrails. Creatures came to feast until there was nothing left of me but a husk of skin, a pole of bones, a cavity where my heart belonged.*

AFTER O'NAN GOT CANNED, the marketing department became a mellower place to work. Amy got her allergies under control, Barbara's health improved, and it had been ages since Jasper or Kyle pulled a prank. There was even talk of bringing Cassi back. The office was calm but dull and Pemberton wasn't sure he preferred it this way, especially on days like today when he was beer-sick, brain-boggled, and finally, tragically, all out of cocaine.

He'd organized his days around the ritual of getting high for so long he was having difficulty accepting it was over. He couldn't believe it was all gone. He'd stashed baggies all over the cabin and he'd spent hours hunting them down. The notion that he must have misplaced one was proving to be impossible to shake. The convenient truth was neither; Pemberton needed a new supplier.

Midmorning, he left his desk and made his way to the chow hall and bought a bottle of orange-pineapple juice, which he promptly doctored with an airplane bottle of Estonian vodka in a restroom stall in the team member locker room. Pemberton proceeded to the casino floor where he assigned everyone he passed to a tribe. The Filipino guy in the FREE LUMPIA T-shirt with an arrow pointing at his crotch was a dick; the fat lady chewing out her timid husband was an asshole, as was the guy who sent his wife and infant daughter to the lobby to wait for him while he gambled. Pemberton wasn't sure about the white dude wearing a Mexican poncho, but his attention-seeking probably made him a dick, and the tweaker with sores on her lip and holes in her jeans was definitely an asshole and most likely an EDP.

The game had become something of a compulsion with Pemberton, especially when he was coked out of his gourd, but that wasn't the case today, and once he finished his cocktail, he headed outside.

The wind blew. The palm trees bent and swayed. During fire season, guests and team members alike wore the marks of daytime drug users. Watery eyes, pinned pupils, inexplicable sniffles. If the Chairman was in the club, anyone could be. Dick/Asshole turned into Cokehead/ Square. But the Santa Anas were making it hard to tell who was getting their weekend started early and who was suffering the effects of the queer red wind that wrecked sinuses as easily as it spurred fires. And was that a tumbleweed that just tumbled by?

Pemberton went to the coffee cart for a Thunderbolt—an extra-large cup of coffee with three shots of espresso—and slowly, reluctantly took the long way back to the marketing office. He saw a man and a woman walking up the path from the main entrance, squinting into the sun. He pegged them as LCD assholes at a hundred feet, but the real question was whether they had any cocaine to sell.

The man wore a baseball cap and a sleeveless T-shirt to show off a shitty tattoo. A name. Something in Spanish. The words crawled around his arm like the shadow of a dusty vine. He was much younger than the woman. He snaked a naked arm around her shoulders like he was afraid she would shake it off. She could be his wife, mistress, or mother.

Pemberton sensed there was something wrong. There is always something wrong when a man and woman leave a casino at ten o'clock in the morning. The woman's eyes were red with exhaustion, wet with fear. Not crying exactly, but her face was a raw and squirming thing, like a creature newly birthed. She'd been gambling with money she couldn't afford to lose. Now she was done, and there was nothing to do but go home and fend off the consequences.

Losers in the game of life. Thunderclap was crawling with them.

Pemberton followed the rules for hospitable engagement, flashed a hollow smile, and said "Good morning!" a bit too cheerfully. The woman raised a bronze arm rippling with fat as if she were warding off a blow. The man removed his arm from the woman's shoulder like he'd been caught doing something illegal. It was Pemberton's team member badge. Its cheap authority spooked them. The man was naturally suspicious, naturally shifty, fearful of the ways Pemberton could fuck up his day. The man didn't have any shoelaces, and the tongues of his shoes flopped about like limbs that had had their bones removed.

When he got his DUI, the police took away his belt and removed his shoelaces before they locked him in the drunk tank. They gave them back when they released him, the laces nesting in the bottom of a manila envelope, curled up with his loose change. He never could bring himself to thread the laces through the eyelets again, and he eventually threw the shoes away.

The couple passed and even though it was clear they weren't holding, he stopped to watch them go. They missed the path toward the guest parking lot and continued on past the Bingo Barn, past the training center, past the stop for the Thunder shuttle, and down the road toward the switchbacks that would take them to Falls City. They'd probably gambled their bus fare. Pemberton sensed the cameras watching him watching them and moved on.

Every day, the same three ladies sat at the picnic table outside the team member entrance, smoking their dollar-store cigarettes. Sometimes Pemberton said hello, but only sometimes. Today wasn't one of those days. There was something in the tightness of their perfunctory cheer that put him on edge.

Pemberton bent over so that the Thunder badge dangling from his neck swept in front of the sensor and unlocked the door with a click. Going up the stairs, his phone pulsed in his pocket. An incoming message. His heart leaped. Could it be Debra? Or, better yet, D.D., with news that he was back in town? He fumbled with his phone.

YOU'LL GET YOURS ASSCLOWN!!!

The number was blocked, so it could have been anyone. Anyone who hated Pemberton, which was everyone. He pocketed his phone and navigated a surprisingly crowded hallway buzzing with news. *I can't believe this*, someone said. *This is bullshit*, said another. Pemberton sighed. This wasn't the day for unbelievable bullshit. But a few steps into the marketing office he learned what all the commotion was about.

Layoffs.

Assholes.

Amy and Jasper were the casualties. Amy clutched balled-up tissues in each of her hands. Her eyes filled with tears that she blamed on the Santa Anas. Barbara looked for boxes so Amy could pack her things.

"Let me help you," Pemberton said.

"It's all right," Amy answered.

"No," Pemberton insisted. "Nothing about this is right. Please, let me help."

Fighting back tears, Amy nodded and pulled herself together. Pemberton took the boxes Barbara had found and stowed the framed photographs of Amy's husband and children. Her cubicle, though stuffed with all kinds of personal crap, was remarkably clean. No dust. No dirty coffee cups. Not a paper clip out of place.

"You have a lot of stuff," Pemberton said. He had never been good at small talk.

"Yeah," Amy sniffled. "Half my life is here."

"You'll find something better." Though there was no way for Pemberton to know what Amy would or wouldn't find, he meant what he said.

When they were finished, Pemberton stacked the boxes one on top of the other and carried them toward the exit. Amy looked back at her empty cube. She looked like she needed to say goodbye, or at least be said goodbye to, but there was no one but Barbara.

"What a day," Pemberton said as they emerged from the tunnel and crossed the parking lot.

"Tell me about it. Could it get any worse?"

"I don't see how."

Amy inserted a key into the trunk's lock and popped it open. Pemberton waited while she consolidated piles of her son's athletic equipment to make room for the boxes. He set them down on the pavement and passed them to her one at a time until they were all stowed. Amy slammed it closed, leaving a small handprint on the grimy trunk.

"Well, I guess I'll be seeing you," she said.

"At least you can start happy hour early."

"Oh, yeah," Amy said. "You got that right."

"A little beer . . ."

"A *lot* of beer."

"A shot and a beer."

"Now you're talking!"

"A shot, a beer, *and* a big fat line . . ."

Amy narrowed her eyes, unsure if she'd heard Pemberton correctly. "What do you know about that?"

"I don't know about you, but I sure could use some."

"That makes two of us." Amy laughed, a nervous giggle.

"Can you help me out with that?" Pemberton hadn't felt this anxious since the last time he'd talked to Debra.

"Seriously?"

"I have cash."

"You *are* serious."

Pemberton was certain she'd figured out that this was the real reason he was standing here in the parking lot with her, but there was nothing he could do about that now.

"But how did—?"

"Your allergies? They've been *acting up* forever."

"But I really do have allergies."

"Of course."

"They're terrible."

"I understand."

Neither one of them could look the other in the eye, which Pemberton found slightly less excruciating than the prospect of spending the weekend pacing his cabin, dulling his nerves with cheap vodka.

"Well," Amy said, "if we're going to do this, let's do this."

Pemberton nodded, climbed into her car.

"I know a place," Amy said, thinking out loud.

"I'm currently without a connection."

"Really? I can't get from one end of Falls City to the other without running into one. It's terrible."

Pemberton nodded, though *terrible* was hardly the word he'd use.

"How much cash you got on you?"

"Plenty."

They drove down Thunderclap Mountain and Amy rode her brakes the whole way. She pulled into the trailer park and angled her car into a gravel lot not far from Pemberton's cabin.

"Take off your badge," she said and got out of the car.

Pemberton did as he was told and followed Amy up onto the trailer's porch. A leggy redhead wearing a tank top and sweatpants opened the door. Pemberton vaguely recognized her from the casino. It would be more surprising if he didn't. She looked them over but didn't give anything away.

"Can I help you with something?"

"Looking for a little pick-me-up?" Amy said.

The redhead smiled. "I can get you some, but you gotta take at least two bags, and it's not going to be cheap. You have the cash on you?"

"Yes," Pemberton said, happy to contribute to the conversation.

"Come on in then."

They sat down on a small, faux-leather piece of furniture that was something between a love seat and a sofa. Amy explained her situation to the redhead whose name was Lisa. They negotiated an eight ball: two grams for Pemberton and a half-gram for Amy.

"I'm going to go make the call. If my roommate comes home, just tell her you're here to see me."

"Uh, we can wait outside," Pemberton said.

"Don't worry. She's totally cool." Lisa skipped out of the room to phone in the order. "Help yourself to whatever's in the fridge," she called out.

Amy didn't need to be told twice.

"You drink beer?"

"Yes," Pemberton said.

"Didn't think you were the type."

"I get that a lot."

Amy retrieved two bottles of lager.

"Happy days," Pemberton said.

"Happier, anyway."

Lisa flitted back into the room with good news/bad news. The good news was she could get some; the bad news was they had to wait for it. In Pemberton's experience, this was the way it always went when scoring drugs from strangers. The connection was always at work or at his girl-friend's house or running an errand. That was the nice thing about party-ing with D.D.: He always had plenty of blow. No matter how epic the party or debauched the weekend, the next bag was always close at hand.

Pemberton was fine with waiting, although it was a little awkward sitting in the front parlor of the trailer with an increasingly despondent Amy while Lisa busied herself in the backrooms, talking on the phone, getting changed, doing God knows what. This feeling of awkwardness was amplified when a petite young Indian woman in a Thunderclap uniform walked through the front door.

"Who are you?" she demanded.

"I'm Amy."

The woman looked to Pemberton, but Amy wasn't finished yet. "I work in events and promotions. Used to anyway. I got laid off today."

While Amy babbled on, Pemberton rose to his feet, wiped his damp hands on his trousers. "Pemberton," he said and offered his hand, but she didn't take it.

"What are you doing here?"

"Waiting for Lisa," Amy said. "She's in the back."

"You work at the casino?" the woman asked Pemberton.

He nodded, which wasn't the answer Lisa's roommate was expect-ing. His mouth was dry, and he didn't know what to do with his hands. There was something unmistakably sad about her. Maybe not sad, but disappointed. With what, Pemberton couldn't say, but it probably had something to do with the fact that strangers were sitting in her living room looking to score.

"What's your name?" he asked.

"Alice," she snapped. "Anything else you need to know?"

He shook his head and looked at the floor, not quite able to meet her gaze. A car pulled up. Slamming doors. Male laughter. Alice looked at the door and then down the empty hallway and then back to the door again.

"Nice to meet you," she said with a sigh, making it clear that it was anything but, and disappeared down the hall as the sound of footsteps approached.

The door opened and in walked two Indians. One big and bulky with a physique like a fast-food addict, the other small and energetic with cornrows. Pemberton thought there was something Cagney-esque about the way the shorter one carried himself.

"Where's Lisa?" he demanded.

"In the back," Pemberton said.

He shook his head. "I'm Lil' Smokey. This is Big Pipe."

"Yo, yo, yo, Red Dawn in the house," Big Pipe said.

"You two the ones looking for a little something-something?"

"Yes," Amy and Pemberton answered simultaneously.

"Then let's get to it," Lil' Smokey said. "We got rehearsal tonight."

"You're in a band?" Pemberton couldn't help but ask. The atmosphere in the room kept changing: from the dull purgatory of waiting to the squalor of domestic unpleasantness to this. Whatever this was.

"Red Dawn. Ever heard of us?" Lil' Smokey asked.

"I think so," Pemberton lied.

"Cool, cool."

Pemberton had met Latinos and Asians in the hip-hop scene, but that was in L.A. Who knew that Falls City had its own Native American hip-hop all-stars?

"Who got the money?"

"I do," Pemberton said. He gave the cash to Amy, who passed it on to Lil' Smokey.

"We good," he said after quickly counting the bills and stashing them in his pocket. "That your ride outside?"

Amy nodded.

"Good. Follow us."

"Yo, yo, yo, we out the do'!" Big Pipe said.

Pemberton followed Amy back to her car, feeling like he'd stumbled into a gangland version of a Dr. Seuss story.

"This where we going," Lil' Smokey said to Amy, pressing a flyer into her hand.

"It's a warehouse, right?" Amy asked.

"You got it. That's where we do our thing. Tomorrow night is gonna be all kinds of ca-razy."

"I know where this is," Amy said and confirmed directions with Lil' Smokey while Pemberton got in the car. He didn't think about what he was about to do. He didn't think about whether he would be missed at work. He didn't think about the warrant for his arrest that ignoring his DUI hearing had caused. He didn't think about anything, except the mysterious text message. Was Jasper still pranking him? Could it be Kyle? Not likely after the layoffs. Did someone know something he didn't? Or maybe it was D.D. in St. Louis . . .

Amy got on the freeway and drove toward San Diego, but turned off at the first exit. The warehouse sat in the center of a fenced-in lot between a tire supply store and a moving company. Lil' Smokey led the way to the entrance around the side of the building and punched in the security code on the keypad. Big Pipe opened the door, and they all followed him inside. Mismatched furniture, tired-looking audio equipment, and the remnants of a party littered the crowded room. Lil' Smokey started flipping switches, filling the dark space with pockets of noise and light. Colored beams swiveled and spun atop a portable rig. First, Lil' Smokey blasted them with beats, then bass, and finally an intermittent vocal loop: *Lost in this nightmare!* Pemberton found it uncomfortably loud.

"All right, all right, all right," Lil' Smokey hollered at no one in particular. "This our latest, 'I.T.: Indigenous Terrorist.'" Big Pipe set a tackle box down on the coffee table and started weighing out the coke. Pemberton tried not to stare, but he found the operation fascinating. Every once in a while, a *Lost in this nightmare!* zapped him back into consciousness.

"Fridge back there," Lil' Smokey said with a wink. "Help yo'self."

Amy smiled and went to fetch drinks. She brought back four beers and distributed them. Pemberton was grateful he didn't have to speak. Lil' Smokey was all over the place. One minute he was standing at the console fiddling with various knobs and dials, adding effects and fills, the next he was flipping through a stack of records, and then suddenly he was standing next to Pemberton, handing him a marijuana cigarette, which Pemberton accepted, inhaled, and passed back to Lil' Smokey, cognizant that whatever it was he'd just smoked, it hadn't been called a marijuana cigarette in half a century. The effects were instantaneous—*Lost in this nightmare!*—his legs felt wobbly, his thoughts disorganized. The music sounded like something sent down from another planet. He couldn't latch on to it; the rhythms eluded him. Only the drums, tribal and relentless, were of this world. His crotch trembled, and it took him a moment to figure out it was his phone. Another message.

REAP THE WHIRLWIND, DICKBAG!!!

Pemberton thought he was going to be sick.

Amy swam into focus. He was being summoned to the coffee table. To inspect the eight ball? Complete the transaction? Ah, to sample the product. Pemberton stooped, but the table was too low so he got down on his knees to do it up, and he didn't know if it was the drugs or his anxiety or the music—*Lost in this nightmare!*—but if he didn't get some fresh air soon, he really would be lost.

"Everything okay?" Amy asked.

Pemberton wanted to leave, needed to go home, but he couldn't quite form the words.

"You don't look so good. We should go."

Pemberton nodded emphatically. He tried to hide his anxiety over the way Lil' Smokey and Big Pipe kept looking at him by finishing his beer, but when he brought the bottle to his lips it was empty. Amy gave Lil' Smokey and Big Pipe a hug and steered Pemberton toward the door.

Lost in this nightmare!
Lost in this nightmare!
Lost in this nightmare!

Back in Amy's car, Pemberton had to reassure Amy that he was fine several times before she cranked the ignition and drove back to Falls City. Pemberton had never been so relieved to be back in this shitty part of the world he called home. Amy pulled over in an abandoned gas station and parked the car by the restrooms. The doors to both bathrooms had been chained shut.

Pemberton cut up enough coke for two short lines and laid them out on a Thunderclap Club Rewards card, which got a laugh out of Amy. They each rolled their own bills. Amy went first, then Pemberton. The coke shot up his nose and into his brain where it toggled the switch marked "more alcohol." Pemberton had spent the day in pursuit of the body's wants, and what this body wanted was more. But not here. And certainly not with Amy.

"What am I going to do?" Amy asked while Pemberton tore off a corner of the baggie and divvied up her share. She repeated the question over and over again. To the rearview mirror, the steering wheel, the empty space between the cracks in her windshield until it got on Pemberton's nerves. *If I don't have an answer for myself,* he thought, *what makes you think I'll have one for you?*

Sensing that she had gotten all the empathy she was going to get, Amy laid her head on the steering wheel and began to sob. Pemberton placed the half-gram bag of coke on the dashboard and quietly slipped away.

There, Pemberton thought while walking toward the Trading Post, *that wasn't too terribly awful.*

"LET'S TALK ABOUT YOUR MOTHER," Dr. Marcus announced at the beginning of their session.

Well, shit. There it was. The words Alice had been dreading since she'd first started coming here.

"What do you mean?"

"Alice . . ."

"Sure. Scold me. The whole stern father bit."

"Alice, this isn't a punishment. We're just . . . talking."

"Well, my mother was an alcoholic. We can start there. We can stop there, too."

"Why did she drink?"

"Why do you?"

"On days I don't meditate, I permit myself a cocktail."

"A cocktail." Alice snorted. She carefully removed a strand of hair from the left side of her face and tucked it behind her ear to give her hands something to do. "Let me ask *you* something," Alice began, but didn't wait for a reply. "Did you know that Indians are three hundred percent more likely to die in alcohol-related incidents than whites?"

Dr. Marcus whistled.

"Tell me about it. Why do you think that is?"

"Lack of economic opportunity, substandard social services . . ."

"It's in our blood."

"And that's why your mother died?" Dr. Marcus asked. Alice could feel the challenge behind the question.

"She drank herself to death."

"Did she?"

"What would you call whoring yourself out for a liter of vodka every day?"

"You always say that," Dr. Marcus said. "Whenever you talk about your mother, you always say she drank herself to death."

"Well, it's the truth."

"Tell me how."

Shit, shit, shit. Alice's vision crosshatched with tears. "She . . ." and that was all she could get out.

"Take your time," Dr. Marcus said, and just that little bit gave her the courage to go on, to get off her chest what she'd been holding back for so long.

"She walked in front of a train."

"Was she drunk?"

Alice laughed. "She was always drunk." But that's not what Dr. Marcus wanted to know.

"Was it an accident?"

Alice shook her head. "She left a note. She had it on her. She totally did it on purpose."

"Alice," Dr. Marcus said, "I'm deeply sorry."

"Well, I'm not. I know that's a terrible thing to say, and it makes me an awful person for saying it, but I don't care." And that was the truth. She really didn't care, and to prove it, she'd tell Dr. Marcus what she'd never told anyone before. "You know what the note said?"

"Tell me."

The note was torn to pieces, just like her mother, but the police put the pieces back together. Alice could still see the bloodstained pages in a plastic sleeve. The words that were written for her to see.

"She said I was the worst daughter in the world. She said I didn't deserve her. She said"—Alice willed herself not to cry—"I was a mistake."

"Alice . . ."

"Let me finish. When I was a little girl, all I wanted was to be with her. She was all I had. Did I ever tell you my mother wasn't from the reservation where I grew up?"

"No."

"I never knew my father. When my mother got pregnant, he took off, but she stayed with my father's people. They didn't want her there, but she stayed anyway, in a place where she wasn't from, wasn't wanted, and didn't belong."

"Is that why you think she drank so much?"

"She always drank, but it got worse after I got kicked out of the tribe."

"You mean off the reservation?"

"No. Disenrolled. Off the books. Wiped off the tribal registry."

"They can do that?" Dr. Marcus's surprise was genuine, and his astonishment—so weak, so genteel, so *white*—spurred her on.

"After they opened the casino, they got a genetics expert to study the tribe's DNA and make sure everyone was legit. That's when they found out my father wasn't my father."

"You mean your father wasn't who your mother claimed he was?"

"Right. At least that's what the paperwork said."

"Who was he?"

"I don't know. My mother wouldn't tell me. I don't think she knew. But whoever he was, he wasn't one of them, and neither was she. So they kicked us out."

"How did your mother take the news?"

"Not well. She blamed the tribe. She went on and on about how they paid someone off to say I didn't have enough Indian blood just to get me off their books. They wanted to purge me from the registry so they wouldn't have to cut me a check."

"Do you believe that?"

Alice shrugged.

"Did your mother?"

"She was devastated."

"But she didn't leave?"

"No. We moved, but we didn't leave the reservation. She rented a trailer way out in the boonies with the rest of the tepee creepies."

"That must have been hard."

"Her drinking got really, really bad. When she drank, her spirit went away. She wasn't really there. At some point, I got used to it. I mean, I had no choice. But after a while, I just wanted her out of the trailer so I could get my homework done, clean up a little, live a normal life."

Alice drew her legs up and wrapped her arms around her knees, just to have something to hold on to.

"Why did she stay?"

"Where else could she go?"

"*You* didn't stay."

"I had no choice."

"You had the same choice as—"

"Look at me. Look where my choices have gotten me. Crying in a shrink's office, loaded on so many drugs I can't keep them straight anymore, talking to ghosts."

"Wait, you *talked* to her?"

Oh, shit. Now she'd done it. Alice had never lied to Dr. Marcus before. Misled? Yes. Lied? No. It seemed pointless to start now. "I can't believe I'm telling you this, but yeah."

Dr. Marcus thought this over. Or maybe he was trying to figure out what to say next. What did one say when the person you're supposed to be helping admitted to having conversations with spirits?

"What did she say?" he asked.

"Don't be afraid."

"That's good advice."

"I can't believe this."

"Believe what?"

"My doctor is telling me I should listen to the voices in my head."

"I didn't say that." Dr. Marcus smiled.

"You think she's a symptom, don't you?"

"Possibly. Probably. Okay, yes, I do."

"I knew you'd say that, but can I ask you a favor?"

"I don't do favors."

"Okay, okay, let's say, it is a symptom, do you think maybe we can keep my medication the way it is?"

"So that you can see her again?"

"Does that sound crazy?"

He removed his glasses and rubbed his eyes. Alice guessed it would not be a meditation day for Dr. Marcus.

"I think I can live with that, if *you* can."

"If I can what?" Alice asked, but then she figured it out, and it took everything she had not to burst into tears. For like the millionth time, she wondered why she held on so fiercely to this shitty, shitty life.

THEY SAY NO ONE KNOWS their fate until it's too late. Lupita could go along with that, but she knew when fortune was smiling down on her, and tonight was the night. She was only going to stay a couple of hours, burn through her Thunderclap Club comps so they wouldn't go to waste. She didn't want to play Golden Gizmos, Donkey Stompers, or Cashylvania Castle. Lupita went right to Loot Caboose, and the second she sat down, she knew it was going to hit. She could feel it from her feet to her fingertips.

Still, as the reels spun, she couldn't help but wonder about the things Mariana had said to her at the hospital. Her sister had always been cruel, but never like this. Alejandro wasn't the kind of person to put his feelings on paper, and his relationship with his father had always been strained. She didn't believe Alejandro would have shared his secrets with him any more than she would share hers with Mariana. He was too macho for that. It was one thing to lie to spare someone's feelings, but to make things up just to hurt her? Who did shit like that?

Lupita needed to let it go. She was here, so she might as well enjoy herself. Just savor the moment because she wasn't coming back for a long, long time. Maybe forever. And then it happened: The wind blew, the thunder rumbled, the sound system crackled to life. *Thunder Cash is coming!*

Lupita pressed the button, and she knew: This was it, the jackpot to end all jackpots, the last bet she would ever make.

The first reel showed the Locomotive.

The Cash Cars came up next, a quick sequence of three. *Thunk, thunk, thunk.*

The fifth reel, finally, incredibly, pulled in the Caboose.

Jackpot.

The whistle screamed. The electronic display exploded with graphics. Screeching wheels and howling sirens let everybody in the casino know she'd won. *Thunder Cash jackpot winner! Thunder Cash jackpot winner!* Lupita lost herself in the frenzy. She screamed, she yelled, she wept, and when it was over, she was $667,000 richer.

The slot rep wanted Lupita to take a check, but she told the rep to bring her the cash. Keep your pinche check. It was called Loot Caboose, right? Well, her train had come in, and she wanted to bring that jackpot home and never, ever come back.

Only it wasn't that easy. The Indians made it hard on her. They smiled and offered her dinner in the Chop House. They comped her a VIP Bungalow at Falls City Vista, whatever that was. They told her the Santa Anas were blowing so hard they'd closed the freeways. Anything to get her to stay!

"I live right over those hills," she told them, pointing at the Sisters on the mural painted on the wall. They looked at her like she was crazy. Men with badges told her to think it over, to reconsider, to choose wisely. They were worried she was going to take her winnings and never come back. They should be worried!

Some pinche cabronas from the events and promotions team asked if they could take her picture, which she refused. First, they acted all concerned about her safety, and then they wanted to put her picture in the paper so that everyone in the county would know how much she won. No, thank you! Guadalupe Garcia knew better than that.

"What do you think I am?" she asked. "A fool?"

The women ignored her while the men with badges told her how wonderful it was that she'd hit the jackpot. She told them it *was* wonderful, more wonderful than they could ever know, which was maybe too much, but they should have treated her like a grown woman and not some child going to the market with her mother's purse for the first time.

The big chief, Chairman Cloudshadow, emerged from his office where he probably sat counting his money all day. He popped open a bottle of champagne and poured glasses for both of them.

"On behalf of Thunderclap Casino and the Yukemaya Tribal Council, I offer you our warmest congratulations for your good fortune!"

They drank their champagne, and the Chairman personally escorted her to the valet parking lot where her SUV was waiting all shiny and newly waxed. Armed men loaded a pair of large black duffel bags embroidered with the Thunderclap logo into the back of her truck. Lupita was bursting with joy. She got behind the wheel and waved at the people. She always knew this day would come, and it was every bit as magical as she'd dreamed it would be. Only one thing would have made it better, and that would be to have Alejandro at her side. They'd had their troubles, but he'd loved her when no one else did. If only he could see her now . . .

The wind! She didn't notice it until she left the parking lot. She could feel it buffeting the truck, whistling and whirling. Even the wind didn't want her to leave! She took it slow as she corkscrewed down the mountain, where she presumed things would be better, but it was even worse in Falls City. Mucho, mucho peor. The Chairman wasn't lying about the freeway; the eastbound lanes across the desert were closed and the truckers had three options: turn around, wait on the access road, or spend the night at Thunderclap. The casino provided shuttles to take the truckers up to the casino. Pinche Indians! They didn't miss a trick!

Lupita drove slowly, carefully. It had been a long, long day in a long, long week and she was exhausted. Such was her concentration that she managed to forget all about the bundles of cash in the back. Lupita thought about her favorite games. Donkey Stompers, Castle Cashylvania, Golden Gizmos. She tapped out their songs on the steering wheel and the immensity of the moment came back to her all at once.

"I won! I won! I won!"

But she'd never seen such wind. As she turned off the freeway, she could see a beat-up pickup blown off the road, half on the pavement, and half in the ditch. A large man with a flashlight tried to flag her down. Ordinarily, Lupita would stop and see what could she do, especially for a poor Mexicano, but she wasn't taking any chances tonight. The Santa Anas made people do crazy things. She was grateful she couldn't hear the man cursing at her over the wind as she passed. She didn't look at the man's wife or his niños in the truck. She kept her eyes on the road until she reached her turn.

In her driveway, Lupita said a quick prayer of thanks to St. Anthony for guiding her home. She got out of the car, and it took all of her might to close the door against the wind. She retrieved the duffels from the trunk—so much heavier than she imagined—and waddled up the walk, astonished by the wind that shook her truck, her trees, her world.

PEMBERTON WAS MAKING A LIST. A list of things he could do to make his life better. He hadn't gotten very far. He kept fondling the baggie so he could get a sense of how much he'd done versus how much he had left. He wondered if it was too soon to do more. The wind had been blowing hard all day and all night, and the bag was already starting to feel light. An eight ball wasn't what it used to be.

Or perhaps the problem was Pemberton had too much time on his hands. He watched the razor glide over the glass, organizing his future into neat, precise rows. Never one, always two. But he wasn't going to do the lines. Not yet. Several things had to happen first: The album he was listening to needed to finish playing and the numbers on the clock had to read twelve zero zero. Then and only then would he do the coke. There was also the matter of the mysterious bottle of Chadwick's Unadulterated Irish Whisky he didn't remember buying. The whisky was excellent, smooth yet robust. Goddamn ambrosia was what it was. Nearly half the bottle was gone and Pemberton pledged to be . . . not careful exactly, but selective with his consumption.

He set the razor down and picked up the dollar bill. He pulled it tight, took aim, fired, and chased the line with a slug of whisky. Yesyesyes. Why did he do that? He didn't knowknowknow. His chest felt like a goatskin drum going *thumpity thump thump*. It was the wind. It was really blowing! The way it shook his shitty shack was really something! It kind of freaked him out. The cabin creaked like the house on stilts in the Hollywood Hills where he'd partied a lifetime ago. A night like this night, the wind blowing, and nothing underneath but miles of glowing lights. Jenny looking so willowy and beautiful. No, not Jenny. Someone else. Kiki. Kiki and Ricky, the cokeheads from Koreatown. No, this night wasn't anything like that night.

He pulled open the fridge, inspected its bright interior. A piece of meat he'd cooked last week sat in a blue plastic tub. He retrieved a beer, opened it, drank half, and put it alongside the last beer he'd begun in this fashion and then forgot to finish. He stood, stretched, touched the ceiling. He took a few practice swings with an imaginary tennis racket. It felt like years since he'd properly exercised. Pemberton wandered about the cabin, trying to remember the name of the song he was listening to, a song he had listened to many hundreds of times. He intended to look out the window, but first he stopped to refill his drink and flip the record. Priorities! It helped to have them. But he had forgotten to look at the name of the song, and now he was going to have to wait until the B-side played all the way through. There was a warm tumbler of whisky in one hand, and a cold can of beer in the other. How had that happened? And why wasn't it open? He rectified this with his teeth and spilled beer down the front of his shirt. Party foul. Unacceptable. Time to chop up more lines and cut through this confusion.

ALICE PUSHED HER CART through the Forest of Fortune, counting the hours until the end of her shift, which was bad news since it had just started. She blamed Mike for this new development. The first time Alice let him drive her home she made him drop her off at the entrance to the trailer park because she didn't want him to know exactly where she lived. If he had any inkling of the sorts of things that went on in her trailer, he might have second thoughts about her. Though he wasn't a cop, he thought like one and, in a vital part of his imagination, he believed he was one, which sent her into a panic whenever she thought about Lisa dealing drugs in their trailer.

These were the things Alice liked about Mike:

His eyes were the brightest blue she'd ever seen.

When they were in bed, he raked his fingers through her hair like a comb.

She'd always wondered what it would feel like to be picked up and made love to against a wall. Now she knew.

He was polite, but not too polite.

He said *Excuse me* when he didn't have to but never said *I'm sorry* for something that didn't deserve an apology.

He'd never, not even once, brought up the seizure.

He had tattoos, but didn't talk about them.

He didn't bite his nails.

He made love like he hadn't done it in a while and didn't expect to again.

He chewed with his mouth closed and pissed with the door open.

He talked to his parents on the telephone nearly every day.

He didn't drink or use drugs.

When he came, he cried out in a voice that not even the roar of falling water could drown out.

Mike was a sweet guy, but she was afraid of how badly he could mess things up for her and she for him. She wondered if he would turn a blind eye to Lisa's drug-dealing if she asked him to. The tribe owned the trailers, so technically they were tribal resources. It was right there in their lease: no controlled substances. (*What about out-of-control substances?* Lisa had asked when Alice showed it to her in the rental agreement.) Alice didn't want to get her roommate into trouble, but dealing drugs out of their living room to Thunderclap employees was brazen and stupid. She'd tried to confront Lisa about it a couple of times, but Lil' Smokey was always skulking around, watching everything she did, listening to everything she said. Alice didn't know how Lisa put up with it. Alice could feel her heart hardening against her roommate, a feeling she suspected went both ways. She didn't want this to happen, but Lisa was running out of chances.

"Well, if it ain't the Garbage Lady!"

Alice snapped out of it and found Lil' Smokey and Big Pipe standing in front of her cart, blocking the path out of the Forest of Fortune. They were decked out in oversize jeans and NFL jerseys with gaudy medallions. Lil' Smokey held a stack of postcards advertising an upcoming gig. Big Pipe sucked on a giant daiquiri in a plastic glass shaped like a lightning bolt and stamped with the Thunderclap logo.

"You straight, girl?" Lil' Smokey asked. "You look like you asleep on your feet."

"Just tired." Her voice sounded feeble and small.

"Officer Friendly must be putting in work!" Big Pipe said.

Alice blushed while Lil' Smokey and Big Pipe bumped fists.

"Here, take some of these." Lil' Smokey tried to hand her some Red Dawn postcards, but Alice refused.

"You already gave me some. I have, like, a hundred already."

"You can pass 'em around as you make your rounds," he said. "Represent Red Dawn."

"You know I can't do that," she said.

"Won't is more like it."

"Fine." Alice took the cards and tossed them in the trash. She pushed her cart forward, but Lil' Smokey grabbed the edge of the trash barrel.

"I always thought you were an apple," he said. "Red on the outside, white on the inside."

"Oh snap!" Big Pipe exclaimed.

Alice kept pushing, but it wouldn't budge. She picked up a spray bottle of heavy-duty cleanser and aimed it at Lil' Smokey, the nozzle inches from his eyes. She felt as ridiculous as she must look. This wasn't her. This was something her mother would do.

"Whoa. Do you have a permit for that?" Lil' Smokey laughed.

"Let go or I start screaming. You can *represent* to security."

The Loot Caboose went off with a blast that made Alice jump. Lil' Smokey moved away, shaking his head as if trying to come to terms with something he couldn't quite believe. "You don't wanna play Red Dawn like that. Ain't that right, Pipe?"

"Sho nuff." Big Pipe finished off his daiquiri with a slurp that echoed in Alice's ears and got stuck there. She pushed her cart toward the falls, but she could still hear the slurping sound, an endlessly repeating loop, the percussive force of it worming through her ear canal, penetrating the depths of her consciousness, over and over again. This hadn't happened before. She didn't know what to think, what to do. She was close to panicking. Is this what the rest of her life was going to be like? New symptoms popping up every time she got stressed?

Well, fuck *that*.

Alice abandoned the cart. She was done with it. Now and forever. She'd wiped down her last machine, bagged her last trashcan, vacuumed her last football field of carpet. Time slowed down as she crossed the casino. The guests were especially strange-looking tonight. All the crazies came out when the Santa Anas were blowing. A black man dressed in a silver tuxedo with a checkered waistcoat and matching shoes consulted a ticket from Off-Track Betting and shook his head. A pair of hookers—plump and curvy and audaciously augmented—stumbled down the aisle in high-heel boots and glittering cowboy hats. Cocaine cowgirls who only cared about not having anything to care about.

"Hey, baby doll," one of them asked, "where's the party?"

Without her cart, Alice was no longer invisible. Panic swept through her. It wasn't a presence she felt closing in, but the absence of one. There was no illness to address, no ghost to blame, just her. *She* was the one causing all this chaos and confusion. It was all in her head. Like those dumb elephants. Like her seizures. Like her mother—even after all this time.

Her mother, she couldn't protect. Her mother, she didn't deserve.

The ghost wasn't gone because the ghost was never there, which was somehow worse, and she felt the loss as profoundly as if her own mother had abandoned her all over again. She was a fool for thinking she could ever be well, for fucking around with Mike and flirting with Dr. Marcus and fighting with Lil' Smokey, for hanging all her hopes for a better future on a man, and now she was going to lose it. Right here at Thunderclap Casino with all these addicts, imbeciles, and thrift-store bimbos watching, egging her on, she was going to completely lose her shit.

LUPITA COULD NO LONGER KEEP her good fortune a secret. She phoned her sister, but Mariana didn't answer. It was late, but so what? Lupita hung up and dialed again. This time the call went straight to voice mail, and when the voice asked if she would like to leave a message, Lupita gave her an earful.

"Mariana! This is your *sister*. I have something very important to tell you, okay? Something that will affect the girls and their future for a very long time. So get off your high horse and call me!"

Lupita scrolled through her messages to make sure she hadn't missed any calls, when she found a message from the day before from a number she didn't recognize.

"Hello? Lupita?" Lupita thrilled at the sound of Denise's voice. "I'm sorry I had to pull up stakes without saying goodbye, but I was taking a beating, and I needed to change my luck in the worst way. So I got the hell out and came here to Albuquerque, yes, fucking Albuquerque, but the homeopaths up in Santa Fe and Taos are amazing. I'm getting better. I'm sorry if you worried about me. I don't know why you would, but . . . Well, that's not true. You're a sweet gal, and you always treated me tiptop. I should have called you sooner. Why don't you come out and see me some time? I'll make it up to you. They've got a shitload of casinos out here. I'm in one now! Big surprise, right? But it isn't the same without you. Keep spinning and winning like you always do, and call me tomorrow, okay?"

Lupita wept tears of gratitude and relief. Her friend hadn't forsaken her. She'd moved to Albuquerque. Albuquerque! She sounded so much better and Lupita didn't have to be lonely anymore.

Lupita dialed the number and it went straight to voice mail. She ended the call. What she had to say was too important. She didn't want to get her signals crossed again.

Lupita dried her eyes with a tissue. This was no way to start a party. She went to the pantry to retrieve her best bottle of wine. She pulled the cork loose and spilled merlot on her blouse. She had trouble working the buttons open and was about halfway done before she realized she didn't have to work like a peasant to get pinche wine stains off her blouses anymore. She tore off the blouse, but she couldn't get the damned thing over her wrists. When she'd finally freed herself, she tossed the blouse into the fireplace. If she'd had the makings of a fire, she would have burned it. She would have built a fire and cleansed the house in preparation for her new beginning.

Lupita sauntered into the living room to turn on the stereo, caught her reflection in the mirror, and damn if she didn't look good. She hadn't been eating much these last few months and it had helped melt away some of the fat she'd put on from all that rich casino food. She took another look at herself and wished there was someone, anyone to share the moment with her. If she couldn't have company, there was always music, but the second she pushed the button on her CD player, the doorbell rang. She sashayed to the door without putting on a blouse and threw it open to shock her bitchy sister—for who else could it have been?—and a large man with a black bandana over his face hit her in the head with a tire iron.

Lupita staggered backward into the house, but didn't go down. Her hands fluttered to her face and came back with the bad news: mucho sangre. Both her hands were covered with it, and the struggle to keep her balance was connected to the struggle to keep the blood from sheeting into her eyes. The man entered her house. Shouted something at her, but her ears were ringing and the music was playing.

Alejandro?

No, not Alejandro, except in the sense that all men who did her harm were Alejandro. Lupita thought there must be some kind of explanation. A misunderstanding, a trick gone horribly awry. But it wasn't a trick. This was her punishment, her just reward.

A second intruder entered the house. "Damn, man!" he shouted. "Why you want to fuck her up like that when she's looking so fine?"

"But you told me to hit her, Smokey!"

"Shut the fuck up and don't hit her no more!"

Lupita didn't want to be hit again, not in her own home, not ever. She fled to the kitchen, where the money was, the reason these bad men had come.

"See, I didn't fuck her up too bad . . ."

"Shut up and close the door."

She didn't hear the door close, but the wind cut off and the music surged. She made it to the kitchen. The money sat on the counter. She was surprised to have made it this far. She wished she had a dog or a gun, but all she had was the Lil' Sure Shot air rifle that couldn't even kill a squirrel, and that was up in her bedroom. She should have gone upstairs. That's what she should have done. Why hadn't she gotten a dog? A dog would have been a comfort to her these last lonely months. All she had was her loneliness. Her only hope now was to give them the money and pray they went away.

One of them called out from the living room. "What's that bitch doing?"

A shadow appeared in the doorway. "Yo, yo, yo. She's in here."

Lupita steadied herself by holding onto the counter with one hand while pressing a dishcloth to her head with the other. The blood ran down her neck and seeped into her bra. The big man came for her again. He brandished his weapon, threatening to strike.

"Gimme the money!" he shouted.

Lupita did what he said and shoved the duffel off the counter and it burst open on the floor, spilling money across the blood-splattered tiles. The second man came into the kitchen. He seemed familiar somehow, and then she had it: It was the man who'd helped her put the picture in her car, the mixteca from the casino with the cornrows.

"Aw, fuck! What did you let her do that for?" he asked.

"I didn't let her do anything!"

"Shit, now you're standing in it, too!"

"What do you want me to do? This bitch's blood is everywhere, yo!"

Lupita backed toward the garage. She felt the doorknob in her hands, but she couldn't open the door. It was too slippery. She slammed into it with her shoulder and forced it open. She remembered the step down—too late—and tumbled into the garage where she crashed into the picture. Pieces of shattered glass fell on her, but she didn't move. She kept still, played dead.

Lupita waited for the bandits to come looking for her—they would be here any minute now—but the minute turned to five and five to ten, and no one came.

She could hear the wind and the occasional crash from the kitchen. It was getting harder and harder to keep her eyes open though she knew she must. The light coming from under the kitchen door seemed bright, much brighter than it ought to have been, and she wondered if this heralded her acceptance into heaven, a divine escalator bathed in golden light that would lift her up into the arms of Jesus. That's what Mariana would think. Lupita noticed it was getting hotter, so maybe she was headed in the other direction. She'd been looking forward to seeing her mother and father again, but took comfort in knowing she'd at least have Alejandro to keep her company. *I'm not going anywhere*, she realized, as the flames raced across the ceiling and ignited the garage's insulation. Pieces dropped down on her, swirling in the superheated air. She stole one last glimpse at the photo. The wolf loped toward the canyon, turned, waited for her to catch up, to make sure she hadn't lost her way. It was a gesture Lupita recognized from her dreams, her mother looking back, Lupita struggling to keep up, but always falling farther and farther behind. The wolf had been trying to warn her all this time, only she was too stupid to see the signs. The edges of the photograph began to curl. Lupita felt the moisture leave her body as the roof caught fire. Her anger seethed as the ceiling buckled and heaved, and she went up like a fireball, shooting into the sky with a scream.

PEMBERTON LISTENED TO THE RADIO. He went up and down the dial, looking for anything that would explain the unusual circumstances. The last time he'd looked out the window there was a weird orange glow to the east. A false dawn that messed with his sense of time and space. As if the howling winds that roared through the trailer park weren't enough. He searched the stations for an explanation: aurora borealis, Halley's Comet, the Rapture, but the only thing the radio gave back was static.

Sometimes he caught traces of a signal, snippets of Spanish, ecclesiastical ejaculations, the hollow sound of a country singer going down down down. Fiddling with the dial, Pemberton swore he heard a female voice giggle his name as he cruised past a station. He rolled the dial back and forth, trying to zero in on the faint broadcast, but he couldn't find the station, not even a whisper. He convinced himself it was his imagination playing tricks on him, like the phantom text messages he'd been getting. He'd be doing something at the sink and swear he could feel his phone buzzing in his pocket, but when he checked there were no new messages.

Ramona smirked at his confusion. He covered her portrait with Debra's pillowcase, but as soon as he turned his attention to something else, the makeshift shroud fell away and he covered her up again. This had been going on for hours now.

He was sitting with his ear pressed to the speaker like a safecracker when the radio exploded with accordion music. Loud, jangly, intense. Pemberton was so startled he heaved the machine into the trashcan. Several minutes passed before he was calm enough to retrieve it and plug the damn thing back into the wall socket, when he heard his name again—*Pemberton*. He fled to the living room to finish the coke, wait for the sun to come up for real, and close the books on this horribly fucked-up night.

He couldn't believe it was almost gone. All that was left was a small clump, enough for a bump. He *knew* he had another bag stashed somewhere. He just had to *think*. He'd been racking his brain all night, trying to come up with it. They were like eggs, his thoughts: He couldn't unscramble them. He'd settle for one good idea, but it was no use. His brain was hopelessly hardboiled.

And then he had it: Pemberton had put an emergency baggie in an aspirin bottle, and hid it in his desk drawer at work. It was a small bag, but a bag was a bag was a bag, and he had to have it.

Pemberton took a deep breath, looked out the window, and the reason it was so bright outside became immediately clear.

The trailer park was on fire.

PEMBERTON STUFFED THE EMPTY BAGGIE into his shirt pocket. He grabbed a pair of sunglasses for the glare, a bandana to fend off the smoke, and, of course, what was left of the bottle of Chadwick's for medicinal purposes. What else? His valise. He'd stopped bringing it to work ages ago and retrieved it from the closet. He practically crawled into the refrigerator to retrieve the last of the beer and filled the leather satchel with cold cylinders. He ransacked the cabin, his whole life in a few quick sweeps, but there was nothing else of value except the record player. He decided to take it with him. It folded up like a suitcase and even had a handle though it wasn't the easiest thing to carry. It was actually kind of heavy. He made it as far as the door before he set it down. Taking the record player was a dumb idea. He would leave it on instead, playing his all-time (as of last night) favorite record so that he could hear the music playing as he left, like the soundtrack in a movie. Fire or no fire, he was never coming back.

Pemberton stuck the plug into the socket, opened the lid, fit the record onto the spindle, and dropped the needle. A hush, a whisper, and then the delirium took hold. That he managed to make this happen so effortlessly gave Pemberton hope, and he celebrated with a shot of whisky straight from the bottle. His phone buzzed. It was a trick, he told himself. Don't check it!

He checked it. There were two messages, both from the same blocked number that had been terrorizing him.

BE SAFE!!!

And then.

Arthur.

Arthur, Arthur, Arthur . . . Pemberton didn't know any Arthurs, but he appreciated the sentiment. Better than *assclown* or *dickbag*, anyway.

Pemberton went to retrieve the pillowcase from Ramona. The ragged gray thing had lost its shape and most of its scent, but it retained some crucial essence of Debra. It made no sense to take it, but it was all he had left of her, of his old life in L.A. It was going with him. He pulled the pillowcase away and a savage face blackened with filth leered at him from behind the glass.

Pemberton screamed and fled the cabin, tripping over a husk of palm on his stoop. He rose to his feet, still clutching the pillowcase and the valise, and ran clear of the patch of bare earth he thought of as his yard, past the Trading Post, and didn't stop until he'd cleared the entrance to Falls City Vista.

Had the whole world gone haywire? The sky looked strangely sub-terranean, underlit, like when he used to drive by LAX on foggy nights and marvel at the way the runway lights illuminated the marine layer. This was different; there was no edge, no limit, no horizon. It was as if the sky had been lowered somehow and now up-close it was shitty to look at, a washed-out smudge of smoke and ash roiling with heat. But the wind was fierce, the wind was for real. Pemberton's eyes immediately started to water. His sinuses were clogged from weeks of epic cocaine consumption so he couldn't smell the smoke. His smeller was out of whack. His senses were unreliable.

Pemberton slipped on the shades and wrapped the bandana around his nose and mouth. Even though it was already unbearably hot, he turned up the collar on his coat and hunched into it. As he headed up the road into town, he took one last look back and was astonished to see the palm tree next to his cabin was on fire, not just softly burning, but really going, like a giant matchstick, a smoky locus of churning embers. A cluster of burning fronds landed on the roof of his cabin. Pemberton expected the whole thing to go up like kindling, as if he'd arranged the whole thing to make his leave-taking as dramatic and irrevocable as possible, but nothing happened. He could still hear the music, the demonic saxophone, playing on the turntable. The cabin looked brightly lit, he didn't remember leaving so many lights on, and then it occurred to him that his shitty little domicile was on fire. As soon as the realization took hold, the curtains went up, fed by the winds and embers blasting through the open door. And still the music played, atonal and herky-jerky, now you hear it, now you don't, and during one such lag, a half measure when there was nothingness where a note would have fit nicely, the cabin exploded. Slowly, ever so slowly, like in a dream, his shit crashed down around him. A small motor the size of a tattooist's machine crash-landed at his feet, and he knew it had come out of the record player. So why could he still hear the music?

It was freaking hot. Embers swirled. Pemberton tried to make himself as small as possible as he hurried down the road. He could *still* hear the music playing, repetitive and insistent; no one could tell him he couldn't. And then he realized his mistake. The horn he heard belonged to a car, not a saxophone. It was Sam from the liquor store. He stood, half-in, half-out of an old Japanese hatchback, waving at him with one hand and honking the horn with the other.

"Get in!" he shouted as Pemberton approached.

He climbed inside and collapsed in the passenger seat. He clawed at the bandana, sucking in the cool air as if it were water.

"I came as soon as I could," Sam said.

"You came for me?"

"I told you I would."

"You did?"

"Yes, at the store!"

Pemberton had no memory of such a conversation, but there were lots of things he couldn't remember, like who the fuck was Arthur? It didn't matter. He was deeply moved that Sam had come for him. It was the nicest thing anyone had done for him since he'd moved to this hell on earth. If he could have wrapped his arms around Sam, he would have. Instead, he laid his hand over Sam's, clutching the gearshift knob, a gesture that made Sam uncomfortable, Pemberton even more so, and he was relieved when Sam quickly withdrew his hand.

"Are you okay?" Sam asked. "Where are you going?"

"I don't know." Pemberton let the answer stand for both questions. Honest either way.

Sam put the car in gear and turned the vehicle around. There was flickering on both sides of the road now. High on the left, low on the right. Pemberton had a hard time accepting the danger as real.

"I will take you with me," Sam said. "We will go to my cousin's house in San Diego. Very big house. My family is there now. Plenty of room for everyone."

Pemberton struggled to make sense of this information. He wanted nothing to do with Sam's family. With women and children and plates of food and loud televisions and hours of speculating about where the fire would go next. He could see it so clearly, like a play he'd read and had no desire to see performed.

"I can't . . ." Pemberton said.

"It's nothing," Sam said. "Everything is taken care of."

"No, I mean, thank you, but I can't go to your cousin's house."

"Of course you can. You're not thinking clearly, my friend."

"I have to go back to the cocaine."

"What?"

"I said I have to go back to the casino."

"The casino is closed."

"I must"—Pemberton searched for the right word and found it—"I'm obligated." It was a lie, of course, but since when did that matter? When did the truth factor into Pemberton's accounting? Sam had never asked him what he did at the casino, and Pemberton hadn't volunteered the information. Sam looked at him like he was seeing him through a new set of eyeglasses, noticing things he'd never noticed before. It wasn't a particularly pleasant feeling for Pemberton.

"But you are a blackjack dealer, no?"

"No. I have something important to do. Very, very important."
Pemberton prattled on like this as they passed through Falls City. He
had no idea what he was saying. He could feel his words slipping away
from him, and he was powerless to call them back, steer them toward
meaning, corral them into common sense. This seemed to be happening to him more and more. Pemberton speaking, Pemberton watching
Pemberton speak, oblivious to how the words were being received. He
knew the more he said, the less likely Sam would believe him, that he
was in fact beginning to sprinkle seeds of doubt in what was a perfectly
good lie. Sam, decent fellow that he was, nodded. He would take Pemberton to the casino.

Pemberton could feel the cans of beer in his valise getting warmer
and warmer. He licked his lips, eager for a taste. Sam steered his car up
the road toward Thunderclap. He drove slowly and with care, and as
they climbed the switchbacks, Pemberton could see the fire advancing
from east to west. It looked like the fire had started at the Sisters and
burned a path to Falls City where tribal firefighters were already on the
scene. Could they stop it? He had no idea. Heading for higher ground
was the right move, but you never knew how people would react in
a crisis. People do all kinds of crazy things. He imagined a Thunder
shuttle barreling down the mountain and smashing them to smither-
eens. He closed his eyes, squeezing them shut to push the possibility
of death out of his imagination. He felt like he could sleep. He heard a
sound, a breathy kiss of air that his exhaustion neatly transformed into
the sound of an arrow whizzing past his ear and thwacking into the
headrest. Pemberton's eyes snapped open and he saw what Sam saw:
Up ahead a Thunderclap tribal security vehicle blocked the road, lights
flashing.

"Stop the car," Pemberton whispered.

"It's a roadblock."

"Yes, I see that, but I need you to stop."

"We'll ask them if you are needed."

"Stop the fucking car!" Pemberton shouted.

Sam jerked the automobile to a halt. Pemberton put his hand on the door handle. He owed Sam an apology, a word of thanks, but nothing came. "I must go" was all he could muster. It would have to do.

Pemberton slipped out of the car and scrambled across the road and over the guardrail. Many thoughts flashed through his head. *This was dangerous. This was dumb.* But these warnings weren't enough to stop him. The spirit of gravity was upon him; it carried him across the rez. He was like a character in a movie, a hero of the Wild, Wild West. Was this what the native peoples of long ago felt like?

Probably not. He wondered what kind of drugs the medicine man would whip up when he didn't like the way he felt. Peyote? Coca leaves? The Yukemaya got off on sleep deprivation, to which Pemberton could most definitely relate. Maybe the sun on their faces or cool rain after a drought felt like drugs to them. When was the last time Pemberton took satisfaction in something so simple?

He looked back to see if he was being watched or followed—surveillanced, surveilled, whatever the word was for that—by tribal security, but there was nobody there. He was alone in the semiwilderness. Impressed with how far he'd come, he popped open a beer and drank half the can in one go. The smoke was much worse now. A haze had descended, blanketing the sky. He could no longer see the Sisters, which was disconcerting, because he was pretty sure they were *right there* just a few minutes ago. Pemberton set off across the sparse meadow. It was thirsty work, and he finished the beer.

His heartbeat chugged along. It was so loud he started to get nervous. Was he having a heart attack? A horse galloped past, a freaking horse, a big lumbering paint. Pemberton couldn't tell if it was one of the wild horses that inhabited the reservation or a privately owned animal from the ranches that surrounded Falls City. There was something the matter with the horse. The way the paint pulled up and jerked its head and then broke into a gallop again didn't seem right. And then he saw the trouble: The horse was on fire. Pemberton wished there was something he could do, but it had already disappeared behind

Dodge 'Em City. With the smoke and the heat and the ash buffeted by the wind, the place almost resembled Old Baghdad or whatever it was Chairman Cloudshadow wanted to call it, but as Pemberton approached the paintball facility he realized he was being watched. He crouched in the scrub, but it was too late. Whoever was standing in the window of the saloon had already spotted him. Pemberton cursed, but the man just stood there. Pemberton waited and then he waited some more. Neither man budged an inch. Perhaps his eyes were playing tricks on him. His knees were most certainly getting sore. Pemberton got up from his crouch and resumed his trek, walking slantwise toward the flimsy structure, but the silhouette in the saloon remained perfectly still. Pemberton crept closer, his eyes fixed on the window until he was just a dozen yards away. There was someone there, his face marked with blood: an injured fireman, a wounded Indian, a bloody ghost?

None of the above. It was Pemberton.

Someone had taken the Pemberton cutouts from the anniversary celebration and set them up as target practice on the paintball course. They were everywhere, propped up in all of the windows. It looked like an army of Pembertons had taken over the compound.

Pemberton pushed through the bat-wing doors of the saloon. The odd light filtered through the windows revealing thick drifts of dust on the floor. More Pembertons were strewn about the saloon. Some stood at the bar while others waited by the windows. Still more were stacked by the door. All wore battle scars from the paintball course.

Metaphor, Pemberton thought as he set the whisky, a beer, and what was left of the cocaine on the bar. He inspected the bag to see how much residue he could scrape out. Not much. Barely enough for a bump. He should just get it over with and finish it right here and now. What the hell, right?

Thankfully, there was no response from any of the Pembertons.

The bar in the Dodge 'Em City Saloon was dusty with ash and soot. Pemberton diligently cleaned off a spot with Debra's pillowcase before he realized what he was doing. The realization brought no regret.

He made sure the bar was as clean as he could get it and cast the pillowcase aside. The Pembertons glared at him. *Are you really going to do
this? Snort more toxins up your nose with all this shit flying around?*

Yes, as a matter of fact, I am.

This was the new Pemberton: resolute in a crisis, cool under fire.

He scraped the bag and tapped it out on the bar. He made a short,
stubby line and did it. He slit the side of the bag with his key and licked
it with his tongue until it was completely clean and washed it all down
with Irish whisky and warm beer.

It was time to get the fuck out of Dodge 'Em *(Harf harf harf!)*
and seek shelter in the casino. He'd left his team member badge in the
cabin, which might cause problems when he tried to enter the casino.
He decided to bring along a cutout to serve as his life-size picture ID.
What better proof of Pemberton's Pembertonness than Pemberton?

The logic was irrefutable.

He staggered across the reservation with the replica under his arm.
All was quiet on the rez. The Indians had left or taken shelter. The
neon signage and video billboards had gone dark. An ominous plume
of smoke rose from the casino. Pemberton followed the road the Chairman had taken when he brought him to Dodge 'Em City in his Hummer. The road was long, the incline steep. The coke up Pemberton's
nose countered the crud clogging his lungs, but still the going was slow.
The wind intensified as he climbed higher up the hill. It tugged forcefully at the other Pemberton, attempted to wrestle him from his grasp.
If he let go, the cutout would go sailing into the air with the ashes and
embers and burst into flames. He couldn't let that happen.

Pemberton crossed the deserted parking lot and entered the Thunder tunnel. He stopped in front of the supergraphic of Jenny Parks. He
set down the cutout and his valise and tried to catch his breath. Her
beauty was intoxicating. It was amazing how much better he felt just
looking at her. She seemed cleaner and prettier than ever before. Prettier than Debra. Prettier than . . .

It was only a flash—now you see it, now you don't—but Pemberton was 99.9 percent positive Jenny had just smiled at him.

Smoke crept into the Thunder tunnel. He couldn't stay here. But he couldn't leave. Not now. No way. Something magical was happening. Something deeper than magic. Spiritual maybe. Pemberton wasn't qualified to say. But he felt *this* was where he belonged. He wasn't thinking coherently. He knew this. Deep in his brain, he understood staying was foolish and dumb. The wind called his name.

Pem-ber-tonnnnnnn . . .

The tunnel thickened with smoke. There was still time to get out. He needed to leave. He needed to get out of here. Jenny's smile turned into a frown, a slight tightening of the muscles, a turning down of the mouth. When the fuck did that happen? Pemberton didn't know. Jenny's eyes filled with tears that bubbled up and scorched the walls, pushing Pemberton toward the casino entrance. How did O'Nan refer to Jenny? *The Asian chick that got smoked?* He wished he'd punched him in the face when he'd had a chance.

When ghosts cry, they weep fire. Pemberton oozed regret.

He reached for the whisky, but the whisky was gone, and he opened a beer instead. He tipped the can back and drained it in one go. That's when he remembered that O'Nan's first name was Arthur. Arthur Chichester O'Nan. He was the one who'd sent the texts. He'd gloated over the layoffs, but then he must have seen something on the news that made him concerned for Pemberton's safety. That was almost decent of him, almost human. Pemberton wouldn't have thought it possible. Somewhere in the universe, Arthur O'Nan was worried about him.

Now Pemberton *really* needed a drink, but he was out of beer and the whisky was all gone. This was not good. This was a disaster. This wasn't just a fire; it was the freaking apocalypse.

RAMONA FLOATED IN THE CENTER of the chamber atop Thunderclap Mountain, her dark halo devouring the light. Her hair was an oily black, her skin a lurid white. Alice could feel the ghost's eyes on her, her expression triumphant.

You've come back.

Yes, Alice thought.

Why have you come?

I need to know what's happening to me.

What do you think?

I told you, I don't know. Alice sat down on the floor. She was so tired. Tired and confused. She was ready for this dream to be over. Seizure, symptom, side effect, whatever. She just wanted it to end.

You believe I'm real, don't you?

Yes, but . . .

You want to know if I am real to others.

Yes.

I am real to all who need me to be.

But can they see you?

What is seeing?

If you're not real, then what's the point?

You want answers, but ask the wrong questions.

I want to be well.

Your actions say otherwise.

I'm trying.

Alice's legs felt flimsy. Her neck could barely sustain the weight of her head. She felt like all the energy was being sucked out of her.

There are those who cannot hear and those who will not listen; which one are you?

Alice wished Ramona wouldn't speak in riddles. What do you want?

I want what you want, to be released from this haunting, to be free.

Alice was so tired. She couldn't figure out what the ghost was trying to tell her, and the more tired she became, the clearer Alice could see herself on the floor. If she didn't know better, she'd think she was already asleep, dreaming about a spirit named Ramona.

Do you miss your mother?

I don't know, she lied. Sometimes she missed her more than anything. Sometimes not at all. Her mother could be tender and sweet, especially when she sang. She used to tent Alice's face with her beautiful hair and pretend to steal her nose. Alice remembered the soft splash and feathery tickle of her kisses. She always let Alice eat off her plate if she was hungry and insisted on fixing breakfast in the morning, even if it was just instant oatmeal, swaying in front of the stove to some unheard music, last night's fun leaking out of her eyes. On the days her mother's head was clear, she'd make up stories about the secret life of missing socks. There wasn't a knot she couldn't untie or a time she couldn't find a piece of tape or a pair of scissors or a last drop of glue when such things were needed. Alice used to think she could pull string from her hair and pennies from her ears, and she knew more songs than anyone. She knew the secret of the hills outside her window, how at night they turned into elephants and marched up and down the reservation, from one end to the next, and in the morning, they turned into mountains again. So many things about her mother lurked at the edge of Alice's memory, a rich reservoir of happy thoughts, buried deep in her past that Alice could no longer reach. Every time she got close, a seizure stopped her.

She didn't want me. She abandoned me.

She loved you.

She said I was the worst daughter in the world.

Not true.

I saw the note. The words were all in pieces, but their meaning was clear.

Words can be made to say many things.

"Worst daughter in the world" is pretty clear.

The words you read are not the words she wrote.

Alice imagined the pieces of the note laid out on a stainless steel tray in the coroner's office. The words moved around, forming different combinations. What if Ramona was right? What if her mother didn't blame her for everything? What if the note was an apology? What if her mother had written that she was the worst mother in the world and that Alice deserved better. That would change . . . everything.

What does your heart say?

My mother wanted a better life for me, but she knew I'd never leave her, that I'd stay with her no matter what. So she took matters into her own hands.

Yes.

But that's not a suicide, that's . . .

A sacrifice.

The vibration of some vast machine turning on somewhere in the casino shuddered through her. It was the Loot Caboose. She could hear the damn thing all the way up here, deep inside Thunderclap Mountain. Was there any place in the casino she couldn't hear that fucking train? A train that went nowhere, but was always arriving. A train with no departures and no passengers. A train stuck in time. A train that triggered . . .

That was it. The train was the trigger.

Yes.

Alice couldn't believe she didn't see it sooner. She wept the tears she'd kept bottled up for so long. They poured out of her and she didn't know what to do. She was so strung out with grief she didn't even see the figure come up the ladder until he was crouching at Alice's side. She let out a silent scream. It was Mike. She couldn't let him see her this way.

What's he doing, Ramona?

What do you think?

Mike gathered Alice in his arms and lifted her up. He couldn't see Ramona. He looked right through her as if she was a camera, swiveling and zooming and capturing everything it saw but powerless to act or interfere. Is that what it was like to be a ghost? A camera from the spirit world?

Mike carried her to the ladder. He held her tight. Alice felt her heart beating through the muscles in his chest. She looked up into his blue eyes, bright as the desert sky.

I'll save you, he said.

Ramona drifted in the other direction, toward the falls, beckoning her spirit to follow. There were no lights. The casino had gone dark.

Alice had to make a choice. Mike whispered a promise to take her someplace safe. Safe sounded good. But this was the moment she'd been afraid of her whole life, to be completely at the mercy of another, vulnerable and exposed and out of control. If she went with Ramona, she would be rid of this sickness once and for all. If she went with Mike, who knew what would become of her. It wasn't really a choice. There wasn't a decision to make because her fucked-up, broken mess of a life wasn't worth saving. Alice went to the edge of the platform and plunged over the falls.

THE FOREST OF FORTUNE WAS ABLAZE. The trees were giant torches, singed leaves made of fire-retardant fabric drifted in the not-so-fortunate furnace. All of Thunderclap's creatures burned. The eagle was scorched down to its armature. A cyborg elk wore a sash of flaming insulation draped across its antlers. The bear wobbled, its circuits frozen midroar, its fake fur afire; it teetered off its pedestal and splashed into a steaming pool by the falls. Alarms sounded and sprinklers gushed. Pemberton wandered through the flames, zigzagging between rows of blazing machines. A wall of fire blocked the stairs to the management offices. His stash of cocaine secreted away in an aspirin bottle in his desk drawer was lost forever.

Pemberton headed back to the Forest of Flames, the Furnace of Fortune. There was nowhere else to go. He hurried through the heat and the smoke and the darkness, trusting his fucked-up instruments to guide him to the main entrance. He could no longer feel the heat, and the smoke went right through him. The deserted casino was lit by emergency lights and pockets of flame. It looked like a circus after a riot. The closer he got to the lobby, the worse the damage. The machines smoldered. The Thunderclap Club Rewards kiosk looked like a bomb had hit it. The desk was destroyed, the computer terminals burned out, boxes of club cards melted into the singed carpet.

Near the front entrance, a young woman stood before the Loot Caboose, stopping Pemberton in his tracks. For a moment, he thought it was Jenny. That she'd come back from the dead to guide him out of here. But it wasn't Jenny. It was the coke peddler's roommate, the sad Indian girl, Alice.

She stood there, staring at the Game, which had somehow escaped being damaged by the fire.

"Are you okay?" Pemberton asked.

Alice twitched her head. It was the faintest of gestures, the look of someone troubled by a bad dream.

"Come on," Pemberton said. "We're not safe here."

Alice shook her head again, a bit more forcefully this time. The Loot Caboose sprang to life, its multiple screens flashing a strange pattern that held her in some kind of spell. Pemberton reached for her, but his hand went right through her, which gave him a very bad feeling. Was she real? Was he hallucinating? Or was this something else?

Pemberton had no idea, but he'd had enough of that fucking game.

He wrenched a war ax from the wall and positioned himself between Alice and the machine. The Game spat sparks and belched steam. Its screens flashed gruesome scenes of blood and gore as it blasted him with a hellish screech. Pemberton swung the ax, a real Yukemaya ax, and it didn't matter that he wasn't an Indian, or that the leather handle was glued on with chemicals manufactured in Taiwan. The feathers came from a hawk that made its home in the mountains from which the sharpened stone of the ax was hewn, and the machine was no match for this marriage of spirit and stone.

The first blow shattered the main screen. The second demolished the belly glass. Pemberton kept hacking away. Glass shattered, screens went dark. He swung and chopped and chopped and swung, until all that was left of the Loot Caboose was a cabinet of twisted metal and severed wires. Game over.

It was ten thousand degrees inside the casino. His lungs felt as if they were burning up on the inside. He looked for Alice, but she was gone. Maybe she had never been there in the first place. The ax slid from his hand. He made his way to the falls. Were they healing waters? He didn't know, but he needed to cool off, clear his head. But he was too late. The falls had been turned off. Water no longer cascaded down the fake mountain. The façade looked slimy and gross, but the water was clear. He climbed over the edge of the pool where a singed wolf perched on a rock. Pemberton slipped into the water as the ceiling shifted and gave way with a roar that let the wind and fire inside the casino and then it all came crashing down in a curtain of flame.

PEMBERTON WOKE TO A STRANGE SCENE. A familiar-looking tribal security officer leaned over him, but he was wearing mirrored shades so that when Pemberton tried to see who was behind the glasses he saw himself. For a moment, he wrestled with the possibility that the other Pemberton, his doppelgänger, had somehow come to life.

"Are you real?" Pemberton asked.

"Don't be an asshole, asshole." The gruff voice snarling out of the truly massive fellow towering over him could only have come from one person. D.D. had returned. But what was he doing here at the casino, and why was he dressed in the uniform of a tribal security officer?

"I thought I was a dick."

"People change." D.D. pulled Pemberton to his feet.

"What happened?" Pemberton asked. His throat was parched and dry, and the words had difficulty straggling out.

"I dragged you out, homie. The ceiling collapsed. What the hell were you doing in there?"

"I don't remember."

"You look like shit," D.D. said.

"Bad day at the office."

D.D. laughed. "You are one seriously ate-up individual. Did I ever tell you that?"

"About a million times."

"I could use your help, amigo." D.D. nodded at a pile of duffel bags stacked by the lobby door. It took Pemberton a long moment to process what he was seeing, what it meant.

"You're robbing the casino?" Pemberton asked.

"More like an early withdrawal."

Pemberton was feeling woozy and out-of-sorts, which wasn't necessarily a bad thing, woozy and out-of-sorts being his preferred state these days, but it told him the worst was still to come. He was going to crash. It wouldn't be long now. He probably wouldn't remember any of this.

"Did you start the fire, too?" he asked.

D.D. grimaced. "After all we've been through, it hurts that you think I'm capable of such a heinous crime."

"Well, did you?" Pemberton asked.

"I'm an opportunist, not an arsonist. A house caught fire over by the Sisters. The wind did the rest. But is this really what you want to talk about? The *weather*?"

Pemberton shrugged.

"Come on. Let's get these into my vehicle."

Without waiting for an answer, D.D. draped the duffel bag's strap around Pemberton's neck. The bag was heavier than it looked. Pemberton would have loved to know how much money he was carrying.

"Can you manage?"

Pemberton nodded, though he was having trouble keeping his balance. In fact, he could barely stand. D.D. scooped up two of the bags and exited the lobby. The wind blew, buffeting Pemberton with stinging grit. He'd lost his sunglasses and he squinted into the wind. He didn't have far to go. A tribal security vehicle idled in front of the entrance, lights flashing. They loaded the bags into the back of the truck. They made three more trips. Just as they were finishing up, a casino cop emerged from the lobby, carrying Alice in his arms.

"We have a situation," the tribal security officer said.

Pemberton thought he recognized him. His team member badge said Mike. What was Mike doing with Alice?

"You show up ten minutes late with a dead Indian chick? No shit, we have a situation!" D.D. shouted.

Mike shook his head, frantic with worry. "She's not dead, but she's in real bad shape."

"What's wrong with her?" D.D. asked.

"I don't know. I think she had some kind of a seizure."

"We can't take her to the hospital."

"I know that," Mike said.

"Put her in the truck," D.D. said.

Mike eyeballed Pemberton. "What about him?"

"This is the guy I was telling you about. He works here, too. He's with us now."

"Maybe I don't want to go," Pemberton said.

"You're going," D.D. answered. "You and me have some catching up to do."

"You and I."

"Same difference." D.D. smiled.

Maybe D.D. was right. Maybe they were more alike than different. He was right about one thing: It was time to go.

D.D. drove. Mike climbed into the back with Alice. Pemberton slid into the passenger seat. D.D. gunned the gas and spirited them away from the casino.

"Alice, talk to me," Mike pleaded, sick with worry.

"You love this woman, Miguel?" D.D. asked.

"Yes," Mike said.

D.D. whistled.

One of the duffels lay open at Pemberton's feet and he flipped through a bundle of bills, not counting the money exactly, but enjoying the way it felt. The sound, the smell. Mike tried to rouse Alice but wasn't having much luck. He was going about it all wrong. Alice's spirit was elsewhere. Her body and spirit needed to be reunited or else they would lose her.

"Tell her she needs to come back," Pemberton said.

Mike repeated Pemberton's words and Alice murmured.

"Now what," Mike pleaded with Pemberton. "Tell me what to say."

There were things he'd like to say to Alice about what had happened in the casino, but knew it would sound like craziness to D.D.

and Mike. Pemberton leaned back, closed his eyes, chose his words very carefully.

"Tell her that her body is here with us, safe and sound, but it needs her spirit to live."

Pemberton almost laughed. It was so *obvious*. The body needs its spirit to live. He didn't know where his had gone, where he'd left it behind. Maybe he'd let Thunderclap take it from him. Maybe it was back in L.A. Wherever it was, he needed it back, and he wasn't going to find it in a bottle or a baggie.

"Tell her that they tried to take our spirit," Pemberton continued, "but we fought back and we won."

"I don't know where you're going with this, amigo," D.D. began before Mike shushed him.

"She's trying to say something."

"The train," Alice whispered.

"That's right," Pemberton said. "The train. But it's gone. It can't hurt us anymore."

Alice opened her eyes as if the effort was almost too great to manage. "Where am I?"

"Leaving Thunderclap," Mike said.

"Good," Alice answered as she closed her eyes, her voice sounding far away.

"You should probably keep your eyes open."

"Just talk to me," Alice said.

"What do you remember?" Mike asked.

"I don't know. Tell me what's happening."

"There was a fire at the casino."

"Is it bad?"

"It took out the trailer park and spread to the casino."

Alice opened her eyes. "Really?"

"Gone."

Alice considered the news. Her eyes drifted to the front of the car. "Who is that?" she asked.

"He works at the casino," Mike answered.

"Not anymore," it gave Pemberton great pleasure to say.

"Where are we going?" Alice asked.

"To a place where we'll all be safe," D.D. answered.

Pemberton had no idea if this was true, and if it was, where that safe place might be, but it sounded good. It was probably best not to mention that they were, technically speaking, accomplices in a felony robbery. That could come later.

"Oh, good," Alice said. "Safe is good."

D.D. turned on the radio. A familiar jingle floated through the speakers. It was Pemberton's commercial, the spot he'd recorded with O'Nan. *Thunderclap Casino. A roaring good time. Harf harf harf.* Out on the freeway, emergency vehicles rushed toward the burning casino. Ladder trucks. Police cruisers. Ambulances. All too late. The mountains dissolved into restless shapes. Colors shifted as the hills receded and went elsewhere. The gray haze gave way to blue skies, clean air, and, beyond that, an infinite expanse of ocean. Waves dropped out of the sky. The surf sprung from the soil. A cool mist settled sideways over everything. Pemberton felt himself drifting toward the outer limits of consciousness, edging closer and closer to the blackout he'd been flirting with for so long. There were so many things about his life that he wanted to change, and even though the odds weren't in his favor, Pemberton liked his chances.

I HAVE WATCHED OVER THIS LAND *for one-hundred-and-seventy-five years. These were my mountains. My canyons. My wind. All of it belonged to me. I dried up the river and silenced the falls. I spoke through thunder and rain and made my moods known through fire and wind. No longer. I have told you the story of how Ysabella and I were brought to this place, and what became of us. My time here is over. I have done my part. Only a spirit can release a spirit, and now you have come to take my place. You have freed me to seek the home I was taken from, the home I have always longed for. Born of fire, you will haunt the houses that went away, those that refused to fall, and those that will be rebuilt. You will be the ghost in the attic, the creature in the canyon, the spirit of the flames that devours places once nourished by the falls. You will watch over those who stay and those who come to help. You will protect the good and punish the wicked. You have much work to do. My hope is you will be a gentle spirit. Bring luck to those who need it. Be the sparkle in the coin, the flutter in the fingertips before the jackpot hits, the feeling that today just might be a lucky day. Guadalupe Maria Garcia, this is your haunt now. Thunderclap belongs to you.*